Also by David Cook

Albert's Memorial
Happy Endings
Walter
Winter Doves
Sunrising
Crying Out Loud
Second Best

Missing Persons

David Cook

HEADLINE

First published in 1986
by The Alison Press/Martin Secker & Warburg Ltd

First published in paperback in 1988
by Arena

Reprinted in this edition in 1996
by HEADLINE BOOK PUBLISHING

10 9 8 7 6 5 4 3 2 1

ISBN 0 7472 5346 3

Typeset at The Spartan Press Ltd,
Lymington, Hants

Printed and bound in Great Britain by
Cox & Wyman Ltd, Reading, Berks

HEADLINE BOOK PUBLISHING
A division of Hodder Headline PLC
338 Euston Road
LONDON NW1 3BH

For Dorothy and Brian Phelan

Contents

Contents

1

Neither In Nor Out

Sepia postcards didn't lie. The world had been that colour
then, everything blurred, a heavy clinging atmosphere,
heat before a storm. Men had worn creased baggy
trousers to cover their undernourished bandy legs, strain-
ing waistcoats over their pigeon chests, and bowler hats
which made them prematurely bald. And her baby had
died on the hearth-rug. A boy.

Sepia. Even grass then was of an ungrasslike rusty
colour, and there had been more of it. Slim women had
worn layers of faded amber petticoats to make them look
plumper, and plump women had worn the obligatory two
and felt undressed. Physical contact had been better then,
more exciting, not only because she had been young but
because the risks were dramatic. Her mother had
forbidden the baby, had threatened not to lift a finger, and
had carried out her threat, keeping both hands hidden
under folded arms.

The sepia room, heavy with dying plants and dusty
velvets, had seemed like a cold uncaring womb from

which she was being expelled without a character. But the boy in her own womb had struggled for his freedom too soon, and had died of it on a rug by the fire which was neither in nor out. That boy would have been nearly fifty now. The cord had been cut, and his face, neck and shoulders wiped clean with her handkerchief. The rest of his body could not be touched, not modestly, not then, though she had noticed that it was all there. Her child had been physically perfect, although dead. By now, nearly fifty years on, that perfect body would be past its best.

She no longer thought about it much. One can expect no more of people than that they should keep their word, and her mother had never faltered from hers. Even the burial of the tiny body had been achieved alone. Cycling from Clitheroe to Penwortham the day before, she had told herself she wasn't pregnant. Lies to oneself didn't count as real lies, or how else could she have managed all these years?

There had been no more children after that, none of her own at least. Evacuees didn't count; they arrived wreathed in sulks and suspicion, and left calling you 'mother' and swearing to write. She had been twenty-eight when it happened, and still wearing plaits; it was not long before she was past the age. Frank had known nothing about the baby when he married her, bigamously as it turned out. Her mother's hands had been revealed long enough to point the way to the door, and she had not seen the velvet-curtained womb with the reluctant fire again. The afterbirth, she supposed, had ruined the rug.

She had lived in re-creations of that room in houses as far apart as Preston, Aylesbury and Westcliff-on-Sea, always with Frank. On the twenty-first of September 1947, when the boy who had died on the rug would have been eleven, she had told Frank, in response to his irritated entreaties, why she was crying, and why she refused to move from her own hearth-rug, which was placed before a blazing fire. Thus encouraged, Frank had told her about his own son, and the wife he had left when the child was three years old. He had never bothered with a divorce, but had married her bigamously.

Edith had known already. Hetty had told her eight years earlier. She had wondered when Frank would get round to telling her. They had sat in silence, moving only to feed the fire with choice lumps of coal, until he said, 'It's time we got some colour into this room, Edith. It's like a funeral parlour. We need some pinks and a spot of kingfisher blue. What's past is past, you can't go back, and anyway we have each other.'

Now she was seventy. Seventy something. She didn't lie about it, even to herself; she just couldn't be bothered with the odd years. Eighty would arrive or it wouldn't. Her only hope was that once she was dead, that was that. She didn't want hereafters, thank you, no judgements being made.

This morning a letter had arrived. It was in Hetty's handwriting, addressed to Frank, not to them both. She had watched him open it, and waited. Finally he had told her that Hetty, after four months of trying, believed she was on the track of his son, the son he had abandoned fifty years ago, a son now aged fifty-three. The trail seemed to lead to Halifax in Yorkshire. The boy was thought to be married and to have grown-up children. Hetty had made these discoveries at Frank's request.

Hetty the foolish, Hetty the scatterbrained! Best friend, only friend, younger than Frank and herself, and with expectations of inheriting most of what they had managed to save over the years. Now there would be other claimants. Blood, even after a fifty-year separation, still clots. Hetty was the biggest clot. Poor Hetty!

So Frank had found a son, and she herself was no longer bigamously married. Hetty wrote that Frank's first and only legal wife had died in 1983. What did that make Edith now? Was she stepmother to a warehouse manager of fifty-three?

Hetty's letter ran to five pages of minute detail in tiny neat writing, each page ending with the reassurance that the information it contained had been acquired without the subject's knowledge that his daddy was alive and well and living in Westcliff-on-Sea. At the end she asked for further instructions. Did Frank wish to make the first contact with his son himself? Should she, as a third party, write to ease the way? And how would Edith feel about it?

She didn't know how she would feel about it. They had had no one close but each other for almost fifty years, not family; Hetty was her friend, but she was not family. Edith could not begin to contemplate carloads of grandchildren and great-grandchildren arriving from Yorkshire to view Frank and herself as if they were historic buildings. They would park their charabancs in the narrow street, and she would be expected to provide tea and fancies. Well, she would not do it. She and Frank had a routine, which had taken years to perfect, and could not be altered now.

Frank had left her the letter to reread. He had refilled her teacup, placed in her hand the magnifying glass which they always seemed to be losing, and had kissed her forehead before putting on his cap and muffler. In those far-off sepia days, he had worn a bowler; she was sure of it. They had argued this point many a long hour, he saying that it was nonsense, he would never have been seen dead in one, and she remembering vividly his round little face like Stan Laurel in a shiny black bowler hat.

Now she imagined him striding out towards Southend, cap pulled down, muffler done up tight against the sea breeze. The walk he took for his bowels' sake would now be a thinking walk, a walk back through fifty years to whatever memories he could muster of a three-year-old playing on the hearth-rug, being tickled and running away, wriggling and fighting for freedom, with small teeth, long eyelashes, all pink and white and blond, she supposed. All three-year-old boys looked the same to her. All three-minute-old babies, she also supposed, must be much of a muchness as well.

No, she could not swear on the Bible to a bowler hat, but it was firmly there in her mind's eye. When he took it off there had been a mark on his forehead and an indentation all around his tow-coloured hair. Short in height and long on lechery, that was Frank Cross, known for it. He had not jumped out on her from behind a tree and taken her like an animal, had not gathered her up like an untidy parcel on the crupper of his white horse, but had wooed her in a casual, take-it-or-leave-it, matter-of-fact sort of fashion. His expression had been that of a cherub who had only recently discovered sin, and was determined to enjoy

5

it, and she had found this attractive since her own life up
to that time had been anything but enjoyable.

She had been taught that life was a punishment for
some crime too terrible to mention, which one either
endured with a good grace and was rewarded in the
hereafter, or else one went to the bad by kicking against
the pricks and earned an eternity in Hell with no remission
or parole. Frank believed firmly in the here and now. She
had been too formed by her upbringing to change at once,
but they had allowed each other their different opinions,
and the years had worn away at hers.

Frank had run away from a pretty wife. She, Edith, was
not at all pretty, nor had she attained prettiness or allowed
it to be thrust upon her, not even by Hetty. The two
waist-length plaits, which her mother had removed with
scissors while showing her the door, had been thick
healthy hair and a lustrous black in colour. They had been
sold, she discovered later, to a wig-maker who had paid
seven shillings and sixpence for the pair, half a week's
wages. Ever since she had worn her hair short and straight
with a straight fringe. It was a muddy silver now, and her
skin dark and tough-looking. People had called her skin
olive, in an attempt to be kind, but since the only olives
she had come across were black or green, she considered
the kindness misplaced. In her early middle age the three
small bumps on her chin had sprouted hair which, if
removed, returned more abundantly. Hair was a plague to
her. Her upper lip, although well shaped, also had its
thatch of dark oily hair, and the black hair on her legs
showed through all but the thickest and most matronly of
stockings. She had even become convinced that her back

and shoulder blades were only awaiting an opportune
moment to sprout. There seemed to be little point in
aspiring to prettiness unless it could be achieved by fur.
The forty-shilling permanent wave she had undergone in
1945 to celebrate VE Day had been her first and last; its
permanency had proved a fiction. She was one of life's
aunties, created to be mocked or pitied, encouraged to be
eccentric, and she no longer cared.

The tea was cold. She placed crockery in the sink, and
allowed lukewarm water to cover it. He had certainly
worn a bowler; her mind's eye was usually reliable. They
had enjoyed physical contact because of the amount of
clothing which had required his negotiation, not in spite of
it. Toast crumbs and tiny globules of Blue Band margarine
floated towards the overflow outlet. When he returned
from his thinking walk, he would require her to have
decided what she felt about the discovery of his son. She
would certainly be expected to feel something. What? If
they were allowed to visit, what would they call her?
Step-gran? Mrs Cross? Or by Frank's real name, which
was Shawcross? If all these irregularities had occurred a
few years later, they could have been blamed on the War.
Many strange things happened then. She poked at jam
with a sponge on a stick, to loosen its grip on the plate.
Her mind's eye showed her the Sewage Farm where Frank
had once worked, the sprinklers circling with their
fountains of water like rows of small boys, Wolf Cubs, all
sitting on a roundabout and peeing, seventy-two arches of
liquid from seventy-two giggling outlets.

Dermatitis prevented her from placing her bare hands
into washing-up water, and she had never mastered the

use of rubber gloves. She cleared away and soaked; Frank washed and rinsed; she stacked the dishes when they had drained, and dried glassware and cutlery. When reading library books she wore cotton mittens with a small hole cut for her left index finger to turn the pages. She had no wish to pass on whatever she had or to contract anything new; one always caught the strangest things from books. Cream which smelt of camomile was applied between her fingers morning and night. It did no good, but couldn't, she supposed, do actual harm, and as punishments for old age go, she considered hers to be light.

Every memory she had of her early life contained within it her conviction then that she would never grow old. To be fifty had been unthinkable, and she would certainly never be so inconsiderate as still to be using up air, space and food at sixty. Fifty had come and gone, and sixty, and seventy, but she had not grown old; only her body had done that. Her body had always betrayed her.

2

Making Waves

He had never in his life worn a bowler, even when hats were an expected part of a man's uniform. It irritated him that he couldn't bring to mind a picture of how his son might look now. All attempts failed. The three-year-old face was blurred and incomplete, and refused to age fifty years. If he concentrated he could persuade himself that he remembered individual features – a pair of eyes, a nose, lips which were sometimes open and sometimes closed and turned down at the corners. Each feature remained in close-up, a little out of focus, refusing to be assembled, refusing to age.

'More Life Myra' had been pretty, the daughter of a publican, who left him minding the baby while she served behind the bar next to daddy. She had said she wanted marriage and children, but having sampled both, decided that she preferred pulling pints and the company of regulars.

'More life.'

'Why?'

She had shrugged. 'I'm young.' And for her age, it is true, she was young.

Life consisted of pouring and pulling, of smiling and shuffling her tiny feet (always in carpet slippers) between bar and crates, tables and bar, collecting empties and wiping smelly ashtrays, with daddy watching, daddy smiling.

'More life?'

'Yes.' Her shoulders always shot up whenever he asked a simple question. He should have hung ten-pound weights on them, front and back. 'Conversation. I like a good chat.'

Three conversations at once, that was Myra's line. 'How's the dog?' – with a pint of mild and bitter under a picture of General Smuts. 'Have a nice dirty weekend?' – with Gladys from the laundry, sipping her port and lemon to make it last. 'My, you have got a nasty one. Don't you go giving it away.' – with the red nose and watery eyes, snuffling into a Whisky Mac. But for him, when she did get home, it was, 'Done the ironing? Here, move your hams; I'm nearly dead.'

For five nights running, he had stood at the bar with a half of black and tan, watching her move her slippered feet, lifting one out of its cocoon to rub against the ankle of the other. 'Chilblains? What an idea! Certainly not.' Only lazy women, those who sat with their legs apart, mottling their thighs against roaring fires, got chilblains. 'Anyway it's only a tiny one. Just on the little toe.' Then away to Gladys, who was wondering whether the stains of port wine could be removed with a little salt, and back again. 'Tried wintergreen?' She had added the conversation with him to the others, making it number four. 'Everything.' 'The love of a good man?' 'Hard to come by.' 'Very hard!' That had made her blush. Two beautiful ripe tomatoes, separated by a turned-up nose, and above it a pair of brown shiny conkers which blinked at him in disbelief. It was the way he told them, husky-voiced, eye to eye, leaving no doubt. So his wooing went.

She hadn't been easy, by no means a pushover, not like Edith later. Having a father-in-law who was the landlord of a pub, that was like marrying a Rothschild in those days. What went wrong was sex. That was new to him. No one had ever told him to keep it until Christmas before, and that had happened *after* they were married. He had been twenty-five, with more than his fair share of urges, all of them normal, but double the average allotment. If he'd put up with that kind of talk, he might well have found himself accosting children on Shaftesbury Recreation Ground.

His son's eyes appeared in sepia, and disappeared. Why was there so little Technicolor these days? Walking was good for you, even if it did make him liverish. A pair of lips, turned down at the corner, threatening to bawl. Bernard, that was the name; Mandys and Elvises weren't allowed in those days; they'd have curdled the water in the font. Bernard Shawcross, son of Francis. When Frank had left, he'd just dropped the Shaw and kept on being Cross. The joke never ceased to amuse him. A really good joke can last fifty years. Like marrying Edith.

He leaned on the promenade rail, and looked out over the waves, wondering not for the first time how many there were and whether anyone was keeping count. All

11

those urges, double the average allotment, all used up by time. Waves, on the other hand, kept coming. He had never expected to see his son again, and even now was not sure he wanted to.

Perhaps he should not have allowed Hetty to go so far. He had confessed it all to her ten years earlier during a bout of bronchitis, and she had pestered him about it on every one of her many visits since. 'Nobody holds a grudge for fifty years. Imagine if you didn't know who your father was.' Well, he had imagined, and decided that on balance he would have managed without the knowledge, but Hetty was like a gramophone needle which had mistaken its function and was trying to slice through the record. 'No harm in me finding out, is there? A discreet enquiry wouldn't commit you, would it?'

He should have known better; least said, soonest mended. He had hoped that Hetty would tire of her Sherlock Holmes act. To have tried and failed, there was honour in that. But not for Hetty. There would not be a stone in the northern counties left right way up, so determined was she to prove her disinterest in his money. He could see her in his mind's eye, knocking on door after door, downing cups of tea, eating cake after cake, her false teeth rocking and rolling in her mouth like a grand piano in a storm at sea. 'That's right, I'm a Wainthropp really. Now, Cousin Jack was a Windrush, I do beg your pardon; that was on his father's side. Had sugar, you know, very bad; blew up like an airship.' She would forget, at least until the third cup, to reach the point. He imagined himself nudging her. 'Word of my old friend, Myra; full of life, she was. Her father ran The Travellers'

Rest, you must remember it, lovely little boy she had, be a big boy now, has to be fifty, doesn't time fly? Bernard. Bernie, they called him then, only three when his father left. Shawcross. Of course they may have changed it after what happened, you couldn't blame them, now what was her maiden name, it's on the tip of my tongue, Engleton. Ever so pretty and full of life and always had a word for everyone.'

He remembered the nappies, the smell of baby-powder, the bum rash and the vicious-looking safety-pins, but not the colour of his own son's eyes. Too preoccupied with the other end! Later he had become the foreman of a Sewage Farm for the Buckinghamshire County Council. It had been a position of responsibility, but he had never worn a bowler. Wonderful vegetables he grew on that land. The work was a doddle, watching the sprinklers go round, and unblocking the occasional pipe. It wasn't often they had a run on. Forty thousand customers, and all of them content, with nothing sent back. What's My Line? had replied politely to his letter, BBC notepaper and all. The producer thanks you for offering yourself as a contestant, and feels sure your occupation would have given the Panel something to think about. Unfortunately our schedules are complete for the foreseeable future.

Life had not been without its moments of interest. There were the greyhounds. A kennels close to the Farm. He'd always called it that. 'I run this Farm for the Council.' 'What do you keep there?' 'Nothing if I can help it.' White City every Thursday sometimes. His Lucksdown Gal got as far as the semis for the Derby, and his Mister Snitch had sired a flyer in Little Snitch, which he'd let go for a hundred pounds, fool that he was. He'd been lucky with the gee-gees as well. Careful too. Kept his winnings separate, never broke into capital for his betting. His total winnings now stood at £24,627.50, all in the house at this very minute, no banks, no pack drill. Not everyone had as much to show for thirty-odd years at a hobby, and he hadn't finished yet. The Old Age Pension, Supplementary Benefit for extra coal, meals on the skids four times a week, a bus pass, and a nest-egg sewn into cushions which the busybody assessors from the Social Services regularly sat on when paying one of their impromptu visits. This government wanted locking up; they couldn't run a three-legged race.

Hetty knew, of course. She knew everything, thanks to Edith – not the amount or where it was, might as well take an advert in the *News of the World* as tell her that, but she knew there was a good bit put by. 'You won't be short of a little money when we go,' Edith had told her, patting the cushions around her like the great stupid Jessie she was, and Hetty had demurred, had become noble and self-denying, had sworn she couldn't; it would burn her pocket, knowing how they had scrimped and saved for it. 'Money come by that way never brings happiness,' and all the time she had been trying to guess a figure, her eyes circling the room as she tried to remember what she knew of property values.

Now the silly bitch had found his son. A warehouse foreman. At fifty-three. Not much of a career, then. Surely a son of his might have done better than that for himself? Even Hetty's son was an out-of-work actor, seen on the television in a commercial for dog-food. He had stayed with them rent-free for six weeks, while playing a poof at the local Studio Theatre. Went around smelling like a chemist's shop, never made his bed, and seldom left it before midday.

He, Frank, had fathered a child, and Edith had watched hers die on the hearth-rug. That would also have been his, another boy. She had never been with anyone else, not before, and certainly not since. She had allowed him to take her virginity during the first hour of 1936 only four hours after they had first met, and they had stayed together ever since. Few women as plain as she could have gambled so much and ended up winning a partner for life. It amazed him that in all those years he had never attempted to hot-foot it to the nearest railway station, had never ceased being Cross in order to return to Shaw. Often he had sat watching the sprinklers play over the sewage at Wendover, and imagined what he might do as Frank Shaw arriving in Harrogate or Hull to start a new life.

He could have gone; he'd had no family commitments; he and Edith had preferred financial security to children. At first he had thought that all the fiddling with French Letters and collecting threepenny bits in a tin to cover the expense of them was paying dividends. Later when they were safely on their feet and had been able to give up the French Letters, but there were still no children, he had resented the fiddling and the expense. He had thought Edith barren until she had told him of her little drama on the hearth-rug. But neither of them had been all that keen, if the truth were known. They'd had evacuees during the War, but one never got too close to someone

15

else's. London lads were always three jumps ahead; he'd had to watch them. They were old enough to earn a bit of their keep by digging the allotment, walking the greyhounds, by paper rounds and fetching coal, and went home the healthier for it, but the closest he'd got to any kind of relationship was smuggling them the occasional crust when Edith had put them on short rations for insolence.

A discreet enquiry did not commit him. He need not do anything at all. If he pushed himself back from the rail now and started to walk, he could write to Hetty before lunch and stop her going any further. Safer to do that. One thing led to another with Hetty. As she got more and more used to the chats and the free tea and cakes, always getting closer and closer to the object of her quest, sooner or later she'd find herself talking to the man's wife, and where would discretion be then? Discretion and Hetty were as far apart as Shirley Temple and Lady Macbeth.

3

Apple Strudel

'I'm his sister-in-law. He only lives four streets away. What did you say your name was?'

'Wainthropp. Hetty.'

'What a small world! You knock on my door, trying to find Bernard, and him married all the time to our Doreen.' Hetty swallowed. The sister-in-law noticed that Hetty's eyeballs became unusually active, darting from side to side in an attempt to hasten the processes of thought going on somewhere above them. 'Are you all right?'

Hetty nodded to reassure her, but too vigorously, causing a chunk of apple strudel to lodge somewhere one side of her uvula.

'My word, you've changed colour. Is it the pastry?' The sister-in-law had large hands, made all the heavier by cheap and noisy jewellery. She used one of them to strike Hetty several times on the back, making a sound like hail on a tin roof. Hetty, her air supply restored, attempted to backtrack, to divert, allay, confuse, muddy. It was only a

17

casual enquiry; she had often wondered what had happened to her old friend, Myra Shawcross, Engleton as was, and the little baby. Time was heavy with her now that her own children had grown away. One was an actor; the sister-in-law might have seen him on television; did it under his own name, Steven Wainthropp. He had trained at a place called Rose Bruford, not a village in Kent as she had at first thought, but a real person, now passed on, and had left her name to an Acting School. The girls were both married, one to an airline steward, the other to middle management, lovely families, very muscial, and heaps of coloured snapshots. Smoked salmon and malt whisky sent by mail order every Christmas without fail; they were all very good. Hetty was soon to be a great-grandmother, made you think your time was nearly up, didn't feel her age and never tried to act it; she couldn't sit around all day, she'd sprout, so thought up adventures for herself, trying to trace old friends, that's what had brought her, that and her Senior Citizen's Gadabout Card, what a blessing that was. A Number Forty-Three had dropped her at the Post Office, and she'd enjoyed her day out so far.

'You must have known Bernard's father, then.'

Hetty smiled, one of those long smiles intended to give nothing away which are thwarted in their intention by revealing almost everything.

'You do, don't you? How exciting!' The sister-in-law poured more tea, but was too busy hugging herself to offer strudel.

'He's not supposed to know. Frank's a very old man now. The shock might kill him.'

'What about our Bernard? What will he say? He's not exactly expecting his daddy to turn up after fifty years.'

Hetty noted the 'our' Bernard. Fatherless men suddenly appreciate in value if the father reappears like a Dickensian benefactor.

'What does he do, Bernard's father?'

'He's retired, of course. Been very steady. Lived very quiet.'

'What did he do before?'

'He worked for the Council, ran a farm, rose to be manager. But sport was his main interest. He did quite well at that, I believe.' Hetty found herself patting the cushions beside her.

'But what about sex? He couldn't keep it to himself from what I've heard, and his son's quite the contrary. It's bound to come out. Did he go all . . . you know . . . or what?' The sister-in-law seemed to assume that Hetty would not know, for she flapped her enormous jewelled hand in a downwards motion, imitating certain comedians she had seen on television, and causing bracelet on bracelet to collide. Hetty took a slow sip of her tea, and waited for the clash of cymbals to die away. She was sixty-five, and had been for at least seven years, and would not be harassed into discussing the sexual preferences of a man of eighty-one.

'He was always very much a real and proper man.' She quelled the memory of Frank's hands wandering around inside her blouse and straying up the lining of her skirt that time when Edith had shingles. In her mind's eye there ran and re-ran as if on a loop the commerical for

19

Dogomeat in which her own son had pretended to be not an actor but a successful breeder of long-haired wolfhounds or some such. Chopped liver had been placed in his hip pocket, and he had walked away from camera, followed and sniffed at by six very large dogs, their heads moving rhythmically to the movement of Steven's bottom as he walked. The film company had paid for the trousers, which could not safely be worn again.

'Free as a bird, and all man? He must have had the time of his life.' Did the woman think of nothing but sex? There is a limit to the obligations imposed by the acceptance of strudel. The Dogomeat commercial was displaced in Hetty's mind's eye by the memory of Edith before and after her forty-shilling permanent wave. She remembered long discussions with Edith about facial hair, and Edith's insistence that Frank didn't mind it. Meanwhile the woman prodded on. 'Expect he's lonely now, though. Old age is when you pay for all those wild oats, don't you think?'

'Did you ever meet Bernard's mother?' Hetty had decided that questions were easier than answers.

'No, but I've seen photos of her when she was young. Very attractive for the nineteen thirties. Difficult to tell with all that sepia, though, isn't it? Everyone looked half-caste and half-cut in those days. Photography being so rare, I think people must have gone a bit silly when they were being shot. We couldn't really have had that many village idiots.' The woman must be an idiot herself. Photography was not rare; had she never heard of a Box Brownie? Hetty herself had always practised her smile so as to be ready for snapshots, particularly on holiday. Her best side was the left. There was nothing silly about presenting the world with your best angle. 'Nowadays,' the sister-in-law said, 'if you're anything like our lot, you've got drawers and drawers full of colour photos, enlargements, negatives, slides, you name it. I think you'll find three slide-projectors in this house if you were to institute a search,' and then, without the slightest pause to indicate a change in subject, 'So he just kept playing the field, then?'

'Yes, he was quite successful at it. Never broke the bank, of course, but he's always kept well ahead over the years. He never backs favourites.'

'I meant women.'

Hetty shook her head demurely. It was her often practised imitation of Joan Fontaine in *Rebecca*. 'He's lived very happily with a good friend of mine for many years now.'

'Our Doreen said he was a randy old sod. She got her mother-in-law drunk one night, and it all came out. How he'd left her with a three-year-old because she wouldn't let him have his oats five or six times a night after she'd been on her feet all hours serving mild-and-bitter to our lads on leave.'

'On her feet she may well have been, and mild-and-bitter is what pubs usually serve, I'm told, but what our lads thought they were on leave from in nineteen thirty-five, when Frank left Myra, is a puzzle.' So sucks boo to you, bejewelled lady, who serves tea to guests out of chipped cups on wood-grained formica, and go and wash your mouth out with soap, which is what I intend to

21

do the moment I get home, after drinking out of this. And Hetty raised her chin in a way which might have caused Bette Davis, had she been present, to consider legal proceedings.

Ninety minutes and two buses later she discovered that she was still shaking. Meeting that woman had quite unnerved her. What a stupid person to give herself such airs! 'Can't have had that many village idiots'! Hetty had simply knocked on that door at random. How could she have known she would be waltzing into the bosom of Bernie's family? 'Institute a search for slide projectors'! What did she think she was on about? Then all that probing for details about personal matters was salacious, no other word. At least she'd not given the woman Frank's address, though she hadn't been able to get away without leaving her own. Thank God she hadn't mentioned that she was on the phone. She hadn't seen a telephone in the woman's house, and nothing had rung except the jewellery. Perhaps Bernard wouldn't even bother to write to her; he might not want to know; often people are funny about their parents. Particularly after so many years. Her heart was still thumping. There was no way she could have explained the real situation, not to a perfect stranger, that after walking out on a pretty wife Frank had bigamously married plain old Edith three years later.

They were passing the football ground; she must watch out or she'd find herself carried on to Morecambe, hot flush and all. 'Half-caste or half-cut'! Well, there were plenty of both walking the streets these days; you didn't have to dig out old photos. What a close shave she'd had! Adventure and the excitement of the chase, that's one thing; dropping yourself right in it is quite another. She could imagine the embellishments which the sister-in-law would be making, bracelets going ten to the dozen, heavy hands flapping about, crumbs of apple strudel flying every which way. Who in her right mind has apple strudel on stand-by just in case of visitors? A few biscuits maybe, a slice or two of home-made Madeira cake, not shop-bought strudel; it's Bohemian, is that, must have been on some package tour, it's surprising she didn't make a point of it.

Kilvert's Garage. Watch out, Hetty; you've done enough walking for today. Four more stops, that's if he doesn't whizz past the schoolchildren waiting at the corner of Holy Margaret's. She might just treat herself to a Dubonnet if there was any left. She'd need all her wits about her if she were to write to Frank before bed. She daren't even think about it. What should she tell him? 'Dear Frank, something terrible has happened.' 'I'm afraid, Frank dear, that we've been found out.' Somehow she must remind him subtly that she was cutting her own throat, chasing around half Lancashire and Yorkshire, looking for his son. All that patting of cushions and vague promises! Edith had a bit of her own too; it was difficult to put a figure on what all those economies in the housekeeping might have added up to. Fifty years of pretending you like sour milk and rancid butter, of boiling sheeps' heads with lentils and bartering for cast-offs at the bring-and-buy stalls, just so you could see your will printed in the local paper when everyone knew you'd been collecting Supplementary Benefit!

If Bob was back from the allotment, and had got his own tea, she'd plunge her feet into some Radox, and watch a few adverts. Steven might have done another, although he did say he'd signed away his life for Dogomeat. She wished he'd be more exact; she didn't know what he was talking about half the time these days. Hers was the next stop.

'Dear Frank, I'm awfully sorry, but accidents will happen.' In her mind's eye she could see his face, watch his lips tighten. God, he was mean-looking when he was thwarted. She wouldn't have taken him on herself, not for half a dozen nest-eggs and a gold watch. He might well have been as sexy as a billy goat and not as prone to preferring a good night's sleep as her Robert, but that kind of thing wasn't the be-all and the end-all. Mr Balderstone would have been more to her taste, when he was thirty, that is; a bit of refinement goes a long way. Some might have thought him a bit theatrical, but envy's a funny thing; he'd certainly had a voice you could listen to for hours. A few caps on those teeth, and if she'd weaned him away from loud check shirts and mustard bow ties, rationed him with the hair oil a bit, oh yes he'd have been worth a little effort; there was potential in Mr Balderstone. Just imagine waking up to that voice, coming at you ever so softly from over the rim of a tea-cup.

Damn! She was there! How did they expect old folk to

get to the front when they drove so fast?

'Next stop, please! Have a little thought for a Senior Citizen!'

4
Betrayal

The commercials never lasted long enough, and it seemed to Hetty that the same man's voice was being used all the time. Steven had explained to her that, in order to make it fair, several actors were employed, but that they all had to imitate the voice of this one man, who was nowadays too rich to sing the praises of cough syrup and such, but spent his days buying oil paintings and antique Japanese daggers. There was a Dogomeat advertisement, at which she leaned forward attentively, but only to be shown a middle-aged woman with a squint and a stupid laugh, surrounded by dachshunds. It was alleged that she had been best in her class at Crufts' or somewhere. What lies they tell the troops! Hetty knew that this woman would just be an actress, who either happened to have a squint, or was clever at assuming one. And anyone could do stupid laughs.

Robert was sprawled in his chair, letting the fire go out as usual. The allotment took it all out of him, although it rarely yielded more than a couple of onions or enough

sprouts to fill a colander. He would wake in time for his
Ovaltine and biscuits, walk to the door into the hall, open
it, turn his back on it, break wind, close the door and
return to his chair. That would be Robert's contribution to
the evening's entertainment.

The notepaper before her seemed to have a blankness
the like of which she had seldom before encountered
in notepaper. She remembered that she had half
composed the letter while sitting on the bus, but her sub-
sequent argument with the driver (who also took the
money) about the nature and timing of the emergency
stop he had performed on her behalf, which had ended
with her sitting untidily in the lap of a Pakistani youth
who had treated himself to a handful of her left thigh, all
this had quite driven what she had composed out of her
head.

It was a muddle. She couldn't imagine how she had
allowed herself to be drawn into it. Somehow she had to
explain how it was that Bernard Shawcross, warehouse
manager of fifty-three, now knew that he had a legiti-
mate father who had been hiding from him for fifty
years, and presumably now believed that his father had
sent an old friend across two counties to find him. Frank
had been promised a discreet enquiry, and now, thanks
to the woman with the cheap jewellery, everything was
out in the open.

Edith was her real friend, Edith had been her friend for
as long as she could remember. She had been very sly for
years, had Edith, about why her own mother had thrown
her out. Just arrived at the door with a small suitcase and
an expression on her face which would have made little

Orphan Annie seem like Mary Poppins. She'd known that Hetty's mother was a soft touch, of course, and she had been soaked to the skin; it had been raining, a cloudburst; she couldn't have been refused. Much later, in 1951, Edith had confessed that she'd been waiting in a doorway down the street for that cloudburst, guessed it was coming, and knew it would help her get to stay, since she'd be bound to have to get out of her wet things, and there's nothing like borrowing a friend's skirt and jumper for breaking the ice. Then later, after tea and toast, she had simply announced rather loudly, 'Mother won't have me back in the house. We've had a bit of a disagreement.' She always had spoken in loud gushes, as if testing out a voice which had only been given to her that very minute. If 'a bit of a disagreement' was what Edith considered a fair description of giving birth on the hearth-rug to a dying baby while her mother turned up the radio so that the neighbours shouldn't hear, then it was not surprising that Edith had always considered Shakespeare wordy.

It might never have come out at all if Hetty had not been summoned by Frank to nurse Edith through pneumonia, and she had been a proper pest, wanting this and fancying that, and all of it having to be smuggled past Frank, since she wasn't supposed to smoke or drink, even when in perfect health. But Edith had got it into her head that she was on her last legs, and had decided to try all the things she had never done – purple nail-varnish, Craven-A filter cigarettes and gin-and-lime, an attempt at sophistication twenty years too late which had given her terrible heartburn.

Hetty had simply had enough. She had never liked gin

anyway, considering it common. She had said, 'Pity it's too late for *one* thing you haven't done,' and Edith lowered the tooth-mug from her lips, rubbed at a cigarette burn on the eiderdown, and asked what that was, and Hetty had continued, 'Surprising really, with all the attention Frank pays you,' attention being their private word for you-know-what, and Edith had blushed while Dutch courage wrestled with embarrassment, so that her olive complexion was suffused with pink and her face looked like a Cox's Orange Pippin, and then said, 'I think Frank and I have exhausted the different ways attention can be given and received, and I'm now refusing to accept any more. It all gets sent back whence it came before it comes.' This had sent them both into gales of giggles, partly at Edith's wit and wordplay, and partly at Edith's new ginny voice, of which she was proud, and which Hetty herself certainly preferred to the usual loud one. Then Hetty's thoughts had turned to her own Robert, snoring next to her in bed at night, and how he had not paid her any attention at all after the arrival of her third, and she had said, 'That's what you've never done. You've never had a baby.' And Edith had stopped laughing, and poured herself another gin, but without the lime this time since it only gave her heartburn, and then after a long silence of staring at the window opposite her bed, had said, 'That plant is dead. It needs throwing out.'

'What plant?' There had been nothing on the windowsill but two hairbrushes and a glass fairing of Bambi, which had lost a leg and lay on its side.

Edith had made a noise which signified that Hetty's question had no meaning for her. Then she had returned from her trip down Memory Lane. 'What was I talking about?'

It had begun to seem to Hetty that the topic was a dangerous one, and that she had better avoid the word 'baby'. 'Giving birth?'

'Why do you think my mother threw me out?' Hetty had shrugged her shoulders. Then Edith had said in a voice neither loud nor ginny, 'My only baby died on the rug before the fire,' and added after a pause, 'We were saving coal at the time.'

After that the rest had been told, how the baby had been Frank's but he had not known until 1947, how it had been alive at birth and stone-dead a few minutes later. Its screaming little face had been all screwed up like a monkey's, and had then just stopped still like a photograph. Then nothing.

Three days later Hetty had returned home to Robert and what was left of her family. The coach ride north had seemed to take no time at all. Hetty could not read on coaches, and had devoted the journey to thought and memory. Edith's description of the baby's death had been so cool. After the silly remark about the dying plant which was not there, she had become detached, even cold, had not seemed to care or even to realize that she had betrayed a lifelong friendship by keeping quiet on such an important matter. How could Hetty or anyone continue to think in the same way about a person who had kept such a secret for almost thirty years, and then casually revealed it over gin-and-lime? Edith had simply used Hetty all these years, and given nothing in return. It was upsetting. Hetty had felt as if it were in some way she who had killed the baby, and somewhere between Luton and Watford Gap she had become aware that her folded arms were moving from side to side, to the discomfort of the passenger next to her, and that cradled within the arms was her handbag containing the twenty pounds which Frank had pressed upon her for her trouble in nursing Edith. She had been nursing her second-best handbag, rocking it like a baby. How ridiculous!

The pangs of betrayal, of emptiness and loss, had lasted for at least three months. Hetty had looked into prams again, had chattered wet-eyed to young mothers, all of whom had assumed her to be depressive or drunk, had talked softly and kindly to her, but had watched her as one would watch a pickpocket or bag-snatcher. The Covered Market and the Shopping Precinct had seen her more often, always with empty carrier-bags flapping, always searching for the youngest baby she could find.

Taking upon herself someone else's worry or pain had not been a new thing. She did not recognize it as such, just thought of herself as a bit of a softy, and classified it as a weakness of which she was proud. Hetty found it impossible to exclude her own life from those of other people. We are not separate, not meant to be. Secretly she suspected that her own life, if it were taken and placed apart for inspection, would appear dull, drab and ordinary. She would not allow that. The prospect frightened her. She had to be interesting. What else was there?

Her mother had been a saint, and her great-great-grandmother had walked the length and breadth of England with a troupe of show people. That woman, only four generations removed from Hetty, had been widowed at sixteen, taught poor people to read and write, become one of the leading female reformers of the Blackburn area, and spoken publicly at Chartist Meetings. Hetty did not agree wholeheartedly with her great-great-grandmother's politics, but the inspiration and energy of the woman had to be admired; it was a difficult act to follow. It was not Hetty's fault that the late twentieth century offered little scope for the individual to cause a stir. At least she had never succumbed to playing Bingo or watching Blankety-Blank.

The name of the television programme reminded her of the sheet of blank notepaper she had managed for the last few minutes to forget. Well, she would not write a cringing apologetic letter, and she would not be blamed. If people did their own dirty work, things would be a lot simpler. Why had Frank taken it into his head after all these years anyway that he wanted to know about his son? She wondered whether she herself might get strange whims when she was old. She knew exactly where all her living relatives were; some of them were best forgotten. Frank couldn't very well have walked the streets of Lancashire and Yorkshire, hopping on and off buses, but with his much-talked-of nest egg, he might have hired a professional detective.

Until her little setback today she had done very well. A professional detective would have booked his hours, claimed for fares and refreshments, and been denied the use of a Senior Citizen's Gadabout Card. A professional detective would have worked out expensive for Frank, who was a great one for getting everything at cut price. Hetty had notched up quite a few miles with that Gadabout Card, and had enjoyed most of them too. Wriggling her toes in the now cold Radox, the empty Dubonnet glass clutched in her fist, she imagined herself in trench-coat and trilby confronting the sister-in-law. 'Strudel? Do I smoke it, or use it to keep the door open?'

Was there a market for such a service? Would the local paper take an advertisement? 'Lost Ones Found! Reliable and Discreet Mature Female Detective.' She worried about that 'female'. Would 'Lady Detective' be better, or might it suggest one of the aristocracy slumming or even out for a bit of a lark? It was all 'person' nowadays, another of their stupid laws. Yet the people who read the paper would need to know she was a woman; she wouldn't touch anything sordid. 'Let me find your kin. I have a nose for it. Modest payment only by results.' Perhaps the last sentence had better be cut. It suggested a lack of confidence.

It would certainly be interesting to see what response there was. If she were flooded with customers, Steven would always help out, provided he could telephone his agent twice a day. The exercise would do him good; he was getting a bit too rounded. He wouldn't have stood for the airs and graces exhibited this afternoon. 'Strudel?' he would have said. 'How very nouveau!' Of course she would have to pay full fare for him on the buses.

'Unattached? Pregnant? Worried? Then phone this number. Let me find your lost loved ones. I have a nose for it.' Perhaps her advertisement should come before the one for Pregnancy Testing. She would leave it to the editor. He'd know best.

5
Love-Bites

Five days later three envelopes fell on to the mat behind
Hetty's front door. The first envelope bore the name of
the midweek local paper, and was a typed acknowledge-
ment of her advertisement. The editor had added a
personal touch in handwriting at the bottom, 'How very
interesting! Perhaps a Profile of you soon.' Hetty was not
sure how to respond to this; usually she knew straight
away if someone was taking the micky. After thought she
decided that the editor's enthusiasm was probably
genuine; he had precious little else of local interest to
print.

The other two letters were not so welcome. One was
postmarked Halifax. She studied the handwriting, and
decided that it was over-careful, with the neatness of
someone who doesn't write often. She held the envelope
up to the light, for no good reason that she could think of,
except that perhaps now she was a semi-professional
detective, she ought to get into the habit of looking for
clues. The envelope was cheap and white, and there was

the thumbprint of some person unknown in one corner. It contained a single sheet of blue writing paper. She opened it. The paper was an azure blue, and lined; an address somewhere near Halifax had been printed at the top. She read the letter:

Dear Mrs Wainthropp,
My sister in law tells me you visited her asking about my mother Mrs Myra Shawcross. She also mentioned that you knew the whereabouts of my father Mr Frank Shawcross. I should be most interested and grateful if you could let me have an address for him, so that I can write and make myself known. He must be getting on in years.
Yours sincerely
Bernard B. Shawcross
P.S. Sadly, my mother died in October 1983.

Here was a letter which, if ignored, would be followed by a visit. Hetty's instinct about such matters was foolproof. Her stomach rumbled its agreement with her instinct, and she closed her eyes, trying to assess how much grace Bernard B. Shawcross would give her before he appeared on the doorstep asking awkward questions.

The third letter was addressed in Frank's handwriting; the postmark included a bearded old gentleman frolicking with bucket and spade. No other clues were needed. This could not be Frank's reply to her explanation and apology, since she had put off writing it, and had only half an hour earlier given it to Robert to post.

Frank's handwriting, though clear and always to the

point, danced on the page no matter at what distance she held it from her. She was forbidden to continue with her enquiries. Edith had been so upset by the news contained in Hetty's last letter that her health was now at risk. Nothing more must be said or done on the subject, or Frank would not be held responsible. Hetty put Frank's letter down, half covering the letter from his son. It was the closest the two men had been for fifty years.

She packed a suitcase, and scribbled a note to Robert, who would by now be on his allotment, having posted the letter she would give her right arm to retrieve. She had been summoned to nurse Edith, who was not well, and would phone, reversed charges, every evening after six to see if anyone had replied to her advertisement. Oven chips, fish, steak pie, Brussels sprouts and a pea soup marked 'London Peculiar' could all be enjoyed from the freezer if it was remembered that three hours were needed to bring them back to life before heating, and there were tins of baked beans in the kitchen cupboard.

She would leave at once and arrive in Westcliff before the letter. She would creep downstairs in the morning the moment she heard the postman, take the letter from him, and destroy it. She would write to Bernard herself as soon as she could. Already the letter was forming in her mind. It had all been a terrible misunderstanding, for which she was sorry. Yes, she had known his father, Frank, but that had been ten years ago when she was living near Bletchley in Buckinghamshire and working for the local council. She had lost touch after that, with not even a Christmas card for the last three years. Certainly Frank must have retired

by now, had been past retirement age when they had last
met, but because of the nature of his work being manager-
ial and not strenuous he had been allowed to work on.
That kind of small detail, Hetty thought, would make the
letter sound plausible; she must think up a few more. If
she insisted that the sister-in-law had misunderstood, who
could contradict her? 'I do get confused myself sometimes. Mind you, I'm coming up for seventy.'

Hetty flashed her Senior Citizen's Gadabout Card at the
driver as she mounted the bus outside the Post Office, and
chose a seat at the front. As she was leaving the bus at the
terminus, she saw a postman emptying a pillar box, and
realized that if she had stood in front of her local Sub-Post
Office, and accosted whoever came to empty the box, she
might have been given her letter back, thus saving the
time and money she would now have to spend in going to
Westcliff. The exasperation she felt with herself at having
missed a trick no professional detective would have
missed, caused her to shout the word 'Shit!' aloud, and
stamp her foot, so that the other passengers dismounting
from the bus, as well as those about to get on it, looked at
her askance and made the kind of detour which they
would normally reserve for the mentally handicapped or
those suffering from leprosy.

It did not last long. Temper tantrums on the Boulevard
at Bolton were not her style. There was no going back, so
it was 'Forward the Buffs!' At some time before reaching
Westcliff she would write the letter to Bernard B.
Shawcross, keep it hidden, but be able to present it if
Frank should get to the postman before her.

Over the years she had observed the National Coach

Company go through many changes. The cramped hard-seated single-decker coaches had been replaced by spacious double-deckers with toilet facilities at the rear. These top-heavy vehicles had ceased to be mere coaches and been renamed 'Gay Hostesses', and for a while each had actually carried a gay hostess, a young woman dressed rather like an airline stewardess, who seemed to have no specific duties except to be cheerful; it was a Company Rule that a gay hostess must always wear a smile. Most of these gay hostesses had very soon succumbed to melancholia; their turnover in every sense was brisk. Eventually the Gay Hostesses and their gay hostesses had been phased out, and roomier single-deckers with tinted glass shuttled up and down the motorways between termini.

Even so Hetty discovered that all the window-seats were occupied. This annoyed her. The whole point of travelling was the view. Surely it was not beyond the wit of man to design coaches in which everyone could sit next to a window. The tops of heads and the backs of ears were no substitutes for the rolling countryside.

The youth beside her had his nose pressed hard against what should have been her piece of a window, and his breath had misted the glass. Hetty was tempted to lean across and wipe it with her hankie, but the brief glimpse she had caught earlier of his face had suggested that behind the sallow skin and the spots might be a soul in torment. She assessed his age as between thirteen and fifteen; it was difficult to be more accurate these days. Before reaching London she would enquire and check her assessment; a talent for guessing ages might be useful in her new line of work. She would not rush matters. The young nowadays had done to the art of conversation what the US Air Force had done to Nagasaki. Soon language would consist of nothing more than monosyllables for ordering fast foods.

'Would you care for a piece of chocolate? I shouldn't really. Everything worth having is bad for you, so they say.'

The youth's head shook from side to side, but his eyes continued to stare into the mist on the window. Hetty saw no reason why the rest of mankind should put up with such a rude and depressing lack of interest from those under twenty. So what if there were no jobs for them? Even in her own lifetime she had seen that before. The world hadn't stopped then; it wouldn't stop now. It was a matter of outlook, of taking and using what there was. A bit of wood and a piece of string had kept her brothers happy for hours. Singing and dancing and telling each other stories, people talking to each other, living close and going to the cinema once a fortnight, that was what life was about; it was all you needed. It made her stomach turn when children walked around like wizened elder statesmen, just grunting, as if to say one complete word would be a betrayal of their entire generation. Free milk should never have been stopped; that's why they were all dried up inside.

Meanwhile the youth, after what seemed to have been a long afterthought, announced, 'Chocolate gives me asthma.' All was not lost. Hetty dismissed from her mind the indignation she had managed to work up by thinking of her brothers singing and dancing in their old front room, and wriggled her shoulders, making herself more comfortable. 'I have a terrible sweet tooth.' The world she and her brothers had known, with one war behind them and another to come, couldn't be compared with the empty drabness which this pimply heavy-breather had inherited. But there it was. You pays your money, and you gets no choice.

'Was that Keele Service we just passed?' The head of mousy hair was lowered and raised again in the most lethargic nod Hetty had ever seen. 'Not very friendly, are you, chum? It's conversation makes the world go round, you know.' This tone had sometimes worked with schoolgirls who had given her cheek in bus queues, and the girls almost always rose to it, 'What you staring at, granny? Never seen a love-bite before?' Then Hetty would smile and nod, perhaps even wink, responding to the fourteen-year-old in her unflappable woman-of-the-world persona, and guessing the love-bite to have been self-inflicted with a pair of dad's pincers. She knew the tricks, knew the importance of pretending to keep up with the crowd. It was a difficult time for them, and if a little pretence helped them along, what harm did it do, just as long as they washed the wound and didn't get iron filings into it? She could see that the youth's hands, each clasping one of his bony knees, had 'L.O.V.E.' printed on one and 'P.E.A.C.E.' on the other.

'Love and peace aren't going to be much good if people still aren't talking to each other.' It seemed to the youth that he was being submitted to a geriatric version of the Chinese Water Torture. By the time they were passing Cannock he was negotiating a surrender, confessing that

43

he had left school that very day, was deficient in O Levels and had only the most inappropriate of CSEs, that his age was sixteen years and two months, and that he was small for it.

He was travelling to London to find work. His parents were separated, and his objective judgement was that his mother was mentally ill. He was an only child, who hated the North and all it stood for; every time he heard a northern accent on television, he covered his ears. He had read a little about the Hunger Marches of the nineteen thirties, and could not understand why the Revolution hadn't happened then. He was hopeless at every manner of sport, hated computers and Space Invaders, liked smoking pot when he could get it, and had twice sniffed glue, which had given him a splitting headache and caused his nose to bleed. He had nowhere to stay in London, but he would make out. He was wearing two of everything because he disliked to see men carrying bags, and although his financial situation was a close-kept secret, he didn't suppose that the money markets of the world were awaiting his next move.

Hetty left the youth at Victoria Coach station, placing a kiss on his spotty cheek and a pound coin in his top pocket. They had changed places on the coach, and she had warned him of the perils of London inasmuch as she knew of them, which was entirely from the documentary programmes on television which she had heard about but could not bring herself to watch. Her success in provoking him into articulating his thoughts had been greater than she had hoped, and she was filled with a sense of well-being. If the generation gap could be bridged between

Keele Service Station and Luton, there was still hope for mankind.

She had not eaten since breakfast; chocolate does not count. The train from London to Westcliff spent more time stationary than it did in motion. Ordinarily she might have enjoyed an unhurried look at each of the many stations on that line, but it was getting dark. Her fear was that if she were to arrive after Frank and Edith had gone to bed, either they would not answer her knocking, or it would inspire in them a panic so great that one of them would have a turn.

6

A Brick Between the Sheets

They weren't expecting her, of course.

'Did you get my letter?'

'Yes, Frank, I did, thank you.' The exchange was formal. Surprises were not what they liked best. At least she had arrived, and would be able to retrieve her own letter.

'We haven't aired the bed.'

'I shall be all right.'

Edith's hunched shoulders spoke of her resentment as she mounted the stairs, carrying one of Frank's old string-vests as a duster. The spare room had not been looked at since Hetty's last visit. Frank rearranged the fire. To add more coal would be a waste at this time of night. 'If we'd had any warning you were coming . . . ' He left the sentence to die.

'I came to see what you wanted to do next.'

'I told you in my letter. You said you'd had it.'

'Oh, yes. Had it before I left. Came immediately. That's why I couldn't warn you.'

Frank looked at her. They seemed not to be speaking the same language. He tried again. 'Well, then, I want you to do what it says. Nothing. Not another move. Best stop as we are before we live to regret it.'

'You said it was Edith's health holding you back. She looks all right to me.'

'Looks aren't everything. I should have known it would frighten her. All this talk of prodigal sons descending from Yorkshire.' Bernard B. Shawcross had not sounded very prodigal, not from his letter. It was more likely that he had inherited from his father the very opposite of prodigality. Frank saw Hetty's expression, and went on quickly, 'Good thing I realized just in time. Didn't want you getting too close to him. Once he knows I exist, there's no going back.' He poked at the ashes of the fire which was by now neither in nor out. 'Perhaps later. If Edith goes before I do. We shall have to wait and see.'

They fell into silence, and listened to Edith above their heads, moving slowly about the spare room, and collecting dust in the string-vest. Only the sound of the television through the wall from next door reminded them that there was life outside this room. Frank said, 'What do you want to do with your teeth?' Hetty looked at him. 'You'll need a glass. Do you want to keep them in your room with you? If you leave them in the bathroom, we shan't know who's wearing whose.'

The spare bedroom was like ice. A brick had been taken from the side of the fire, wrapped in an old piece of towelling, and placed between the sheets of the bed; it constituted the only bright spot in what had otherwise been a Siberian evening. The draughts and cross-currents had fought with each other for supremacy; to move one foot away from the hearth had been to risk hypothermia. Yet Frank and Edith had appeared to be used to it, he in his waistcoat and shirtsleeves surrounded by a pile of cushions, she sporting nothing more substantial than a twin-set which didn't match. Hetty had longed for her overcoat, and had made a point of bringing it upstairs with her to add to the bed. She imagined Robert at home, the rubber soles of his slippers melting, his snoring gently circulating the warm air.

Not since the Coal Strike had she been so chilled, and that was not the more recent Coal Strike, but the one when she was a little girl. She looked back over nearly sixty years at the queues of bleached faces with their eyes like piss-holes in the snow, pair upon pair of glinting cinders, and perched above each pair a frayed cloth cap, and heard again the sounds of flapping shoe-leather and songs sung without hope. She shivered. The removal of her teeth helped a little. In very cold weather they had a life of their own, and sounded like an excitable foreign radio station.

Frank and Edith had already had their tea when she arrived. They had offered her bread and jam, or bread and Marmite if she preferred. No mention had been made of the fatted calf. She had declined the cup that cheers. The sight of Edith dangling a cut-price tea-bag on the end of a string like a hypnotist, and shouting, 'It's no great trouble really. Just say the word' had brought on one of her stubborn streaks. It had hurt her that nothing more substantial was being offered. She was their only friend. It was not as if she popped in every evening to make demands on their larder. Even the sister-in-law had given her shop-bought strudel and brewed a proper pot of tea. She closed her eyes, and in the darkness there formed the image of a cup of tea strong enough to trot a mouse on, and the steam rising from it.

They had sat in the dark. Even the television had remained off, its screen animated not by elegant and noble hounds leaping at Steven's behind, but by the reflection of the three flames which the fire bravely put out in spite of Frank's discouragement. In the darkness they had shared those three flames, and Hetty had wondered which of them was hers. If the radio (bought in the nineteen forties) had activated itself to announce the start of World War Three and to demand a blackout, they would have been ready; they need not even have left their chairs.

She remembered how Edith had once shown her the secret compartment which Frank had made at the back of the pantry. The removal of a piece of hardboard had revealed thirty-seven tins of pilchards all marked Special Offer, ten tins of baked beans, twelve packets of cream crackers and four tins of cocoa. There had also been candles, matches, two hot-water bottles, a primus stove and two sets of earplugs. They did not intend, Edith had said, to be caught out this time. Would they still be there, Hetty wondered, the pilchards, the baked beans and cocoa?

Not that Frank and Edith had been caught out last time; the need for a secret pantry in their last house had been in response to a different set of circumstances. The idea had come to Edith one night in 1942 in a flash, as she had been sitting up in bed listening for any sound which might indicate that the evacuees were making another of their midnight raids on her food supply in one of their forlorn and increasingly desperate attempts to keep body and soul together. While Frank's Black-Market butter, eggs and cheese came and went and his cast-iron money-box in the form of a grinning negro became heavier, the evacuees had wasted away, and been thought by the local doctor to be pining for Lambeth. The greyhounds they exercised had eaten better and seemed to have more flesh on them. Hetty had incurred Frank's displeasure by asking him if it was his intention to put a muzzle on the smaller of the two boys and place him in the Starting Trap at White City. Edith had maintained that the worming medicine the two evacuees had been given on arrival had cleaned them out so thoroughly that they had not yet started to show the benefit of her feeding, and so finally it had fallen upon Hetty to take the boys aside and tell them their rights, offering to take them to the doctor and obtain diet-sheets against which they could check the daily intake of nourishment provided.

Hetty lay resting the hot brick on her stomach; her feet would have to wait their turn. Her own hunger was growing more urgent. If it were not attended to, it would keep her awake. Would Frank and Edith be asleep yet? Could she find the pantry in the dark? She remembered that her handbag contained a Christmas present which she had been intending to pass on, a combined key-ring, torch and door-lock defroster. To open a door of which the lock had frozen, one first located the lock by means of the small torch, then pressed a button which caused an even smaller spike to emerge from the torch. This spike would be heated by the battery, and, gradually inserted into the lock, would melt the ice. One would then open the door by means of the key on the key-ring. It was a useful and practical gift, and she hoped to find someone worthy of it. Meanwhile the torch, although its beam was no wider than a pencil, would show her the outline of the linoleum-covered stairs, which would otherwise be a death-trap. And if the pantry door turned out to be locked, and the lock frozen, that would not surprise her in this house.

She would not make a pig of herself, but take what had been offered, bread and Marmite, and the trip downstairs would be a practice for the morrow, when it was imperative that she get to the letters before Frank. She must be sure to be up really early. Her microchip alarm would not wake them; she would press the Snooze button before it got louder. Steven's flair for inventive presents knew no bounds. He had said, 'This will remind you of me every morning when you wake, so just go easy with it, and don't start pulling its little attachments off.' He knew she was hopeless with gadgets.

She had been in bed at least an hour. Surely, if she waited another ten minutes, it would be safe to get herself a bite?

7
Bouncing

Sitting by the fire in the dark with Frank and Hetty had reminded Edith of old times. Nothing much had been said; that in itself was a relief. No effort was needed with people you'd grown old with. It was unlikely that anything of real importance had been left unsaid between the three of them over the last fifty years.

Hetty had seemed a little fraught when she arrived. It was unlike her to have come so far without checking that a visit was convenient, even more unlike her to turn up her nose at the offer of food. Bouncing about the country as she did, and being so full of energy, it was only natural that Hetty should eat as if there was no tomorrow; she had done so since 1925, but maintained that her large hips were the result of three pregnancies and that her flabby upper arms were hereditary, though Edith remembered Hetty's mother as a slight and fragile woman with the neatest and most elegant of shoulders.

She had always thought that Hetty was like a multi-coloured rubber ball. Throw it to the ground, and it would come back up at you, bouncing higher the harder you rejected it. Hetty's two elder brothers had spoilt her as a child, giving in to her whims and lavishing attention on her. Bill, the elder, had been the mainstay of a semi-professional Concert Party. They were semi-professional in the sense that they would accept money if it were offered, but it had rarely been offered. Consequently he had found employment as a door-to-door salesman, travelling in everything from insurance to fly-paper. Sometimes he had burst into a snatch of song or a tap-routine on the doorsteps of the district to gain admission, but it was in the parlour at home that his talent had mostly flowered. With the furniture pushed against the walls, and plump little Hetty spinning around him or dangling over his arm with one toe pointed as near to the ceiling as it could safely go, he would be Fred Astaire to the life, and Hetty would be Ginger Rogers. Edith herself had never danced in public. Even at the sixpenny hops, she had stood or sat by the wall. But alone, with only the radio, then she had waltzed and jitterbugged, and sometimes she still did.

All that excitement and love given so early had gone to Hetty's head, rose-tinted her view of life and left her with an inability to take the world's real measure. Alf, the younger brother, had been quieter, but even he had played the piano by ear and attempted to sing like Hutch. He had gone to Australia, and was now in an Old People's Home in a suburb of Adelaide. A photograph sent by the Matron to Hetty showed a wizened old man, sitting on a verandah and squinting into the light. The sun and the farming had dried Alf up, smoked him like a kipper. No more would his rendering of 'I'm Dancing with Tears in my Eyes, Cos the Girl in my Arms Isn't You' be followed by that rapt silence which signifies so much more than mere appaluse. The snapshot, taken in 1974, had reminded Edith of a child's leather toy, a Mister Mole, stitched together from patches and strips of well-used chammy.

Hetty had insisted that a mistake had been made, and the wrong snapshot sent. That tiny shrunken man could never have been her six-foot brother. She preferred to remember him as she had known him, towering over their small piano, his long arms extended and his artistic fingers rising and falling. She had threatened to throw the snapshot away, knowing that Edith would offer to keep it, which she had.

Brother Bill's death had subdued Hetty for a while. His widow had disliked Hetty from their first meeting, and as the two women had walked to the gate of the cemetery, holding hands, she had turned to her and said, 'Please don't come back to the house. Bill was the only member of your family I ever liked,' and Hetty had remained, fixed to the spot, watching the cars depart for the Funeral Tea of smoked salmon and sweet sherry. Then she had walked back into town, and signed up for Evening Classes in Flower Arranging, Keep Fit and First Aid.

Edith propped herself higher in the bed, and listened to the sounds of the house settling down. The question of what she felt about the discovery of Frank's son was still unresolved. She was curious to know what he looked like. Probably like Frank at fifty-three, but since Frank had never allowed himself to be photographed, she had nothing to refer to. Hetty's eagerness to reunite father and son had gone beyond a gesture to show how disinterested she was in Frank's money. Perverse gestures were the kind Hetty made best, but this one was extreme, even for her. She wasn't a relation, so why should she be so concerned? And it wasn't like her to come all this way just to double-check something Frank had written in a letter.

She tried to conjure up a picture of Frank at the age of fifty-three, but it was beyond her. The changes in his voice were easier. The quiet and seductive voice she had first heard that New Year's Eve proved later to be capable of many different tones. Even on entering a shop to buy pipe tobacco, there would be adjustments made according to the sex of the assistant. During the war, when women had come to his allotment by the Sewage Farm to buy vegetables, his tone had been different again, partly because the transaction was illegal, since the allotment came with the job on the condition that it was not used for personal profit, but mainly owing to the fact that Frank took an almost neurotic pride in what he had grown and that his customers were almost always women. Men, if they offered to buy cabbages, Brussels sprouts or giant carrots, were given a lecture about poor little Poland, and asked how their consciences would permit them to take vegetables grown specially for the hospital. It was just as well that no hospital had got to hear of Frank's vegetables.

The War had meant the Black Market, for Frank a source of excitement and finance, for her a matter never to be discussed. The eggs, butter, cheese, sides of bacon, car tyres, chocolates, silk stockings, which she had discovered under the stairs, had been pausing there while in transit; she had thrust them from her mind as nothing to do with her. If she continued to eat no butter and no more than her ration of eggs, to dye her legs with gravy browning and to remain unfamiliar with the sight of a plucked chicken, she was innocent. Whoever had filled and locked the cupboard under the stairs may have had his own reasons for doing so.

That was another of Frank's tones of voice, when customers had come to the house. Edith had gone upstairs, and listened through the floor. Usually the conversations seemed to be in code. Young women would giggle, ask Frank to examine the rash on their thighs caused by the use of dye instead of stockings, tell him their chances of marriage were slipping because they couldn't stop their knees from knocking in the cold. Edith's hearing, assisted by a glass tumbler pressed to the floorboards, became preternaturally sharp until she could hear, below the whole course of the conversation, the wafting of a ten-shilling note to and fro in the air, and this too seemed to her to be a part of the code.

It had all been a game, with Frank thriving on the risks and the profit. Sometimes she had thought that, even more than the money, the satisfied expressions on the faces of his customers as they left put him into such good humour. Of course nobody likes being at war, but Frank had never been so happy-go-lucky after it had ended. And in another tone, totally unlike the last, he had taken to repeating, 'Two more years would have done it. Two more years was all I needed.' He had never explained this remark, and she had not asked him to do so. It had been the end of an era, and its only vexatious week in the whole six years had been one in which he had gone to considerable trouble and expense to procure a forged medical card stating that he had TB, only to find that he was considered to be in a reserved occupation.

No bombs had fallen near the Sewage Works.

Hetty bounced on her bottom down the last three steps, and the sound woke Frank from a dream of inspecting the Guard of Honour. Edith was patting his arm.

'It's all right. It'll be Hetty. I expect she realized she was hungry after all.'

Frank adjusted his feet against Edith's shins, and tried to remember where he had got to in the inspection. In the process of remembering, he fell asleep again, and took up where he had left off. The lines of khaki uniforms stretched out in front of him as far as he could see, their buttons reflecting the weak morning light. The pink newly shaven chins were firm, and the clear eyes above them brimmed with trust and respect. Each man smelled of toothpaste and coal-tar soap. If they came back alive, it would be because they had been given the right example. He moved down the line, nodding his approval at their turn-out, setting his mouth in an expression of dignified pleasure; it would encourage them to know that they had given him pleasure. Then he came to a gap. Someone was missing. He looked at the men on each side of the gap for an explanation, but their heads remained in the eyes-front position, never wavering; they did not seem to know that there was anything wrong, or if they did, were not admitting it. He was about to move on, when a child's voice said, 'Present, sir,' and he looked down into the gap, and saw the top of a small boy's head.

She could find neither jam nor Marmite, but the bread and margarine compensated a little for the stinging sensation in her buttocks. The brick in its towelling cover had now lost all its heat, warming neither herself nor the bed, and the key-ring-torch-lock-defroster had separated itself into its component parts somewhere at the bottom of the stairs. If she closed her eyes and breathed with her ribs extended as Steven had been taught to do at Rose Bruford, eventually the world would disappear and reassemble itself for her tomorrow, when she would feel more capable of dealing with it. Nothing was worth adding lines to one's face for; even psychological stains come out in the wash. If they had offered her a small sherry and a piece of cake in the first place, none of this would have happened. Why had they not seemed pleased to see her?

Hands on diaphragm, shoulder-blades separated. Think of Mr Universe. Neck and throat relaxed, breathe in to the count of twenty and out to the count of thirty. Think a nice thought. Imagine you're sinking. Feet icy, knees still knocking. Hetty dismissed the world with a smile. She would not be put down, not be discouraged; it took more than a slice of stale bread and margarine to do that. The tear on her cheek was theatrical licence.

8

Baked Beans

Hetty had not slept. Her confidence in Steven's microchip alarm clock had been undermined by the fallibility of the key-ring-torch-lock-defroster. Hours had passed as she watched the seconds blinking at her with a regularity which had turned the Rose Bruford breathing exercises into hiccups. She found the clock's silence disconcerting. Perhaps if she had brought a normal alarm clock with a loud tick she might have drifted off.

Waiting for the postman, she fried herself two eggs, opened a small tin of baked beans, and brewed a pot of tea. With the eggs on a plate, the beans in the frying-pan and the tea brewing, she became convinced that if a morsel were to pass her lips, gluttony would overcome her and she would miss his arrival, so she went to stand on the doorstep in housecoat and travelling slippers. She was so tired. The start of a new day usually lifted her spirits, but if she allowed her eyes to close now, she would never wake up. She would insist on an hour under the eiderdown after lunch. Meanwhile there was the problem of controlling the front door, which seemed intent on pushing her out and locking itself behind her.

As the postman appeared at the corner of the street, Hetty heard Frank's dry cough at the top of the stairs. She left the door to look after itself, pulled the houscoat round her, and walked the length of the street.

'Anything for number Twenty-Six?' One of her slippers had submerged itself in a puddle.

'One for Cross. Catch your death.'

'I'll take it. I want to surprise them.' She had certainly surprised the postman. However, he handed the letter over, and Hetty stuffed it into her pocket. She did a three-point turn getting her foot out of the puddle, and only realized as she tossed back her head in a merry laugh that her teeth were still bleaching themselves in the bedroom.

She returned, and knocked at the door. Frank was downstairs by this time.

'What are you doing out there?'

'I couldn't find the milk. I thought I heard a crate rattling down the street.'

'It's all cartons now. Bottles have been phased out. Those beans are sticking to that pan.'

Hetty unstuck the beans, and placed them on the plate next to the cold fried eggs. While Frank was in the WC she tore up the letter without taking it from her pocket. She wondered whether she should eat the fragments before starting on breakfast. She knew from past experience that good-quality writing paper is difficult to flush away, and any attempt to burn them would be noticed. The fragments fitted neatly into the empty baked-bean tin, and once she had bent the lid back into position, it kept them there, safe and sound. She placed the tin with its new contents deep into the rubbish bag, and then washed her hands before sitting down to table.

'Are there any letters?'

'I don't know, Frank. Has he been yet? I'll replace these eggs for you when I go into town.'

'No need.'

'Oh, yes. Only fair. You weren't expecting me, after all. They're not the same, though, are they?'

'What aren't?' The *Daily Express* had most of Frank's attention.

'Eggs. Not like you used to get. Cages aren't the same as running round the farmyard, picking up anything and everything. I don't reckon you'd be inspired to give of your best, sat in a cage all day with a conveyor belt under your behind, just waiting for you to give birth so's it could be whisked away, to be washed, packed and stamped.'

Frank looked up from his paper. Hetty swallowed the dried-up yolk in her mouth. 'They don't stamp them nowadays.'

'No, they don't. The shells are too thin. Do you remember that song. "When, when, when, when, little hen, will you lay me an egg for my tea?"'

It seemed that Edith had been awake for most of the night, listening to strange noises. Hetty excused herself, dressed, and went for a walk towards Southend. She had destroyed the letter to Frank. Her only problem now was to explain convincingly to Bernard B. Shawcross that it had all been a ghastly mistake. That done, she could relax and enjoy herself. Nothing had yet been said about how

long she might stay. Surely they realized it wasn't worth
the fare unless she stayed a week or two? The longer she
remained, the less chance there was of Frank's son tracking her down. She had intended to write on the slow train
between London and Westcliff, but had deemed it safer to
wait in case Frank were to change his mind again. However, he had seemed determined enough last night. 'Not
another move. Best stop as we are before we live to regret
it.' That was clear enough.

As always Hetty's second-best handbag contained writing paper and envelopes. She sat on a bench facing the
sea, staring at the waves, then began to write. 'Dear Mr
Shawcross, Thank you so much for your fascinating letter,
but I do fear there has been a misunderstanding.' The
waves looked back at her, wild and angry. She shivered,
wishing she had packed more woollens. 'I can only assume
it occurred because I was anxious to renew my acquaintance with your dear mother, whom I knew as a young
woman.' No, that wasn't right. It was too formal, too
stilted; he would know that she was trying to cover
something up. She must try again, make the letter more
casual, get the damn thing written, and post it in
Southend, since obviously it mustn't arrive with a
Westcliff postmark.

Then it struck, what she had forgotten. Fool! Fool! She
hadn't instructed Robert not to tell anyone where she was,
not on any account to give away Frank's address.

The pad and envelopes were back inside her bag, and
she was up and walking, almost running, to find a telephone. She could see everything going wrong before her
eyes. Spray from the sea dampened her clothes. The wind

seemed to be holding her back. Bernard B. Shawcross would not have been held back. Flushed with the prospect of reunification with his long-lost dad, he would already have followed up his letter with a visit. He would have caught Robert sleeping by the fire, and that dozy twit would have blinked and scratched himself all over and invited the visitor to share a fry-up. Northern hospitality! She could picture the whole scene, and be sick right here on the promenade, she was so angry with herself. 'Oh, yes, she's nipped down to Westcliff to talk to an old friend about his son. How'd you like your bacon, crisp or soggy? She'll be livid she missed you, but poor old Frank's been living bigamously for fifty years, walked out on his wife and child, what did you say your name was? Now, that's a funny thing, that was Frank's name before he hopped it, calls himself Cross now, and thinks it's a joke. Here, sit yourself down, and get stuck into that.' She could spit; she could spit.

Hetty stood for a moment, holding the promenade rail. She had passed two telephone boxes, both vandalized, and too much rapid movement had given her a stitch.

The Penny Arcades to which she had once been addicted were now Tenpenny Arcades. Children still used them, but so did the unemployed, who stood in groups for the warmth. Hetty walked on. She passed Dreamland Cash Bingo, Sovereign Bingo, Royal Bingo, Regal Gifts and Live Jackpot Bingo. Still she could not find a telephone.

The unemployed watched her. She was going somewhere, and they were not. One saw them all the time at the seaside now, people who had given up trying to get

anywhere. Hotels catered for them. She had seen the
adverts, 'Winter by the sea. Special low rates for the
unemployed.' In summer they were less noticeable among
the few who were on real holidays or the odd day-trippers,
but in winter they seemed to be everywhere, just standing
and waiting. Again Hetty remembered the nineteen
thirties – the overcoats, the mufflers, the black eyes in the
white faces, forever watching what they could not share. It
made her nervous; she couldn't help it, nervous but a little
glad also, glad that she had missed it this time round, was
a Senior Citizen now, with a pension and a Gadabout
Card. She knew that this was a selfish attitude, but it was
the one she had.

At last a phone box with all its bits intact. She heard
Robert being asked to accept the charge, and waited for
what seemed several hours while he made his decision.
Robert disliked the telephone. She had seen him sometimes lift the receiver and replace it, just to show who was
boss. He grunted, and his grunt was taken by the operator
as acceptance.

'Has he been?'

'Who? Has who been?'

'Anyone. Has Bernard Shawcross been?'

'Nobody's been.'

'Has anyone telephoned?'

'Yes.'

'Who?'

'Only you. It's not after six y'know. We're not getting
the cheap rate. It's still morning.'

'Shut up, and listen. And this time, pay attention. It's a
matter of life and death.'

'Oh, aye? Let's be having it, then.'

She spelled out for him all the things he must not say, and then made him repeat them so that she could be sure he understood. If anyone asked, she was staying with a friend in Scotland. (If one was going to lie, one might as well make a proper job of it.) She would phone him again when she knew her real plans. Edith was confined to bed with nervous exhaustion, claiming she heard strange noises.

'What sort of noises?'

'Me falling downstairs.'

'Good job you're there, then. You can look after her.'

Hetty walked slowly back to the house to calm herself, and to enjoy fully the relief and self-congratulation of having spotted a possible disaster and avoided it. A bald-headed man with a cigarette dangling from his mouth moved across the beach carrying a metal-detector. There were yet more people in overcoats in the doorways of Space City, The Rumpy Bar, Sunspots and The Ocean Fun Palace. She and Robert had been lucky. The pension was just enough, and Frank and Edith wouldn't forget her entirely, even if Frank's son did turn up; they'd see her right. Perhaps it would be best if she didn't write to Bernard B. Shawcross straight away, but waited to see how things went; Frank had been known to change his mind. His wishes were what mattered. Old friends ought to stick together in emergencies.

'You were up and out early.' Edith finished rubbing germicidal cream between her fingers, and began to re-place the grubby cotton mittens.

'Do you ever wash those?'

'How can I, when I can't touch water?'

'I'll do them. They'd dry if we could have a decent fire.'

'I'd have come with you if you'd waited.'

'I walked into Southend.'

'All that way?'

'Did some shopping for your pantry. These claim to be free-range, but I wouldn't bet money on it.' Hetty placed the carton of six eggs on the table.

'I hope you didn't bother about the beans.'

'What beans?'

'Baked in tomato sauce. There's no need to buy your own food, you know. We can run to the odd tin of beans now and then. Meals-on-Wheels, though, have to be ordered; they only bring so many round. I thought you could have some soup. Frank's out, so we've to pretend he's upstairs when the woman arrives, and keep his warm for him.'

'I forgot about the beans.'

'Just happened to notice the empty tin. I hope you slept all right.'

'Like a brick.' Hetty pulled the cotton mittens over her own hands in order to wash them.

'Don't do that. You'll catch it.'

'If a skin rash was going to strike me down, it wouldn't have waited until now. Are you really upset about Frank's son?'

'Who told you that?'

'Well, it wouldn't have been the postman.'

'No. Specially as he didn't come today. Frank, was it? You ought to know by now that if he's upset he always makes out it's me.'

'If he's that devious, how am I going to know whether he really wants to see his son or not? Start looking. No, don't. On, off, stop, go; you don't know where you are with him.'

'Looks like he's going to have to now, doesn't it?'

'Saying one thing and meaning another! There's – What?' Hetty stopped rubbing powder into the mittens. 'How d'you mean. "He's going to have to"? And where is he anyway?'

'At the pub. I'm sure you know what that indicates.'

'He fancied a drink?'

'That pub hardly sees him from one year's end to the next, and certainly not at ten past twelve on a Tuesday.'

'Was it something I said?'

'He left here like that tornado thing that used to clean floors on the television.' Edith took a pair of cake-tongs from the cutlery drawer, and lifted a stained piece of writing paper from the top shelf of the larder. Sellotape had been used to stick the jigsaw of pieces together. Laid on the kitchen table it looked like a prop from an over-meticulous production of *Treasure Island*. 'He often checks through the rubbish bag to see what I've spent my money on. Once I bought a box of Black Magic. We weren't speaking at the time, so I ate them all myself.' Soapy water ran down Hetty's arms, and dripped from her elbow on to the table beside the scrap of incriminating evidence. Edith said, 'He shook the bean tin and it rattled. You met Bernie's sister-in-law. She knows that Frank's still alive, and she knows where you live. We couldn't read this bit here because of the tomato sauce.'

'It's about sitting on the lap of a Pakistani.'

'Why?'

'I nearly missed my stop.'

'I don't see the significance. What's this word here?'

'Strudel.'

'What's that got to do with Frank?'

'Nothing. Not everything in this world is to do with Frank. It's what the woman gave me for tea. Apple strudel.'

'Are they very rich, then?'

'No, just showy. I didn't take to her.'

Hetty felt numb. All that effort to save Frank from his own personality defects, the anger, the outrage, the self-absorbed paranoia! She could have taken the scraps of paper out with her, and thrown them into the sea. How could any sane person have imagined Frank bent double with his nose sniffing the inside of a black polythene rubbish bag, rattling tins to see if any beans had been left inside?

She held her hands under cold running water to rinse the mittens. For a while neither woman spoke. Hetty removed the mittens, squeezed them, and hung them to dry by the tea-towels. Then Edith said, 'I wouldn't be at all surprised if he doesn't put a very large bet on today. He's terrified of coming face to face with his son after all this time. If you'd taken the time to think instead of rushing about all over Yorkshire, if you'd put yourself in his shoes, you'd have realised what it might be like to meet a stranger, knowing him to be your own flesh and blood whom you'd abandoned. And now on top of that, our only own friend has lied to us, interfered with Her Majesty's Royal Mail, and let us down.'

Hetty dried her hands. 'I'd better go. I'll write to him, and try to explain.'

'Yes, I expect you will. I'm the one who has to stay. If he loses on Friendly Face in the three o'clock at Haydock, it'll set us back for quite a few weeks. We can't afford that kind of aggravation at our age.'

'What if I went and talked to him?'

'He hates seeing women in pubs.'

Hetty's sense of the unfairness of it all turned to rage, and burst out. 'Don't you stand there, Edith Merryman, with moral blackmail oozing out of your ears!' The use of Edith's maiden name was saved for very special occasions. 'If Frank's put a large bet on Friendly Face or any other face in the three o'clock because of me, I might have done him a good turn, because he never bloody loses; he should be offering me a share instead of stomping off to sulk in pubs. I've written to this son of his, telling him it's all a mistake, and I don't know where Frank lives. How could I know Frank was going to blow hot one minute and cold the next? He's always expected everyone to dance attendance on him, him and his bloody precious nest-egg, holding it over one's head like a bloody great avalanche!'

'Hetty!'

'He's the bigamist, he's the child-deserter, he's the one who's cheating the government and even the sodding Meals-on-Wheels, and I'm the one who gets it in the neck.' She paused for breath. 'Is there any Dubonnet in this house?' Edith shook her head. 'And that guest-bedroom of yours is like a deep-freeze. You're lucky to have anyone at all as a friend, let alone someone who runs about all over the place, and worries herself sick when

things go not quite as planned. I was doing very well with
my discreet enquiry until I happened to knock at the
wrong door and that over-made-up sister-in-law began
jangling her bangles at me. Are you sure you've not even
some cooking sherry? I've had a shock.'

'What would I want with cooking sherry?'

'To sip with bread and Marmite perhaps. And that's
another thing, Edith; you don't have to live as if it was
nineteen thirty all over again. You want putting in a bag,
and shaking up, and always have done. What are you
going to do with your last few years, nurse your dermatitis
and leave Frank love messages in the rubbish bag? What
happened to the gin-and-lime Edith? the Craven-A
Edith? the woman with purple nail-varnish? What
happened to "I'm accepting no more attention; it's all got
to go back"? If my mother could see how you've wasted
yourself after all she did for you, she'd come back and kill
off every plant in this house.'

This was just one of Hetty's sayings. There were no
plants. None had survived the draughts. Edith considered
in silence what had been said, and then replied, 'If only
you'd waited for me to go for a walk with you, Frank
might not have bothered with the rubbish today. Sometimes when I leave the house he settles down straightaway
to counting his money and doing sums about Yankees and
Trebles.'

'You've a little money of your own, don't you?'

'A little.'

'Is it around?'

'What for?'

'To buy us lunch. I'm starving.'

'Meals-on-Wheels will be here any minute.'

'And you know what you can do with it. I'm not coming all this way to the seaside and travelling straight back, on two fried eggs, five baked beans and a can of soup. Get your coat on. We can go to the pub he doesn't like, the one where they charge extra for sitting down. I'll have scampi in the basket and a glass of wine.'

'It's not a fortune I've got, you know. I don't think we should be rash just because you're feeling guilty.'

'Leave me to do the thinking, Edith. It takes equipment.'

'What about Frank's lunch? They won't leave it if there's nobody here.'

9

A Special Favour

He had drunk four pints of beer and two scotches, been to
the toilet three times, and eaten a pork pie which had
tasted of caramel custard. His inside breast pocket contained £500, which he had taken from the paisley-
patterned cushion on the chair by the kitchen door.

After the heat and noise of the Saloon Bar, the sea
breeze seemed sharper and more salty than usual. His
progress from the Star and Shield towards the Betting
Shop was sideways, like a crab performing the veleta. One
hand, like that of the Emperor Napoleon, remained inside
his jacket holding the money, while the other waved at the
traffic to give them fair warning he was crossing.

He was in motion; he could and did move, unlike More
Life Myra, who had, it seemed, become No Life Myra in
1983. The fingers of his waving hand clutched the damp
Westcliff air, and he heard her voice saying 'No.' It had
always been 'No.' Tiny breasts the size of oranges, which
you wouldn't get your hands on for love nor money, not
that he had ever offered her money, or had then much to

offer. He took a firmer grip on the £500. Nipples which jumped back into place, always at a thirty-three-degree angle pointing upwards. Toes shiny red with chilblains, their nails clipped short, hardly bigger than a baby's. He had eaten those toes in the early days, forced them into his mouth, and pretended to bite them off. Having one's own teeth had opened so many doors which were now slammed shut.

So here he was. The wind hadn't blown him away. He was still crossing roads without a white stick, still eating solid foods in the form of pork pies, and suffering for it. Already he'd had two more years of life than she. 'Save it up for Christmas', she had told him. Well, he'd gone ahead and opened his presents without her.

His addiction to the free Biros supplied by the Betting Shop had been noted, and it had become the practice of the regular staff to tidy away as many as they could as soon as he stepped through the door.

'Going broke?'

'No, sir, not yet.'

'What are we to write with?'

'Here, sir! Have this.'

'It's a pencil.'

'Yes, sir. I sharpened it for you myself.'

'Never had any luck with black lead, son. That's why I left school early. Where's all those little blue dinky what-sits?' A Biro was placed before him. 'What's the going like at Haydock?'

'Firm to good, sir.'

'What price Friendly Face in the three o'clock?'

'Sixes.'

'Get me the manager, will you?' The young assistant slid his bottom off the high chair, and smirked his way into the back room, while Frank leaned his back against the counter and tried to bring the other punters into focus.

'Yes, sir? What can I do for you? Everything all right?'

'Could be better. This Friendly Face of yours. Three o'clock, Haydock. What can you do for a large bet?'

'The price is six to one, sir.'

'That's for your tenpenny punters, for your Yankees and your Trebles. I need a bit more encouragement than that. Perhaps you ought to phone Head Office to cover yourself.'

'How large a bet, sir?'

'Five hundred.'

'On the nose?'

'Most certainly.'

'What sort of price were you hoping for?'

'Nines.'

'They'd laugh me right out of court.'

'Then you'd have made someone happy. Me, I'm as miserable as sin meself, with these sixes of yours. Where's the sportsmanship in sixes for a horse that's never been better than third, and hasn't been taken to the gate for a look-see all season?'

Eventually the manager returned, and Frank accepted eights as a special favour to Messrs William Hill and Co. When his shaking hand had written the slip, the money been counted, paid over and counted again, Frank pressed himself into a corner near the counter but facing the door. From here he could see the sky and the roof-tops of Westcliff above the lower windows of frosted glass.

She had taken to sitting closer and closer to the fire with her legs apart, shutting him out, and mottling the insides of her thighs to look like rusty chicken wire. No hand was permitted to touch her; even her toes were out of bounds by then. 'No' to licking and stroking, 'No' to practising geometry with her nipples, 'No' to everything. It was as if the baby had used up all the life inside her, had either eaten it or brought it out with him among the afterbirth. She had said, 'I feel hollow,' and for three years he had saved it till Christmas, had waited while she shuffled from bar to table, from table to the threadbare strip of carpet beside her father, the publican. Even fifty years later, Frank still didn't know what had gone wrong. 'I feel hollow' – he could have filled a hollow if he'd been allowed.

He could not see his son now, could not and would not; it was as simple as that. Suppose the boy's cheeks flushed easily, or his nose turned up at the end and his eyes looked like polished conkers. Suppose Frank found himself longing for the boy to take his socks off, kept asking him about chilblains for want of anything better to use as conversation. Suppose he found himself pulling the boy away from the fire by his hair, and screaming at him to get some reaction.

After the lunch, at which Hetty had grown progressively tipsier, and talked of making something of herself before it was too late, Edith went alone to the Public Library to choose a book in the hope of calming her nerves. At one point during the lunch it had come to her that Hetty might be on the verge of a nervous breakdown; her speech had come rattling out so, with one thought contradicting another, and none of them making very much sense. She was going to start her own Detective Agency, and call it 'Lost and Found'. She would travel the whole country, taking on the Salvation Army at its own game, and beat them by tracking down people who were in hiding. She would use disguise; she would have to invest in some wigs and a variety of expensive outfits. A little capital was what she needed, not much, perhaps a sleeping partner with a little money who could put her down as a tax loss. The publicity would be enormous. She would be photographed in silhouette with a cigarette-holder, and wearing a Christine Keeler wig. British Telecom would have to make her ex-directory, and she would take an office somewhere inconspicuous, like Huddersfield or Barnsley.

It had all been too much for Edith. The ham-and-tomato pizza had frozen on her lips, and the price of the house wine had set her dermatitis itching. She required a nice light read with nobody dying and no social comment in order to regain her equilibrium. The quietness of the Branch Library, with its redundant men in shabby raincoats and the women either waiting for or recovering from the menopause, was sanctuary to her. The quiet coughing and occasional apologetic whispers after Hetty's over-excited jarring voice, piling fantasy on fantasy and expecting her to follow every twist and turn, came like a Chopin prelude after a mistaken burst of Radio One.

She was twelve pounds and fifty-two pence the poorer and still hungry, but it would be a long time before Hetty showed her face again. She had been told to give them plenty of notice next time, warned that Frank's health

couldn't put up with any more surprises. There were to be
no more flying vists, no unexpected arrivals after supper,
no impersonations of Mata Hari with the postman. Frank
and Edith had already used up their three score years and
ten, and were now living on borrowed time. One more
coded message hidden in a baked-bean tin, and the game
would be up. Edith had made her point clearly, even
though Hetty had pretended to dismiss it, throwing her
head back, flushed with three glasses of house wine,
pointing to the sea, and shouting, 'Look at all those forty-
shilling permanent waves, our Edith. It's not a bad life,
and if you don't pick it, it might get better.' Thereafter
Edith had walked Hetty firmly to the station and seen her,
tearful, safely on to the train. She had waited on the
platform until the train actually began to move, and then
headed for the Library.

The station had reminded her of summer, of holidaymakers with noisy children, of all the different summer
smells, of hamburgers, suntan oil, rock, shellfish, wet
bathing clothes, boarding-house breakfasts wafted
through open windows. How foolish that once she had
told herself that she would never use up air and take up
space after the age of fifty! Now she would fight with fists
and elbows flying for both. The sun might turn her skin
olive or green or khaki or even black for all she cared, just
as long as it brought with it those smells. Yet, even as she
stood measuring with a critical eye the amount of dust on
a shelf marked 'Modern Classics', she knew well enough
that this year, next year, some year in the not-too-distant
future, she would have to give up the fight, and discover
whether her mother had been right about the distribution

of punishment and reward in the hereafter. Well, she would take what came only provided that she was not reunited with her only child, still in the state in which she had last seen it, mouth stretched in a perpetual scream, only its face clean where she had wiped it, the rest of its body still stained with her blood and body-fluids. Edith shuddered. The vision was unlikely. An innocent child would already be in Abraham's bosom, where there would hardly be room for her to join it. It was Frank who had this obsession about being reunited with past mistakes. Sanity had always been her main priority. Perhaps she should choose a novel she had already read. Then she would know she was safe.

She reached home to find that the Meals-on-Wheels lady had slipped a note under the door, to say that she was sorry they had missed the liver and bacon followed by semolina, since it had been spoken of highly, and that Thursday was to be ravioli in soya sauce, and she hoped to see them then. Edith spread a slice of bread with loganberry jam from the Women's Institute, and sat by an unmade fire to wait for Frank.

The manager had watched Frank pressing himself further and further into the corner, had noticed the tightly closed eyes which seemed to be watering under the lids, and had sent the young assistant to shake him awake and present him with his winnings. Someone was demanding champagne, and hands of varying strengths and colours were gripping and grabbing, mock-punching and waving. Friendly Face had been placed first after a photograph and a stewards' enquiry, and Frank had missed the whole race, had not heard one word of the commentary.

With four thousand five hundred pounds, less tax, and six blue Biros stuffed into his pocket, he edged sideways towards and through the door of the Betting Shop. Usually his mind would be adding the winnings to what was in the cushions at home, but it lacked the energy, lacked the concentration, lacked even the indignation he usually felt towards the betting tax. His mind was otherwise occupied, just as it had been while the race was being run and throughout the excitement of the photograph and the stewards' enquiry. What his mind had been doing and still did was to replay him a series of pictures of Hetty, stuffing egg yolk and baked beans into her mouth, bouncing downstairs on her backside and rushing into the arms of the postman, vaulting the garden gate in housecoat and slippers. His mind told him that things happened behind its back, and must not, adding for good measure that pork pies which tasted of caramel custard should be avoided. Frank raised his arm to show the traffic what he intended, and imagined that he was climbing up rusty chicken wire in order to expose himself to children in the park.

That boy could not be seen; he could not see that boy. Not now. Not when he felt so empty inside.

10
Cheesecake

'We thought we might do a spread on you this coming Wednesday.'

'That'll be nice.'

'Have you had many replies to your advert?'

'Not strictly speaking, no.'

'Any at all?'

'There was one letter from a gentleman, but he must have got the wrong end of the stick. Wanted a photo of me in leather trousers, practising ju-jitsu. He'd have got that from the television, I expect.'

'Perhaps the Profile will help.'

'Do have another piece of cheesecake.'

'Would you be prepared to go abroad if the job required it?'

'That would depend. I mean, some countries aren't very friendly, are they, hijacking and kidnapping people? You only have to turn your back, and there's a war broke out. I might send my son, Steven. You did a piece about him when he played on the radio once.'

'What do you expect the most common request for your services will be?'

'I hadn't thought about it. I hope there'll be a bit of variety. I won't do divorces, spying on husbands and wives. I suppose it'll be people who've run away from home, children mainly. I find I get on very well with youngsters; they respond to me. My approach will be unique, and since I don't look like a teacher or a police-man, I might have more success than they would. I've got the time to spend, you see. I'm not going into it for the money; I've always considered public service important. Baking cakes for the WI and collecting for lifeboats is all very well, but it doesn't satisfy the more imaginative, does it?'

'What will you wear when you're on the job?'

'Nothing special, not to draw attention, as long as it's comfortable. That's the joy of it. I said to my husband, "I have a wardrobe full of undistinguished frocks that need wearing out." Nobody will look twice at me; I shall be well away. It's a pity you didn't bring a cameraman.'

'Photographer. There's a lot of weddings this week. I thought you might have some favourite photo of your own.'

The Profile appeared with the heading, 'No Black Leather for Supergran Sleuth', and the photograph chosen from those Hetty had supplied was one Robert had taken on the beach at Southend while Hetty was paddling. It was a little out of focus, and Hetty's smile was marred by her having left her teeth in her second-best handbag for safety.

In the Sub-Post Office, one of Hetty's neighbours said, 'There's been a man watching your house. Haven't gone and got yourself in trouble already, have you?' Hetty smiled what she hoped would be her long-suffering smile, but sensed that it came over more as one of the brave variety. There was no need to ask what the man looked like, since a full description was bound to be immediately forthcoming, from the turned-up nose to the style and colour of the man's shoes. Television again, Hetty thought. Since Crimewatch, everyone was shopping their nearest and dearest.

'Did he have a tic or a stammer?'

'I don't speak to strange men. He just keeps walking up and down. Perhaps he wants you to find him a wife.'

There were several immediate applications for this role from the group waiting to exchange their sixpence-off coupons for spray-on window cleaner. This was not surprising, with all the sticky marks their noses made, pressing against the glass. Hetty had expected to get her leg pulled, and had. Various kind people had said, 'Saw your knees in the *Chronicle*,' or shouted across the road, 'Good to see the *Chronicle* with a Page Three Girl at last.'

It crossed her mind to take a bus back to the centre of town. That way she could do some thinking and postpone meeting the man with the belted lovat-green gabardine raincoat and brown Hush Puppies, for she had known at once who he would be. But her curiosity to see what, if anything, of Frank had been reproduced in his son was too strong. Instead she took the longer route home, past the grey pebble-dashed council houses, past the greengrocer who was going out of business and whose wife had run off

with the teenager they had taken on as part of the Youth
Opportunities Scheme to drive their van. She had pretended not to watch the greengrocer silently weeping over
the cauliflowers, and had said nothing when he had
short-changed her by two pence.

She had rehearsed her speech ready for Frank's son
many times. In fact, many different speeches had been
memorized, and were now all forgotten. She must rely on
instinct. Hetty's instinct seldom let her down.

'Are you Mrs Hetty Wainthropp?'

'As I live and breathe.'

'I'm Bernard Shawcross.'

'How do you do?'

'May I come in?'

'Well, I'm not bringing your tea out here for the whole
street to share.'

In situations which required the most delicacy Hetty
invariably discovered that her Lancashire accent became
broader. She recognized this to be a kind of defence. It
was her way of telling those with whom she was attempting to be delicate that she was an ordinary person and
allowances would have to be made.

'So you're little Bernie?'

The man was fifty-three years old, greying at the
temples, with the over-ruddy complexion of someone who
has high blood pressure. His features were neither like nor
unlike Frank's; there was not enough difference for anyone to protest, 'This man is an imposter.' His eyes were
the colour of Frank's, and they were small, but the twinkle
was missing. Dullness was the order of this man's day;
Hetty tried to multiply three hundred and sixty-five by

fifty-three. The clothes, the hair, the skin, all had a matt finish, and although the lovat-green of his belted raincoat was inappropriate to the high colour of his cheeks, all else spoke of conformity and acquiescence. The spark which Frank had once possessed, and which still flickered even now on occasions, was absent.

'Where's my father?' The man blew his nose, turning away politely to do so. That nose was not from Frank.

'That I can't tell you. I've made a promise.'

'He doesn't want to see me? But I thought . . .'

'He wanted to know you were alive and well. That's where I came in. I wasn't supposed to let you know.'

'Why not?'

'It's a difficult decision for him after fifty years. You know he's over eighty?'

'Yes, he must be.'

'I think he needs to get used to the idea. He's not ready yet. Things happened a lot faster than we thought.'

'It's like being rejected twice over.'

'Try not to think about it like that. Tell me about your wife and family.'

'We're separated. She has a little trouble with reality – can't accept too much of it. We've the one boy; he's with her. Just left school. Depressing time all round really.'

Hetty watched the man's eyes. Certainly they were the eyes of a man disappointed by his wife's lack of appetite for reality. Were they also the eyes of a man who had spent fifty years missing his father?

'What's he like?'

'Who? Frank?'

The man nodded, forcing her to consider the question.

Loyalty was important to Hetty, but Frank's recent behaviour, his selfishness and bullying had not inspired it.
His hands inside her blouse all those years ago had done
some damage too; she had fainted away right in front of
her own doctor a few years later, and he had only been
feeling her breasts for lumps. She said, 'He's an old man.
What can one say about old men?' She paused to sip her
tea, watching Bernard fold and refold his handkerchief.
'He enjoys his life on the whole. Likes his own way, but
don't we all, if we can get it?'

The man nodded. It was the hesitant nod of someone
who wouldn't recognize his own way if it fell on him from
a tall building. 'I've had a picture of him in my mind all
these years. Will you tell me if it's right?'

Now it was Hetty's turn to nod hesitantly, wondering
how far both loyalty and honesty might be stretched. The
man said, 'And you must remember that I shall be able to
check your answer, for I do intend to meet him one day.'
It was a tiny flicker of a spark, the minutest smouldering
chip off the old block, instantly snuffed the moment he
added, 'No offence, of course.'

Hetty refilled her teacup. The man's tea was untouched,
and now cold.

'My picture always includes women, never just one, and
they're all . . . you know . . . well proportioned. Dad's
wearing a tweed cap and a white silk muffler. He has a full
healthy-looking moustache, and he's always sitting in a
car, a sporty sort of car, white with no roof. He looks
younger than he would now, of course, but it's summer,
and the women are all . . .'

'What's he doing in a muffler if it's summer? Is he

perspiring a lot? He must be in all that heat. You've a high colour yourself. Do you suffer from blood pressure?'

The man whose wife could not bear too much reality shook his head, dismissing from his mind's eye the white sports car screeching round hairpin bends, while the legs of the well-proportioned models spilled enticingly over the sides and their arms waved towards the cerulean sea. The wind on the bends had blown back the skirts of the models right up to the tops of their thighs, and not all of them were wearing anything underneath. When the car had quite disappeared, he said, 'Do you think if I wrote to him, sent him a photo of myself and one of his grandson, he might change his mind?'

'I really couldn't say. But if you sent your letter care of me, I'd have to pass it on, wouldn't I, otherwise I'd be interfering with Her Majesty's Royal Mail?'

'This is the boy. He's older now.' He proffered a school photograph, and Hetty held it at arm's length to adjust the focus. She had a feeling that she had seen the face before, but pubescent boys were all much of a muchness when placed against a backing flat of HMS *Pinafore*, and photographed full face.

'Isn't it funny the way they all get those spots around their mouths? Is it too many chips, do you think? I wouldn't mention the silk muffler or the well-proportioned women in your letter. He's never driven a car to my knowledge, and the lady he lives with is a little on the old-fashioned side. Try not to sound too complaining, or indicate that you blame him in any way. It's my view that old men are a little like Boy Scouts; they don't like being found out. Oh, and he's not had any more

children; you're his only one as far as I know, which I
think I may say with confidence, though I didn't live in his
pocket all the fifty years you've been parted. Thank God.'
She laughed heartily. The man managed half a smile. 'He
does tend to wear oldish clothes, second-hand usually, a
cap and muffler like you said, except that the muffler's
wool and has more darns than a bishop banging nails in.
He likes a little flutter on the horses, and he . . . ' Hetty
stopped herself, feeling that the addition of the words
'usually wins' might arouse expectations, ' . . . and he
takes a lot of exercise. Oh, and another thing, though I
don't suppose you would but just in case, don't make any
jokes about Sewage Farms in your letters; he used to
manage one. I'm telling you all this because I can't touch
the letter once you've sealed it, and we want you to make
a good impression, don't we?'

'You don't have a photo of him, I suppose?'

'No, he won't allow himself to be photographed. Says
it's against his religion.'

'What religion is that?'

'None, as far as I know. I think it's just his joke.'

When the man had gone, she felt much better, as
though a heavy weight had been lifted from her chest.
Now she had no more secrets, and Frank could do what he
liked when his son's letter arrived. She would forward it as
she had promised, and then wash her hands; it was time
she concentrated on her new career. If only she hadn't
given the *Chronicle* that snap of herself with her skirts
hoisted! No one wants to employ a toothless detective
with flabby thighs. Perhaps if she went on a crash diet
they'd print another one.

* * *

A letter was waiting for Bernard B. Shawcross when he returned to his bedsitter on the outskirts of Halifax. It was from his estranged wife, and informed him that their son had not been home for a week. The boy, who had been induced to remain at school for an extra year in the hope of acquiring at least one O Level (having failed to acquire any at all the previous summer), had endured two terms, left in an orderly manner by the school gates on the final day of the second after participating in the end-of-term celebrations, and had not been seen since. The police had been informed but seemed to be pessimistic about finding him. Their view was that he would either return of his own free will, or else he wouldn't. The letter ended with Doreen Shawcross's returning to her obsession with unreality by asking her husband whether he had sufficient funds to hire a private detective.

11

Clouds Over Germany

Dear Frank and Edith,

Events have moved ahead since I was last with you. Frank's son came to visit me, as I expected he might. He seems a nice steady sort of chap and was most disappointed that I was unable to give him Frank's address. He intends to send me a letter for Frank which I will forward to you. But since he is unlikely to give you an unbiased pen portrate of himself, I will do the honours. He looks a little like Frank might look if he had a turned up nose and very red cheeks. (Blood pressure would be my guess.) Not the most cheerful man I've ever met, but first impressions can mislead, so I'll hold my peace.

Since his visit, which was Tuesday, he has telephoned to tell me his 16 year old son Geoffrey has run away from home. (Geoffrey is of course Frank's only grandson) Bernard and his Wife Doreen are seperated, and the boy had been living with her. The police have been their usual unhelpful selves, merely stating that hundreds of youngsters leave home every week and just disapeare. Bernard has to work and Doreen is unwell with her nerves, so I've offered to try and find the boy. London seems the obvious place to start looking, I doubt if anyone runs away to Middlesbourgh. I'll send you a postcard from Trafalgar Sq.

                    Wish me luck.
                Love
                    Hetty
    P.S. One 16 year old son and a seperated Wife. No sharabangs of toddlers to make jellys for. Think about it, Grandfather.

Having read the letter aloud, Frank handed it to Edith as usual. She waited for him to stand and walk to the door where his cap, muffler and overcoat were hanging, but instead he remained at the table, looking out of the window, watching the blue tits keeping each other from the string to which last Sunday's bacon rind had been attached. She glanced down briefly at Hetty's handwriting, at her use of the large 'W' for 'wife', the letter curling ornately as if wives were the most exciting things in the world. She had no wish to read what he had already read aloud to her. Why did he insist on dragging her into his guilt? These were his son, his grandson; this was his past. She said, 'Don't miss your walk.' If he didn't get out, he would be in a sour mood all day.

Frank remained where he was, as if he hadn't heard. His reverie disturbed her. It was morning, with a robin tapping on the window asking for breadcrumbs, yet his body had slumped, the muscles in his face sagged as if it were one of those early afternoons when nothing moved. She must bring him out of this by conversation. 'It's all excitement, then?' Only his eyelids moved, and only to droop. Let him not close his eyes so early in the day. 'Why would he have blood pressure? You've never been bothered with that.' She waited, saw his mouth begin to move; he was about to speak. Let it be a complaint of some sort, and they would be back to normal. One day she would persuade the robin to take cheese from between her lips. A woman had done it on television.

'His son's run away.'

'That might have given him a shock, but it wouldn't raise his blood pressure, not unless it was already high.'

'History repeating itself.'

'Hardly. To repeat itself, he'd have had to run away from his son. Too late now! The son's gone. The letter doesn't tell us whether he left the wife or the wife left him.'

'What a family!'

'I wasn't going to mention it first, since some of it is flesh and blood of yours, but they do seem to be accident-prone when it comes to sticking together. No doubt the boy'll wander back when he's spent all his money. One of the evacuees did that, do you remember? Started off in the wrong direction with a slice of fruit cake and one of your road-maps. Had to be brought back from somewhere near Bedford. Then there was the little one with his knock knees and his bed-wetting. Hid in the wood above Leigh Bank all afternoon, said he'd rather live on berries and mushrooms than starve on what we gave him; I'm sure he had his rations; I went short myself before I'd let them go hungry; they were food-obsessed, those boys. You carried him home over your shoulder, and he was sick from eating raw hips, all down the back of your waistcoat.' Frank stood up. Good! 'Your grandson won't find anything for nothing in London, and might get more than he bargains for.'

Frank was in definite movement towards his cap and overcoat. 'I just thought for once we could sit here and discuss it. Fat chance of that.'

'Nothing to discuss, is there? When he writes his letter, you'll write one back. Tell him he can come down and see you, just so long as he doesn't expect the Ritz. I haven't the right cooker to lay on five-course meals non-stop.'

He had gone. Their routine had been recovered. Watching him sitting there, so unusually torpid, closed in on himself, eyelids drooping as if to shut her out, she had felt suddenly lonely and the fear of being alone. Nothing must change. Her mittens needed washing again. The brain was a tormentingly complex instrument; she wished she could switch it off. Hetty and her damn letters! Fathers and sons, runaways, deserted wives, and Hetty's neat little pen curling her 'W' as if she were composing an heraldic scroll. Even the 'f' in 'Grandfather' looked like someone with arms outstretched, signalling to an aeroplane.

She turned the tap off. Water covered the plates, and particles of fat floated from them in the direction of the overflow outlet. Some day there would be a blockage. Her own father had been a prodigious writer of letters. He had written from Flanders Field, mainly on the backs of postcards, 'silk cards' he had called them, since they had been embroidered with brightly coloured silks. 'I take pleasure in riting these few lines to my dear daughter Edith.' They were nearly always the same few lines, which was odd, since it seemed to be only the word 'writing' itself which he had difficulty in spelling. 'I'm sending you a silk card my Dear Daughter Edith. Hope it will find you and mother in the very best of health. Dear Daughter, give your mother a kiss from me, your loving father.' The silk cards had been of the same size as ordinary postcards, but had a delicate fabric glued to them, into which silk had been threaded to form such words as 'Mother', 'Dearest Wife', 'A Souvenir from Belgium' or 'Clouds Over Germany', or sometimes the pictures of flowers such as pansies, roses, thistles or fleurs-de-lis, or sometimes crosses or regimental badges, all in neat embroidery. Some cards had contained pockets into which smaller cards had been placed. Always there had been the same messages, repeated on card after card, 'I miss you both, love and kisses, your loving husband, Harold.' More had been said in coloured silks or scribbled in pencil than had ever been pronounced face to face.

The silk cards had lined the mantel, then were moved to the glass-fronted cabinet, to be shown to the very few who visited. 'This is my father.' 'This is my husband.' The door of the cabinet would be unlocked, and a sepia photograph removed of a man posing with delicate hand on hip. It was not a studio photograph, but had been taken in the field; the khaki tunic was shapeless, the khaki trousers crumpled and creased, and the puttees skew-whiff. Edith remembered a wispy moustache, and frightened eyes staring from beneath a cap with a badge. What colour had those eyes been before they became forever sepia?

She must have been eight or nine when the news came that the man in the photograph was dead, the homesick lonely soldier with nothing to say. There had also been a pin-cushion in the cabinet; it was in the shape of a heart, and the glass-headed pins were stuck through beads, fake pearls and small buttons, which surrounded four brooches containing enamelled portraits of famous men, Sir G. White, Sir R. Buller, Lord Roberts and Col. Baden-Powell.

Her mother's name had been Nellie. He had used it in the addresses of his postcards, 'Mrs Nellie Merryman', but in the text it had usually been 'dear wife'. Later, when Edith had reached the age of twenty, she had reread all the silk postcards, and tried to imagine Harold and Nellie making love, had tried to visualize them together, holding hands, being happy. Neighbours had told her that Harold Merryman had been a difficult man, strong-willed and domineering, but the cards contained nothing of that; they were cries for help, pleas for reassurance and love from a shall child who longed to be collected and brought back home. 'God bless you both, my dears. We are still here, but expecting to go onto another front. I can't say where we are going. Please do not worry. I love you both very much.' That was her father at his most informative.

She had often kissed her mother, since her father's written wish had been that she should do so, and her mother had endured her kisses. Later when that same mother had stood with folded arms by the door, Edith herself had asked for reassurance and for help, but the woman whose glass-fronted cabinet still contained all that

98

was left of her husband had only said, 'Thank God your father didn't survive the war to return home to this spectacle.' With the fire neither in nor out, and her child dying on the hearth-rug, Edith had called instead to the memory of her own father, had seen his pencil poised over a silk card on which her imagination now embroidered birds, ribbons, a stork carrying a baby and the word 'Welcome', and had written for him the words she needed, 'My dearest daughter Edith, I take pleasure to rite and congratulate you on the birth of my first grandchild. Please kiss him for me. I hope this silk card finds you both well. Your loving father.'

And then the shell burst open his bowels, and her child died.

12
Lead Soldiers

Bernard Shawcross studied his face in the mirror. That woman had been right; his cheeks were red. His job was to blame. Rushing in and out of the deep-freeze all day was bound to have an effect on one's complexion. Butchers always had red faces, which was not surprising, considering some of the tricks they got up to. However, Bernard was not a butcher, nor had his budget allowed him to eat meat over the last two years, or drink wine of either colour. Therefore it had to be the sudden changes of temperature – huddled over the paraffin stove in his office one moment, wrestling with frozen sides of beef the next.

He was a store-keeper, who counted sheep and the halves of sheep in his waking hours, pigs and the halves of pigs, beeves, ice-sculptures of red and white filled with crystallized blood waiting for the next power-cut and its chance to escape. A whole Cold Room full of frozen chickens, hundreds of neatly folded wings and drumsticks lining the walls from floor to ceiling! There were enough wishbones to build a scale model of the *Ark Royal*, and still all his luck was bad.

He wore wellington boots and thermal socks, a lethal combination for perspiring feet. He wore a white coat like a surgeon, but his had the name of his employers, Lean Price Wholesale Butchery, stamped on it. He wore a hat shaped like a woman's hairnet to keep the stock free from contamination by dandruff. Bernard Shawcross looked at himself in the mirror, and decided that he would not do. Self-study unnerved him.

A pocket note-pad served him as accounts-book. There was room in his budget for neither illness nor accident. He gave his wife £52 a week for herself and the boy, and was left with £36.28 of his take-home pay for his own expenses. His room cost £20. The remaining £16.28 was divided between vegetarian food, fares, clothes and forty pence a week for the Football Pools syndicate at work. The lovat-green overcoat had been reduced to clear. He did not care for the colour himself.

There was no way he could cut down. His attempt to persuade his workmates to try a cheaper perm on the Pools had been overruled. If he returned to his wife, he would save the £20 on the room, but his health would suffer. There was no accounting for high blood pressure, and Doreen was by no means the ideal companion for it. No, he could not be ill. The note-pad accounts-book had become his Bible; his escape from Doreen had been made possible by his continual study of it. Its message was clear. To return would be false economy; it would be angina and nervous exhaustion and all manner of ailments which could not be afforded.

He must cure himself; he must cultivate calmness, and learn to relax. He would think himself paler, draining the high colour from his face with the power of positive thought. His mother's subscription to *The Reader's Digest* had not been a wasted investment. He must stretch his mind backwards, leapfrogging over negative memories to compose a vista of happy moments.

He stretched his mind backwards with immediate success. There was the seaside, and a woman paddling. Closer mental inspection revealed this to be the newspaper photograph of Hetty Wainthropp, with thighs the size of bolsters looming above the terrified waves, and a toothless grin. Back further! The picture melted into his mother's funeral. The yellow clay of the graveyard and the sallow faces of the women who had known her. Heads shaken sorrowfully. Doreen drunk on Mateus Rosé, and sleeping the whole of the following day. His son, Geoff, refusing to wear a suit. Geoff squeezing his pimples in front of the bathroom mirror, and the mirror spotted with the contents of those pimples. Geoff standing beside him at the grave, wearing orange make-up to cover the pimples, and the vertical stripes of dried blood standing out against the orange make-up so that he looked like a clown or a child's toy.

Blood pressure rising! Back further! Taking Geoff to see where he worked. The aroma of wintergreen among the frozen chickens. Geoff picking his nose as they studied the carcasses of spring lamb, his voice echoing through the Cold Room, 'Not much of a career, though, is it?' Back! Geoff and himself sitting together in the park on Sundays, rain or shine, with no money and nowhere to go. Forty-six

minutes of birdsong and silence, suddenly broken by
'How am I supposed to form meaningful relationships
with women, when you've set me such a crappy example?'
More silence, standing together on the towpath by the
canal, contemplating the grey skin of scum on the surface
of the water, then himself asking Geoff, 'What are you
thinking about?' and Geoff's reply, serious and grave and
almost tender, describing his wish to break the skin on the
water by sliding his body through it, and having the skin
heal again over his head, 'Wouldn't even leave a pock-
mark.'

The past was failing him. It was not a repository of
positive thoughts. He would calm himself by thinking of
the note-pad and its carefully worked out accounts. But
even the note-pad was not infallible. There was a sum of
threepence, he recalled, still unaccounted for, and a
search back over the expenditure of the past six months
had not discovered it. Finally he had investigated the
linings and pockets of all his clothes, and found, not three
pence, but his mother's wedding ring.

He had invented the man in the white sports car while
still at school just after the war, had seen in some magazine an advertisement for a new sports car (was it a
Sunbeam Alpine?) being driven at speed along a coast
road by mountains somewhere in the South of France, the
driver's white silk scarf streaming out behind him and the
legs of the models dangling in the air-stream. His mother
had looked briefly at the advertisement, and said, 'Just
like your dad, that.' Even then he had known that she was
referring to the presence of the long-legged women, not to
the physical appearance of the driver, but it had been the

only clue she ever gave him. There were no wedding photographs, no mementoes, just a thin band of nine-carat gold.

Ordinarily this memory of the man in the white silk scarf would have calmed Bernard Shawcross, and lowered his blood pressure for a while, but it had been destroyed by Hetty, and replaced by that of someone who wore a cap and a woolly muffler and liked a flutter on the horses. He must go back beyond Hetty's more recent memories, back to his own as an infant during the days when he had been conscious of a male presence which had suddenly disappeared. More positive; get rid of the negatives. He must remember a comforting male presence, with hands stronger and thicker than his mother's, which had lifted and dressed him, his own face pressed against a cheek which was rough and scratched him. His mother's clothing had smelled of something which he had been later able to identify as Barraclough's Mild & Bitter; the other presence had smelled of sweat, tobacco and sometimes coal, the dust of which had buried itself in the cracks of long thick fingers. This coal was from the fire. His father made fires to keep Bernard warm; those fingers washed him, slapped his legs, spooned food into his mouth. The fingers! he must hold tight to the fingers. They had tied Bernard's bootlaces, buttered his bread, buttoned his buttons. They were the source of all warmth. They had rolled twisted newspapers to start fires, wielded a poker and rattled it in the grate, had lifted buckets of coal. They had spun his top so that it circled the floor before stopping. They had been rough, enormous and unclean, and he had loved them; they had served him. It came to

Bernard that it had been his father, in those days, who had looked after him; his mother had often been out of the house. The problems of his present world, the world which contained his job as a custodian of frozen meat, contained his depressive wife and that walking pile of fermenting resentment, his son, these were nothing to his need to reunite his red cheeks with the hands which had first slapped them.

He supposed that his mother had loved him. If so, she had not allowed that to spoil him. Her own parents had died by the time he was seven, leaving just the two of them in the terraced house bought with the legacy of £600 which was all that remained of the tenancy of the pub. There had been nobody but her son on whom she might then have lavished affection, but she had turned out not to be the lavishing sort.

To Bernard, as later to his schoolmates, his fatherless state had seemed to require explanation. His mother used the word 'disappeared', and refused further discussion. He had searched for the word 'disappear' in the dictionary, and found it next to the word 'disappoint'. The meanings of the two words had merged into one: 'to cease to be visible, to frustrate expectations, to deprive, to fail, to undo, destroy, to cease to be present'. If a bus had knocked his father down, something on his broken body would have identified him. If he had fallen or jumped into a river, his corpse would have been hooked out before it reached the sea. But Bernard's father had disappeared, and Bernard's mother would add to this piece of information only that such disappearances and the disappointments which went with them were by no means unusual.

Frank Shawcross had risen from the bed he shared with his wife at four am one morning in the spring of 1935. He had made his own breakfast, left the house, and had not returned. His mother had continued to work in the evenings; one of the neighbours had come in to 'watch' the three-year-old. After a few months, when it no longer seemed likely that his father would return, they had moved into a room above the pub to live with his grandparents. While his mother washed glasses and chatted to the regulars downstairs, he remained alone in the room. At half-hourly intervals his grandmother, who did not care for children, would come to the door to make sure that he had not swallowed the bleach or hanged himself with his skipping rope. The noises of life and conversation in the bar interested him very little. His world consisted of a toy fort and thirty-two lead soldiers. He had eaten most of the red paint from their tunics, and left various impressions of his milk teeth on their plinths. This was in the days before the sucking and biting of lead soldiers by children was considered to be harmful. The large strong coal-ingrained hands never returned to undress him, never again lifted him on to a trousered lap to sit watching the fire take hold, never built up the fire when it was in danger of dying. At the pub, fire was brought in a shovel from another room, placed in the grate, and a guard set in front of it. At three years old, at four, at five, Bernard Shawcross learned every way there was of treading water and killing time.

So time passed, so childhood had passed. His mother's single kiss was the mark that another day had run its uneventful course. 'Let's see what tomorrow brings, shall we?' Her voice had never conveyed the anticipation that tomorrow would be any different. Her whole life, and then his, had been the tedious addition of one day's passing to the next. While his father had been driving a white sports car along a mountain road above a cerulean sea, with the white legs of fast women beating a devil's tattoo on the gleaming paintwork.

It was not until she knew that she was dying that his mother had spoken to him with any feeling, admitting that she had been a fool, and asking him not to judge her too harshly. 'And you're a sad lot too, our Bernard, staring at my hands all these years as if I were about to hit thee. Is that what he did to thee?' Bernard had squeezed her hand, feeling its brittleness, its smallness, its weakness. 'Bending soldiers in your mouth, and dribbling lead poison down your front. Looking up at me with those bedroom eyes you got off him, as if the world owed you a clean nappie every hour and a shapely woman to cuddle up to. Learning to like people takes practice. You and me, we never applied ourselves.' Then she had died. Of course, by that time Bernard had had a wife and a son of his own.

At the funeral, his wife, having drunk a bottle and a half of wine, had almost fallen into his mother's grave, and his son had refused to wear a suit, and had sported a face striped orange and red like a clown. Bernard Shawcross closed his eyes and strove to think positive thoughts to shut off the sidelong glances of the sallow women who had known his mother. '*Learning to like people takes practice.*' Even at the age of fifty-three, even without the application or the natural aptitude, if he could learn to like people, would it lower the pressure of his blood?

He had liked a pair of hands; he had loved them; he ached to be reunited with them. But they were as far away as ever, his only hope of finding them again in the gift of a woman of seventy who could not even be relied upon to adjust her clothing at the seaside or put her teeth in before being photographed. His own son had walked out of school on the last day of term, and disappeared as successfully as the boy's grandfather had done fifty years earlier. The note-pad accounts-book Bible by which he had regulated his life now showed a discrepancy, and although three pence would not break him, it had sapped his confidence in the value of strict accounting. If even single entry book-keeping went wrong, what could one trust? It was the small things which added up.

13
Two of Everything

Sixteen-year-old Geoffrey Shawcross, who looked thirteen, had once seen a television programme in which homeless people in London had been filmed sleeping in cardboard boxes piled up outside delicatessens. He had also seen an often repeated TV series in black and white (Geoffrey watched a lot of television) in which a deep male voice announced over the opening credits of every episode, 'London never sleeps!' This was all the knowledge he had acquired of the sleeping habits of Londoners, but he was certain that whichever was true, communal kipping in cardboard boxes or mass insomnia, he himself would need his usual nine hours a night.

A bed was not essential; sleeping had never been a problem to him; he could do it anywhere. If he were able to find the cardboard box people, he would ask them politely to make room. On the television they had been woken up to be offered free soup and questioned about their health. He would not object to free soup. And if anyone should ask him about his health, it might be prudent to mention the state of his feet and the shooting pain in his right hip.

Midnight found him sitting on an empty plastic beer-crate in the doorway of the Criterion Theatre in Piccadilly Circus. He had spent many hours trying to find a cardboard box and strike up an acquaintance with its contents, but this was the day on which Westminster Council collected the refuse, and he had found nothing on the pavements of the West End but the leftovers from split plastic bags. The cardboard box people seemed to have disappeared. Perhaps they were lying in wait for the delicatessen people to begin unpacking their deliveries of pickled gherkins, salt beef and roll-mops.

A police constable and a WPC passed, walking in tandem, then turned on their heels like Torvill and Dean, and walked smartly back to make eye-to-eye contact.

'Haven't seen you on the Meat Rack before, have we?'

'It's a beer-crate.'

'Don't get smart with me, sonny. How old are you?'

'Sixteen.'

The WPC requested him to pull the other one, and asked for his name, which was, he told them, Albert Ramsbotham, his address 'north of Watford'. Thereupon the WPC required him to repeat after her a few lines, starting with 'Once more into the breach, dear friends, once more', and by 'Stiffen the sinews, summon up the blood,' she was able with confidence to tell him that he had been in London no more than half a day, and had previously resided within ten miles of Halifax.

He was advised that where he sat was a dangerous place for minors. Since he chose not to give them an address, they would give him one. He made no protest, assuming that he would sleep in the police station, or that they would know where the cardboard box people slept on Collection Days, and would introduce him. And so, at fifteen minutes past midnight, Geoffrey Shawcross was strolling through the West End with a police officer on each arm.

They took him to a Night Shelter for teenage runaways, conveniently situated just off Trafalgar Square. He was made to shower, given a meal, told that a doctor would visit on the following day to hear about the state of his feet and the shooting pain in his right hip, and allocated a bunk in a dormitory shared by seven other male juvenile home-refusers.

From here he would be instructed how to claim Social Security. The Birth Certificate which he'd had the foresight to bring with him would prove that he was due Unemployment Benefit, and would prevent arguments brought about by his happening to look thirteen. Nobody at the Night Shelter asked to see the certificate, or pestered him to return home, their view being that two weeks in London were enough for any young person of intelligence to see what was going on. Most, they told Geoffrey, returned home to endure unemployment in familiar surroundings, and the few who didn't moved on to a life of prostitution or drugs, sometimes both. These were the people who spent their nights either in cardboard boxes or wrestling with sixteen Arabs in one of the smaller bedrooms of the Savoy.

These were the choices, and the organizers of the Night Shelter were mature enough to know that many young persons can be led, but few can be driven. Posters decorated the walls of the Common Room to remind their charges of the delights of the metropolis. Geoffrey, consuming the hot soup for which he had pined, followed by a bacon sarnie, read on the wall in front of him:

Nobody in 1985
HAS
to sell their
ARSE
for food
SO WHAT's *YOUR* EXCUSE?

and on the wall to one side:

Forget about the FUTURE.
Get yourself some AIDS.

Quite quickly Geoffrey became friendly with two fifteen-year-old female runaways from Bristol and their companion, an overweight fourteen-year-old called George. With these three he was to spend much of his time. Since the girls knew a trainee hairdresser who required heads on which to practise, all four had their appearances changed several times during the next fortnight. With each change of appearance, George changed his name and sometimes his gender, but in or out of make-up, with green hair or with blue, Geoffrey always remained Geoff, sensing that his popularity with the two girls depended on it, and anyway so many young men of his generation had taken up transvestism as a hobby; the competition was fierce.

Thus, without ever having to try on a cardboard box for size, Geoffrey Shawcross found his community. The girls had hitched to London with a view to trying their luck at prostitution, but had decided on arrival that they were young enough to wait. Their childhoods would soon be over; they might as well enjoy what was left, sleeping with men of their own choice before entering the world of commerce. Prostitution was always a livelihood they could fall back on. Meanwhile their income came from what they enjoyed doing most, which was shoplifting.

On the third day of his first week in London, Geoffrey lost his virginity to the taller of the Bristol girls, and then again half an hour later to the shorter. George's demand for equal rights was denied. Shortly afterwards, as the conclusion of the ritual of achieving adulthood, Geoffrey wrapped with extreme tidiness every one of the pieces of clothing in which he had travelled south, two sets of each, and deposited them in a litter-bin outside the National Gallery. His new outfit, provided by the Bristol girls, had been acquired at the best shops, and George, who had an eye for colour, expended a great deal of thought over its selection.

During the next fortnight, thanks to the skill and generosity of the Bristol girls, Geoffrey became the owner of many luxury items, including a face sauna and a sunlamp to counteract the baleful over-activity of his sebaceous glands. His face was no longer striped orange and dark red, though his general appearance was in every other respect much more colourful.

One day, having set out with the others towards Regent Street and the Scotch House in search of tartan for

George to make into slacks, he passed an old woman in Leicester Square. She was sitting on a bench, watching the passers-by, intent and birdlike, and writing in a notebook. He recognized her as the old woman who had pestered him on the coach. For a moment he felt a desire to go over to her and return the pound coin she had given him, not least to see her expression when he introduced himself in his new clothes, scarlet Afro curls and emerald eye-shadow. It would certainly have given Supergran something to write home about.

But the desire passed. One never knew when one would need a pound. Life was sweet and easy at that moment, but if the Bristol Countersnatchers moved on without him, he lacked the skill to go into the business of shoplifting for himself. They might so easily tire of him. Or he might; the duties he performed in rota every morning, afternoon and evening were beyond what most sixteen-year-old males were called upon to do, and Geoffrey was small for his age. Besides, the pound had been a gift, a good-luck token; it would be tempting fate to return it.

14

The Detective

Hetty Wainthropp, overweight and on the wrong side of seventy, sat on a bench in Leicester Square, watching four pigeons share a packet of prawn-cocktail-flavoured crisps, and tried to imagine herself into the mind of an undersized sixteen-year-old boy with no money and wearing two sets of unwashed clothes.

When Geoffrey Shawcross's mother (who appeared to have been drinking) showed her a recent photograph of him, Hetty's lower teeth had shot forwards and taken a firm grip of her upper lip, so that her yelp of excited recognition seemed merely to be one of pain. The helpful denture prevented her confessing that she had already kept the subject under discussion company during his journey south, had given him good advice, a kiss on the cheek, and a pound coin for luck, and had last seen him walking away in a state of trance from Victoria Coach Station, in imminent danger of being flattened by a bus. It would not have done to tell her client this; it would have made her task seem too easy.

It would not be easy. London appeared to contain a great many people, very few of whom would remain still for long enough to allow a proper observation. Hetty watched and listened to twelve Japanese tourists, arranging themselves into groups to be photographed queueing for tickets to *No Sex, Please! We're British*. On the bench opposite her, a Welsh lady was attempting to convince her companion that the only show in London guaranteed to be entirely free of innuendo was the one at the Palladium, where Tommy Steele held centre stage.

So far every moment of Hetty's time in London had been an object lesson on the infinite variety and sameness of her fellow human beings. She had stared into their faces, studied the way they walked, had seen them reflected in shop windows, and spied them spying on themselves. She had watched their faces as they approached, and their backs as they retreated. Their faces revealed their aspirations and dreams, and what their backs concealed she did them the honour to invent. She was a late developer. She had wasted decades in unpromising areas, had frittered time away playing one-upmanship games in sub-post-offices or attempting self-expression across the counters of small-town butchers. Now in the metropolis she felt herself flowering. London was important. There were people walking the streets who reeked of importance, and others whose eyes revealed their search for it, desperate, unresting eyes, programmed to be content with nothing but high office.

No one looked twice at her. No one commented on her clothes or hair-style. No one asked how she was, and then proceeded to redistribute their weight while she answered. She was anonymous, a condition she had always dreaded, yet now she loved it. She was as frisky as a sparrow taking a dust-bath.

She had a purpose, not merely that of finding Frank's runaway grandson, but one larger, more far-reaching, all-consuming, ever-interesting. She would learn, watch, study, make notes of all she could discover concerning the way people behaved, man-watching, woman-watching, child-watching. The finest detective since Sherlock Holmes had begun her training, and not a moment too soon. She must establish herself quickly, or she would be over the hill before she reached her peak. Nobody but Ironside did detection from a wheelchair, and look how constipated that had made him.

The Welsh woman's companion, having finally allowed herself to be convinced that Tommy Steele would not stoop to smut, scraped something sticky from her sandals and followed her adviser towards the Angus Steak House. Hetty's keen gaze pursued the two women until they were out of sight, then panned along the queue forming outside a cinema. She had already checked the prices of the seats. Frank's grandson would not have the money to go in there.

In Soho she had been disappointed not to see girls swinging their handbags and winking at men, since she had assumed them to be as much a part of London as the pigeons. The photographs of topless models reminded her of inter-school netball. In 1930, Manor Park High had fielded a quarterback whose boobs would have put to shame anything she could see squeezed together in the windows of Old Compton Street. The sex shops looked very much like Mr Limbolini's, the chemist on Salford Road, and he'd never caught on either. That fourteen-year-old quarterback would be seventy now, and round-shouldered, Hetty wouldn't wonder.

Hetty sat, flicking through the pages of her notebook and wishing she had brought Robert's camera as an added aid to memory. She was trying to convince herself that the last three days had been useful as well as enjoyable. Any hopes of assistance from Steven with her assignment had been stifled. She had phoned him, of course, and he had told her three times that he had a temperature. The basement flat in Earls Court, which he shared with a colleague, had only three rooms, one in which a pair of single beds doubled as sofas, a corridor which doubled as a kitchen, and a bathroom which could have doubled as a horsebox. She had not intended to impose herself, but an invitation to tea would have been welcome. Instead he had spoken as if someone were holding his nose, 'Give us a ring next week if you're still around. I might be over the worst by then. You enjoy yourself, and don't get too tired. God, I feel awful.'

She had intended to ask Steven where in London he would hide if he were an undersized penniless school-leaver, but his insistence on informing her of the statistics of deaths among Senior Citizens resulting from flu passed on to them by close relatives quite put the question from her mind until she had run out of tenpenny pieces.

Yes, she was enjoying herself and didn't mind the tiredness, but was she getting anywhere? Certainly she was not being extravagant, but she would have to contact Frank soon. A withdrawal from a cushion would have to be made. This was not going to be an easy assignment or a quick one.

It was two weeks since she had travelled south with the boy. How would he have eaten, where would he have slept? Could he have already been brainwashed by a religious sect? In her mind's eye she saw him, floating over zebra crossings in his saffron robes, light-headed from hunger, grubby fingernails bitten to the quick as he tapped on a homemade tambourine and faintly mispronounced his leader's name. She remembered his father, the beetroot-red cheeks and turned-up nose, the ready apologies and self-deprecating glances from anxious eyes. If Geoffrey took after his father, this city would swallow him up and spit out nothing but the shoe-laces.

Plimsolls! Yes, that was it. Or were they trainers? Training shoes. Rubber, certainly. The pungent aroma of youthful feet, encased in rubber and pressed against the underseat heating of a long-distance coach, came flooding back to her. She must organize her thoughts more closely; she would start tomorrow when she was less tired. A clue like that could easily have been missed. There were four young people passing the bench a little to one side of her. Extraordinary outfits, the boys more outrageous by far than the girls! One of the boys, who had scarlet Afro curls, had paused, and was staring at her. She considered putting out her tongue, but he moved on with his companions. She supposed that he imagined he was in the fashion, but Hetty had already noticed in Oxford Street that aubergine and emerald were the In colours for hair, and recorded it in her notebook. It was important to write down everything which might be useful, not only to her search, but also for the interviews with the media which would succeed success.

She lifted her nose, and sniffed the air. A colder breeze from the river seemed to bring with it the faint tinkle of hand-bells sounding in her inner ear, and with it, even fainter, like a breath dying in the wind, the words, 'Chocolate gives me asthma.' She must not lose heart; she had her clues. She closed her eyes, and saw in close-up a white-headed spot, protected by four newly sprouted blond hairs, preparing to erupt from a chin which seemed to be trying to bury itself inside the collars of two shirts. She saw an undersized soul in torment, wriggling inside two pairs of everything. Those two pairs of everything would have had three weeks of being worn by now. She had only to keep her nose in the wind, and she would have him.

Neon flicked into life around Leicester Square. The lights were coming on all over London, as afternoon ended and the evening began. She had an hotel to go to, her room paid for in advance; there would be no rebate if she were to freeze to death, her bum encased in a block of ice.

She would treat herself to a small drink, and put in an hour's study of the *A to Z Street Atlas* before she went to bed. A small brandy would help her sleep. Her mind was racing, and decisions had to be made. She must send Frank a Telemessage, 'Please wire two hundred pounds to Trafalgar Square Post Office prompt. Terrible danger to grandson from unknown God Squad. Hetty.' That should get him unpicking a few stitches and dipping his hand in. Three weeks must seem like a lifetime to an undersized sixteen-year-old. It would be worth dropping in to West End Central on her way back to the hotel, to see if he had been handed in.

15
Knocking Together

Wearing an old pair of gardening gloves and holding his breath, Frank Cross rummaged in the plastic dustbin-liner for clues. Edith was in one of her silences. No clues were necessary, as far as she was concerned. The dispute was simple. She conceded that a more secure place than under his pillow should be found for Frank's winnings, and that there was no room in any of the existing cushions for another four thousand pounds in notes, but protested that Frank could no longer expect her to fiddle with kapok and zips at her time of life, when a few pounds would purchase a shop-bought cushion which could easily be adapted to accommodate the money.

Frank said that a shop-bought cushion, plumped down beside all the home-made ones, would look out of place, and attract attention. Edith considered this to be a slur on her earlier needlework. The dispute continued. She would not end it by admitting that threading needles was now beyond her powers. Her hands had not stopped shaking since Hetty's visit, and the last letter containing the

account of Bernard B. Shawcross from his Hush Puppies
to his high-coloured cheeks and his lovat-green overcoat,
had unnerved her; she expected at any moment to look
down and see those Hush Puppies on the hearth-rug.
Clearly Frank anticipated a visit. He had asked her where
she kept the recipe books, and when she had told him that
they had never owned any, had become thoughtful, and
asked, 'Do you mean to tell me that in almost fifty years of
marriage you've never cooked anything from a recipe?' as
if, by not referring to Mrs Beeton, she had betrayed her
marriage vows.

Then a letter had arrived, postmarked Halifax, and
forwarded from Hetty's address in Robert's handwriting.
Frank had not opened it over breakfast, but had slipped it
into his pocket, and taken it on his walk. He had returned
with a paperback entitled *Tasty Dishes for the Budget
Hostess*. Now he was rooting through the dustbin like a
pig for truffles, searching for a grievance to hold over her
while he made his announcement that he had asked the
intruder to visit.

'I need another cushion, Edith.'

'Rackham's Sale is on.'

'Home-made.'

'No can do. I've told you. My fingers are too stiff.'

'Show me how to do it, then.'

'Just to save a pound or two when you've won four
thousand?'

'That may seem a lot of money now, but in ten years'
time we'll be lucky if it keeps us a month.'

'The state will be keeping us then. You'll be well over
ninety.'

'And all that more in need of cushioning.' Neither of them laughed. 'It's not the money, and you know it. It's the principle. Why should big firms make huge profits out of what we could knock together ourselves?'

'You go ahead, then. Knock it together. There's needle and thread in that drawer. You can have that old skirt which is lying on the bedroom windowsill to catch the condensation. Off you go! Go up and get it. Let your fingers do the walking. Mine have got bad joints as well as a rash. I'll supervise; it'll only take you four nights' work. We'll need the electric on to see by, I'm afraid. The skirt's already got a zip in it. We can dry it by this blazing fire of ours.'

Edith's voice trembled and subsided. The game would be over soon. They were no longer talking about cushions or even money. They had returned to the icy living-room. She watched him examine the coal in the bucket, contemplate putting another piece on to a fire which was neither in nor out, then reject the idea. She closed her eyes, and sat waiting for him to make his announcement. He would have preferred to make it, she knew, when she was in the wrong about something which would allow him more of a grievance than her refusal to cobble a cushion together.

After ten minutes of silence she did the unthinkable, picked out the largest piece of coal she could find in the bucket, and placed it on the fire.

'Are you mad?'

'No, just cold.'

'We'll be in bed soon.'

'We'll be in somewhere even more restful than that

soon if you get your way all the time.'

'If you'd told me you were cold, I'd have got you your
coat. That coal's wasted now. You've no cause to make
argumentative gestures this late in the day.'

Again they sat in silence. Had she given him enough of
a grievance to allow him to make his announcement? He
spoke.

'I like home-made cushions, Edith. I didn't mean anything when I said a shop one would look suspicious in
here. I actually prefer yours. It's to do with what we've got
and what we've made of ourselves. It's not the same,
sticking four thousand in a shop-bought thing. If it's in a
cushion you've made, Edith, it seems more ours, don't
you see? All right, so it was easy money, won on the
horses, gained through luck and a bit of good judgement,
but everything else we've achieved, you and me, is from
being careful.'

Edith raised her hand, still marked with coal dust, to
stop him going further. If allowed, he would become
maudlin, carried away into a future of terrors – the
Workhouse, an Old People's Home, the Geriatric Ward.
He would describe them helpless, tied into walk-
ing-frames, being force-fed on semolina and blancmange.
His eyes would moisten as he told her how good they had
been for each other, and how it was his duty to protect her
from poverty, from walking the streets selling clothes-pegs
or sleeping out under the pier in all weathers. All he
wanted was to save her from regimentation by nurses and
social workers, from endless card-games, milk puddings
and Instant Whip.

He obeyed her hand-signal, and turned his attention

instead to the fire, which was now producing heat. 'I suppose I could take that big bit off when we go up, and stick it in the oven ready for tomorrow.'

She could scream. Where was the Craven-A Edith, the purple nail varnish and the gin-and-lime? Why had she spent her life shivering in shadows, waiting for someone else to poke the fire into life? Too late! Her knuckles had locked, and her hands shook beneath folded arms. She supposed that there must be strength of a kind in what she had endured. It must have built her character in some way, though she couldn't think which. She was as she was. All the grand gestures in the world would be too late now. Let Hetty storm the Bastille, let Hetty take the town to her well-rounded bosom – a bosom fingered by Frank at a time when conjugal fingering was being withheld. Edith was tired, seventy something and tired. All she asked now was that her mind should move at the pace of a slow walk, with no novelties, bumps and shocks, allowing the sepia photographs of her memories to saunter gently by. She said, 'What are you going to do about your son?'

At first he did not answer, but seemed to be wondering how much would be left unburned of the extra piece of coal when they went to bed. Then he said, 'I want to see him if it's all right with you.'

He had been able to think of nothing else for weeks. Behind all the fear and rejection there had been the knowledge that he would have to bring himself to see the boy. He had to know what that woman had done to his son during all those years, during which Frank himself, mainly at the back of his mind, had been building up a picture of a Bernard who was very like an idealized Frank.

Perhaps that was why he had been frightened. A younger version of himself, however idealized, would be hard to accept by someone who knew himself to be not at all ideal, a creature of farts and failings and eccentric habits. It had been easier, after Hetty's letter, to accept a different Bernard, a warehouse manager with a red face, high blood pressure, a wife and a son who had both left him, and a nose the shape of which had been attractive on his mother, but would be unlikely to suit a man.

He had to see the boy; he had to recapture the lost years. He would find the paraffin heater, and put it in the spare room. He would cook one of his stews. Everyone liked his stews, and it would do them for two meals.

Edith said, 'I'll need to have my hair done.'

'I'll cut it tomorrow. You said you liked it the last time, now I've got the knack of cutting it level.'

'A proper hairdresser. I want it styled.'

'You tried that in '45. It didn't last.'

'I don't believe they use heated curling-tongs any longer. I've seen women through the window. They wear plastic hoods, and read magazines. They've come a long way since my permanent wave.'

'I'm not having you look like a stick of candyfloss that's had blue ink poured over it.'

'No, I wouldn't let them rinse it. Just the wash and set.'

'We could wash it for you before you go.'

'And celebrate my first hair-do in forty years with a cold?'

'You won't be the same.'

'No, I shall be different. You may go off me. It's a terrible risk I'm taking.'

For a moment he was thoughtful. Then he said, 'It's not a Beauty Contest, you know. Nobody's coming to judge.'

Edith smiled. 'Good! That'll save me darning my bathing costume.' Pictures of Hetty paddling flicked past her mind's eye. She wondered whether all that capacity for enjoyment would ever diminish. 'Hetty'll be enjoying herself in London, I expect!'

'Would you like to read Bernard's letter?'

'You read it to me. I always enjoy that.'

Resting her head against the back of the chair, she placed her feet closer to the fire. Without shoes and stockings, they resembled two lumps of stained alabaster, pitted with time and ill use. As she moved her arms, loose skin flapped at each elbow like puppies trying to shake themselves dry. Certainly there must be no Beauty Contest.

Sometimes Edith imagined herself lying naked on a bed in some foreign country. The walls were white, with no pictures, and the sun streamed through the open window which had brown wooden shutters. Through the window Edith would be able to see a mountain covered with pine forest. Her body on the bed was the colour of clear honey, smooth as silk and in perfect proportion; it had no folds of redundant flesh, no grey body-hair, no superannuated blackheads, no chafing or stains, no liver-spots on fingers and arms. It did not shake. If asked to thread a needle, it could, but was never asked.

Inside this faultless body, Edith lay waiting, not as she had often waited at bus-stops, or in a queue at the Post Office, with those behind her sighing and the buses passing at full speed. There were no schedules, time-tables or

131

Pension Books in this white room, just the reassuring hum of near-silence and the casual swaying of millions of swelling pine cones. She was not waiting *for* anything; there was no fear that when her time was up she would leave, screaming and cursing. The waiting was an end in itself.

The body on the bed was her real body. The body with the flappy elbows and the legs like stained alabaster, leaning back in an uncomfortable armchair against lumpy home-made cushions, listening to Frank read, belonged to someone else. All Edith was required to do was to keep it ticking over until the real owner returned to redeem it. Then Edith would return to her real body in the white-washed room.

Far away she could hear Frank's voice saying, 'Fifty years is a long time for a child to have been separated from its parent.' She closed her eyes.

16
Cake Walk

The Silver Birch Hotel in Pimlico was a Temperance establishment run by a Bangladeshi family, who also owned the Tropicana Club Discotheque which shared a backyard with it, and was not temperance. Automatic free membership of the Tropicana was extended to all guests of the Silver Birch in compensation for the lack of a bar, but the invitation to sit in semi-blackout amidst wrap-around amplifiers in order to drink diluted but expensive spirits was seldom taken up, since many of the guests were retired people on a pension, living there on the favourable terms offered to permanent residents. Time had stopped for these residents. The present perplexed them, and they dared not contemplate the future. Each of the separate rooms in which they passed what was left of their lives was a time-capsule in which the permanent residents of the Silver Birch Hotel endlessly refashioned the past into a shape which would allow them self-esteem.

Hetty had bought a bottle of Dubonnet and half a bottle of brandy on the evening of her arrival. A hand-written notice pinned to the door of her room had informed her that self-catering was forbidden anywhere in the hotel, but as she poured herself the first life-restoring Dubonnet, preparatory to beginning her study of the *A to Z*, she was beguiled by the aroma of freshly ground coffee and toasted-cheese-and-bacon sandwiches wafting in from the landing.

She opened the door. She had not expected to find coffee and toasted sandwiches on the landing itself, and there were none; the aroma emanated from Number Seven. Hetty hesitated. Her instinct was to knock at the door of Number Seven and say to the person inside, 'Are you aware that self-catering is forbidden, and may I have some?' While she hesitated, the door opened, and a most ravishing personage stood in the doorway. She was of Hetty's age, exquisitely coiffed, wearing what may have been a tea-gown. She smiled. It was a smile which had clearly been modelled on that of the Queen Mother, since it was accompanied by a prodigious lolling of the head, first to one side and then the other during which time one hand was raised and the fingers gently twiddled. Hetty, overwhelmed, sank at once into a deep curtsey, said, 'Ma'am, I think your toast is done,' and was invited in.

This personage was Phillida Meadowhite, born Edna Trask. She told Hetty that she had begun her working life as an apprentice manicurist in a West End Beauty Salon, but realized that manicurists were two a penny, and began to spend her evenings at the family home in Battersea reading up on chiropody.

'I was working on this hand, and my eyes wandered a bit, my dear; you know how it is.' Hetty did know. 'And then I noticed that my client was taking alternate feet out of her shoes – slipping them out, you know, one after the other, then rubbing the foot hard against her leg, and putting it back in the shoe, and so it went. Something's not quite right down there, I thought, and then on the way back it struck me like a bolt from the blue that there was money in feet if I was prepared to lower my sights a little. Socially it would be a comedown. A foot-person without a track record gets all the rubbish. If you could have seen some of the feet I had to handle in those days! They would have been more at home clinging to trees than mounted on platform heels. But I stuck at it. There are plenty of dicky feet in London, and in no time at all I was up to my neck in regular clients, none of them the *crème de la crème*, you understand, but it was a good living. Then I met Carlo, and everything changed.'

Hetty reloaded the Breville Toaster with bread and cheese. 'For the better?'

'For the worse, and *then* for the better. He was a clairvoyant. I taught him a little about feet, and he used it with his clients – read their palms and then their soles and doubled his takings, and if he spotted anything untoward like an ingrowing toenail or a verruca, he'd hand them my card. But Carlo's own feet, my dear, were itchy, and also the police were not always kind to clairvoyants in those days, so we were soon on the move. I lost my London regulars, and sometimes we weren't in the same town long enough to merit a second advert in the local paper. Then he left me on Crewe Station, without a ticket or a change of clothes.'

'You must have been all beside yourself.'

'In the depths. I jumped on the London train, rushed into a first-class compartment, and slumped into a corner seat, blubbering my eyes out. Worked wonders. By Bletchley, I'd done four pairs of feet including the ticket collector's and given out eight business cards. From that day forth I rose like a rocket. I was unencumbered, you see, a free spirit. I never quite reached the heights, although it looked for a while, my dear, as if I might be by Royal Appointment, but I did a small circle of ladies-in-waiting for a good twelve years. It's hard on the feet, tramping the corridors of the Big House; you wouldn't believe the condition of some of them.'

That was the story told by Phillida Meadowhite to Hetty Wainthropp, senior investigator, who believed it all. The cheese was plastic stuff, sliced in a packet, but it did for toasting, and the coffee was most welcome after Instant.

'Why did you give it up?'

Phillida looked sadly at her hands. 'Time stiffens all fingers. I still see one or two of the girls for tea at Fortnum's when we can get in. They don't like queuing behind pop-singers and Australian film-directors.'

In one corner of the room, under a signed photograph of Lord Louis Mountbatten, the television images changed continuously. The set was kept on from breakfast to midnight; on many a morning Hetty would wake to the sound of an astrologer, and she would fall asleep at night to the Epilogue. She developed the habit of looking in on Phillida for coffee and toast before she went out, and taking in the Dubonnet bottle for a discussion of the day's progress when she returned. Phillida herself, in spite of all the talk of tea at Fortnum's with Her Majesty's intimate attendants, seldom left her room.

'He'll have gone to ground.'

'I thought . . . some religious sect.'

'Then you'd never find him. They shave their heads. It changes the shape of the face. Or he could have a job if he's prepared to work all night and sleep during the day. You'd never find him then either. Being young, he'd be paid a pittance.' Phillida gazed critically at the photograph of Geoffrey Shawcross. 'Wouldn't be in a bar; he looks under age. He might be selling hamburgers or fried chicken. There was a time he could have picked up a few pounds shifting scenery, but I believe they have a strong union now. They'd take them off the streets in Covent Garden in the old days, straight from the farm or the cotton mill into pushing on the pagoda for *Chu Chin Chow*.'

'What are we looking for?'

'It's not what, it's who; and if I've told you once, I've told you a dozen times. A sixteen-year-old boy who looks thirteen, wearing two sets of clothing and some very smelly plimsolls.'

They were sitting by the fountains in Trafalgar Square. Chalky, who admitted to being sixty and whom Hetty guessed not to be a day under seventy, had attached himself to her outside Madame Tussaud's. No amount of rudeness on Hetty's part had damped his ardour. Every lash of her tongue had heightened the sparkle in his bloodshot eyes and extended the width of his National Health smile. He had said, 'You OK, girl. What I seek is a long and deeply rewarding relationship with a mature woman,' repeating the description several times as if listing the contents of a bottle of sauce. Hetty had replied, 'Look, mister, I'm not standing here for the good of my health. I'm doing a job. Work! Comprenez? So what *I* seek is to see your bum do the Cake Walk.' Thus encouraged, he had attached himself to her. Chalky was from Tobago via Westbourne Grove. He was retired, widowed and very lonely.

'Aren't there any coloured women of your own age in Westbourne Whatsit?'

'Some, but they all gone to seed.'

'You can talk, with that bald spot the size of a Jaffa orange and those National Health choppers. I thought black persons were supposed to have good teeth. And keep looking for the subject while I'm talking to you.'

'Too much sugar. I'm a devil for the honeypot!'

'Well, this honey is spoken for, and has been for the last fifty years. Where I come from, the people have impolite names for gentlemen with dark skins, particularly those who hang about outside Waxworks, chatting up Senior Citizens of the opposite sex.' Chalky rolled his eyes, and ran the tip of his tongue over his upper lip. 'And if that's an obscene gesture, you can put it away for starters.'

'We should eat soon, eh? Keep up our strength for tonight.'

'I've decided to miss lunch. These thighs have got to be solid muscle next time I venture on to a beach. I must have walked the breadth of the earth.'

'I shall carry you to Hamburger Heaven.'

'You and whose army? We could do with one or two

like you back home. We've got the coalman of course, but it's not the same. His hand only knows two positions, one held out for money, the other scratching his surgical support.' Chalky placed one of his own hands next to Hetty's in the centre of her lap. She studied the contrast of colours for a few moments, then picked up and removed the collection of warm curled fingers as if discarding an oily rag. 'Now, stop that, Chalky, or I'll begin to get serious.'

He followed her up one side of the Strand and down the other like Burlington Bertie, and Hetty's will-power became undermined by the sight of chickens turning slowly on a spit. They ate lunch together after all, and Chalky paid. Hetty drank from what seemed to be an inexhaustible supply of carafe wine. 'You haven't bought my body for a mere chicken 'n chips, you know,' she said, and they returned to Soho, leaning on each other for support, in their unremitting search for the subject, Geoffrey Shawcross.

Stepping carefully over the fallen fruit and vegetables which littered the narrow streets, Chalky grinned and nodded, bowed and waved in his pleasure at showing his new companion to the world. Hetty kept her eyes lowered, and this was taken as shyness, but in fact, as well as the rotting vegetables, there were patches of wet pavement to be negotiated with caution; the last thing she needed was a broken leg. Music blared from Strip Joints and Strip Booths. It seemed to Hetty, herself a little blurred, that the tempo had been slowed in order to enable the tired legs on display to bend and stretch in time.

Standing in a doorway, a wizened old woman the size of a small child peered out at the world from the depths of an old army greatcoat. Her unstockinged legs had been planted in a pair of fatigue boots. She tilted a miniature bottle of whisky to her mouth, shouting, 'Go on, Blacky! Give it to her' in a high shrill gurgle as if each word was painful to produce. Hetty turned to reprimand her, but the face into which she looked was dead, the eyes stared past her, and the miniature bottle was empty; it dropped from the woman's fingers without her even noticing. Hetty stared at the old woman's steel-grey hair, which had been piled on top of the head in a pyramid of matted curls, until Chalky led her away.

On a bench in Soho Square, Hetty leaned her head against Chalky's shoulder, and willed her eyes not to close. Tourists and kitchen porters sucking in air after the lunchtime turmoil sat on the other benches. Business people, shoppers and non-stop showgirls between shifts came and went, but none was Geoffrey Shawcross.

They left Soho Square when a very drunk wino, attempting to comb his shoulder-length hair, collapsed at their feet, and put their shoes in danger. In Tottenham Court Road they saw plenty of young men walking alone, some with spots, some undersized, a few with haircuts which might have been created within ten miles of Halifax; these last, said Chalky, were probably on leave from the armed forces or recently out of prison; he recognized the cut. Most of them mooched aimlessly, some even furtively, but none was the one whom Hetty sought.

They parted at Holborn Underground, with promises to

meet again. Chalky had business, he said, or he would have seen her back to the hotel; he was not prepared to admit to Hetty that he had spent more than his day's allowance on spit-roasted chicken and carafe wine, and would have to walk to Westbourne Grove. It occurred to neither of them that rush-hour is not the best time for an elderly lady from the North to travel by the London Underground.

'Room, please! Accident! Mind your backs! Gangway! Senior Citizen! Give her air!' A gentleman in a grey trilby and fawn mackintosh placed his clenched fists under Hetty's arms and dragged her backwards through the crowd on the southbound platform. She had fainted. She had only recently grown used to travelling on moving escalators with any degree of confidence, and the experience of walking down one while it was stationary had quite robbed her of any sense of balance. On reaching the bottom she had staggered towards a wall, and tried to find some protuberance on its tiled surface which she could grip to steady herself. There was none. Hetty became driftwood in the tide of rush-hour commuters, moving to and fro, still touching the wall whenever she could, with those who came and those who went and those who were merely changing lines, but always in the direction of greatest thrust, which was the westbound platform of the Piccadilly Line.

There the crowd was even thicker. A train arrived. Passengers pushed to get out, and passengers pushed to get on. Hetty was caught in a swarm of disgorged passengers, and forced to walk backwards towards the escalators. It was as if she had strayed into a marathon performance of the Gay Gordons. Then the renewed thrust came from behind her, and she had found herself back on the platform, pressed shoulder to shoulder, front and rear. One train after another had arrived, all packed full; she could see through the windows the desperate waving and open mouths of those being carried past their stop. Only those at the front of the platform were able to board a train, and then only if they were standing by a door when it opened. Hetty maintained her place, and prayed for an open door; she had gone too far to turn back. Now she was at the front, with the crowd like a giant's fist pushing behind her. She dug in her heels and leaned all her weight backwards against a pinstriped waistcoat. A train. She was between doors. For a moment the pressure eased to left and right as those on each side of her struggled to reach the doors before they closed. She reached out and touched the window in front of her. As she did so, the pressure built up again, stronger now as it seemed from behind than at the sides, and she realized that she had lost the strength for a backwards push, and with both strength and balance gone would be flung forward as soon as the train moved out, to lie with antique toffee-papers and empty crisp-bags on the line below. She fainted.

Seconds were stretched into infinity. She saw herself falling from her pram as she leaned forwards in an attempt to reach the brake. She saw herself screaming, her head secured between the bars of her play-pen. She saw Hetty's fingers scratching in a flowerbed, searching for worms to slip into her sleeping brother's mouth, Hetty walking down a street with a brother at each side, each gripping a wrist to prevent a repetition of the time when she had run ahead, removing all her clothes to astonish passing cyclists, Hetty again between her brothers, a sack of potatoes squeezed into pink organza, singing and dancing in the front room, doing side-steps and trying to keep up. Hetty watching Al Jolson with tears in her eyes, feeling fingers which are neither hers nor her mother's touching parts of her body she is not allowed to name. 'Shouldn't we loosen her clothing? Was it a fit, do you think? Amazing how tough some of these old girls are!' She opened her eyes to discover that she had been propped against an air vent, her skirt adjusted to conceal the large expanse of mottled thigh, her teeth removed from her mouth and placed inside her second-best handbag, and that a gentleman in a grey trilby and fawn mackintosh was slapping her cheek with one hand while using the other to fan her with his copy of *Sporting Life*.

She was placed in a taxi. For most of the time occupied by her journey to the hotel in Pimlico, the taxi seemed to be stationary, and when it did move, seldom progressed more than a few yards. Meanwhile the meter ticked, converting pence into pounds at a rate which could deflate all the cushions on Frank Cross's sofa in no time at all. In order to distract herself from watching it, Hetty decided to show the taxi-driver Geoffrey's photograph. She did not expect that Geoffrey had ever taken a taxi, but, if so much of a taxi-driver's time in London was spent waiting in traffic, he must see a large selection of the passers-by. Then she discovered that she no longer possessed the photograph or her second-best handbag in which it was kept.

It seemed to Hetty that it would be better not to communicate this discovery to the driver until they had reached the hotel.

17

The Prodigal

Flushed with a little too much of Sainsbury's Pink
Champagne, Hetty placed one hand on the mantel to
steady herself and used the other to grip Geoffrey's right
shoulder. They were being photographed for the local
paper.

'How did you find him?' It was the same young lady
reporter; that gave continuity. She leaned forwards over
her lined reporter's notebook and helped herself to
another slice of Black Forest Gateau.

'It wasn't easy, I can tell you. Three weeks I spent
combing the West End, up one street and down the
other, round all the alleyways and in and out of the
lanes. I'd followed so many dead ends, you see.' Hetty
paused to give the young woman time to enjoy her cake
without diminishing the accuracy of her shorthand. 'I was
forever looking over my shoulders. There are places in
London it's not safe to stand still. I could always feel
the vultures snapping at my heels. Pimps, prostitutes,
pornographers, pickpockets! Everyone's got something

to sell. I had my purse snatched twice.'

'Gosh! What did you do?'

'Snatched it back, of course. It wouldn't have gone with what he was wearing.' Hetty's laughter started her off into a coughing fit, and she began to sweat. Glancing sideways at herself in the mirror above the fire, she saw that her carefully applied make-up was cracking, with large areas of red skin showing between the cracks. 'They're not in colour, these snapshots, are they?' The photographer shook his head. 'That's all right, then. Only you did do a front page in colour once. For Royalty.'

'You were telling me how you found Geoffrey.'

'Well, it was a Wednesday, just after midnight. I'd been walking the streets since six that morning, and I was passing this alleyway near Soho when I thought I heard something moving among a pile of rubbish.' The re-porter's pencil raced and symbols like the footsteps of birds in snow crowded the pages of the lined notebook as Hetty assembled word-pictures of the dark alleyway, il-luminated only by the neon signs of Strip Clubs in the streets at each end, the piles of rejected prawn shells and chicken bones spilling from black plastic bags, the rain falling sideways in bursts and drumming on the lids of dustbins like the sound of Whiplash, the pools of greasy water in the blocked gutters, the stench of decaying vegetables and rotting fish, and above all the cold penetrating every layer of protective clothing and striking at the marrow of one's bones.

'It was the sort of place you'd pass by in a hurry before you began to feel poorly, but me being only elevenpence to the bob wrapped a scarf round me face and started rooting. It was funny really, but I just had this feeling in me water.' Again the Lancashire accent was becoming broader, as Hetty the ordinary person for whom allowances would have to be made was brought into the service of Hetty the performer. 'And I hadn't been at it for more than twenty minutes when I shoved some cabbage leaves to one side, and there he was. His tiny white drained bloodless features and frost-bitten fingers were all I could see protruding from this soaking wet cardboard box, but I knew at once I'd found him. There he was, just clinging to life.'

Removing her hand from Geoff's shoulder, Hetty waved it towards the camera, and turned her face away while she wrestled with her emotions. Geoff offered her his handkerchief which, surprisingly, was clean. The photographer stopped his clicking, and the young woman reporter said, 'It's a wonderful story. I am glad you remembered my name, and asked for me.'

In fact, Hetty had discovered Geoffrey Shawcross sitting next to her on the coach coming home.

'And, Geoffrey, what did you feel when Mrs Wainright rolled the cabbage leaves to one side and said she'd come to take you home?'

Geoff knew that whatever he said would be taken down and repeated back to him for weeks to come. This was a moment for the considered response.

'It's all a bit confused now. At first I thought I was hallucinating, you know, not having eaten for three days. I didn't say much, did I?' Hetty confirmed this with a shake of her head. 'I do remember trying to concentrate my mind on the twenty-third psalm. Oh, and I said,

"Thank God!"; I repeated it several times, "Thank God!" It was so fantastic; I just couldn't believe it. I'd been at death's door, almost stepped over the threshold. How do you say "Thank you" for that?'

The reporter made a special note, and circled it. 'Youth thanks God and seventy-year-old Hetty for his resurrection from slime of Sin City.'

She had lost her second-best handbag; she had lost the photograph of the subject. Frank had finally sent her fifty pounds, which had been just enough to pay the bill at the Silver Birch. At the Victoria Coach Station she had bid tearful farewells to Chalky White after supervising his placing of her suitcase in the rear of the correct coach. She had kissed his old black balding head, and had turned to mount the steps with a feeling of desolation and failure. As the coach door closed, and the vehicle backed, she had waved at Chalky as if she were some memsahib waving from an ocean liner to the family retainer after the Dissolution of Empire. Soon she would be back in the North, in front of her own fire, watching Robert's nostrils dilate as he slept away the hours between tea and cocoa.

All but one of the seats in the coach had been occupied. She would not normally have chosen to sit beside a youth in ripped black and silver vest, metal-studded belt with another stud in his nose, baggy tartan jodhpurs and Chelsea Football club socks, whose hair stood up on top of his head in three multi-coloured horns like upturned icecream cornets, but she did not have that choice. Distractedly she had lowered her weight down beside the youth. The cornet of hair closest to her was visibly melting, and blocked her view of the window. As a preliminary to asking whether it could be tied to its companions until the journey was over with a ribbon which she herself would be prepared to supply, she had broken off some chocolate, and held it out to him.

'Chocolate gives me asthma.' The words had been addressed to the steamed-up window, and Hetty had popped the chocolate into her own mouth, and replied, 'Seems to be a lot of it about' before the significance of what she had heard exploded in her memory and travelled as pins and needles to every extremity of her consciousness. Those words in that thin throaty voice had been playing like a loop in her head for the last three weeks, each time more faintly, less well remembered, and suddenly the loop had been refreshed. She had reached out a hand, grasped the youth's chin, and turned it to face her. The spots were there beneath a covering of orange pancake, partly washed away by tears. Lilac eye-shadow and eye-liner of burnt gold had become mixed, forming khaki blotches around red-rimmed eyes. She had said, 'I've just spent three weeks searching for a school-leaver with two sets of everything, and you sit there looking like something out of a nightmare.' She spat on her hankie, and began to wipe his face. 'How are those spots going to breathe if you smother them in muck?'

'They're not supposed to breathe. They're supposed to die.'

He had endured her wiping his face in public, passive in his sorrow. He owed her a pound, and might go to prison without passing Go unless he could find another hundred. In prison he would encounter worse than having his face wiped by a Senior Citizen, much worse. His youthful appearance would place him at the bottom of a very active pecking-order. He said,' Why were you looking for me?'

Hetty spat, and rubbed harder at the butterfly on his left temple. 'Your dad engaged me to find you and bring you home. For some unaccountable reason he wants you back.' A fresh burst of tears made any further spitting unnecessary. In a voice which caused the driver of the coach to glance over his shoulder, putting the Mini Metro in front of him in jeopardy, she said, 'I expect you've caught the clap or something, haven't you, is that why you're bawling? One can't go into the Ladies down in London without reading all about it on the walls.'

She had asked him if he was hooked on H or coke, and had thrust his chin backwards and squinted up his nose for signs of glue burns. When he had kept shaking his head, she had said, 'It has to be sex, then. Come on, you can tell me,' and he had turned his head away, and after a long silence asked her if she had ever been in love.

'Is that all?' Then he had turned, and looked straight at her, and asked the question again, so that she had been forced to consider it. Of course she had. She was married, wasn't she, with children? He had kept looking at her in silence while Hetty had felt herself to be increasingly on the defensive, and the passengers both in front and behind and across the aisle had been obliged to control their impatience to hear her reply. Finally she had said, 'Well, I enjoy my life, don't I? You could say I'm in love with that. It's not what it's cracked up to be, you know, love; it's not all wine and roses. I always think of that film with James Mason and Ann Todd, where he keeps slamming the piano lid down on her fingers to stop her practising her scales. That's a bit like love. One moment you're tinkling away nicely, the next – ooh! Love's not that hot.'

Gradually the story of Geoff's involvement with the two Bristol girls and George had been told. The girls had led him on, giving him their bodies to pleasure three times a day. 'That should have cured your spots,' Hetty said. Then they had left George and himself to look after a room full of consumer durables, until the police had broken the door down, to find the two of them sitting in front of the telly wearing stolen dresses. George himself, Geoff explained, often wore a dress but he himself had been wearing one for warmth, since George was adding chains to his only pair of trousers, and to sit for any time with only underpants for protection was too much of a test for George's self-control.

At first the police had thought that these were the two girls they sought, who had been photographed leaving Harrods with a bottle of crusted port for which they had not paid. Only a body-search (much enjoyed by George) had persuaded them to a different view, for the girls in the photograph had both possessed cleavages deep enough to conceal a hamper, and Geoff's chest was clearly not up to that. George said that he and Geoff were a gay couple, looking after the flat while the girls were away at a Protest March against the Church of England's refusal to ordain women; nothing in it belonged to them, and they had no idea where any of it had come from.

Unfortunately the fur-lined bedroom slippers and pink candy-striped button-down dress Geoff was wearing had been on the list of stolen property the police were carrying, and the shop's label was still on the dress. Geoff might not have stolen the articles, but he was in possession, whereas George's outfit defied identification, since he insisted on re-modelling everything before he allowed it next to his skin, and his use of sequins, ribbons, buttons, broderie anglaise and slits in unexpected places could transform a quite ordinary frock into something only seen in the Sunday Colour Supplements.

The store had agreed not to press charges, provided that Geoff paid a hundred pounds into a police station within three weeks, and obtained a receipt. He and George had waited in the room, but the girls had never returned, and since the only places in which they were likely to be found were large department stores, it seemed to be tempting fate to look for them. They had returned to the Night Shelter. George had pointed out that there was a very easy way of earning a hundred pounds in very little time and at the cost of what Geoff would soon learn to consider only trifling inconvenience, but Geoff had looked at the posters on the walls of the Night Shelter about AIDS and Arabs, and had felt the call of Victoria Coach Station. He had left George there, with a kiss on the cheek and a pound coin for luck, and had mounted the coach in which he now sat.

'So it's Face the Music time?' Geoff had nodded. 'Your dad hasn't got a hundred pounds to spare, I suppose?' He had shrugged. If the Sunday afternoon outings with his father were anything to go by, a hundred pence would be just as hard to find. Hetty said, 'Pity you never met your granddad.'

Hetty applied a hairpin to the destruction of the offending cornet of hair, and for a while they sat in silence, admiring the verge of the motorway as it passed the window. Slowly an idea had begun to form in Hetty's mind.

Geoff had said, 'What will you do now?'

'Now that I've found you?'

'That's right.'

Hetty's knowing smile had been vintage Rosalind Russell, inclining a little towards Mae West. 'I shall soak my feet for a whole week, and wait for the fan mail to roll in.' He had not understood. Men so seldom understood. 'Because we're not going to let on that I found you on this coach sobbing your eyes out, are we? Not if I promise to find you that hundred pounds before they cart you away.'

By Knutsford they had worked out the details. Geoff had stated his preference for being found in a cardboard box off Wardour Street. Hetty had added the three days of starvation. Both sets of his own clothes had been stolen while he slept, and what he now wore was all that Hetty had been able to collect together quickly. The icecream cornets of hair had been constructed by the liberal application of soap and hair lacquer, and could be demolished by placing his head under the tap in the wash-basin of the coach's WC. Only the studs in his right nostril and left ear-lobe would be difficult to explain, since their removal would be painful and might lead to infection. He would have to say that he had been terrorized into having them inserted, and had only narrowly escaped being tattooed from head to foot.

Now, as they stood in Hetty's front room entertaining the press and waiting for the car which would take them to the local television station to tell their story again, their mutual delight at being celebrities was only slightly marred by their knowledge that, if Geoff did not present himself and a hundred pounds within the allowed time at a police station well outside the area, then a quite different story, involving fur-lined slippers and a pink candy-striped dress, would have to be told.

After the television interview had gone out live, their story and photographs had appeared in not just one local paper, but had been syndicated throughout the northwest. Hetty's feet had been pampered until they puffed up, and her delight in opening letters was also given full expression. The postman complained that the sudden deluge of correspondence was adding half an hour to his round.

Hetty would sit at the bottom of the stairs, watching the flap of the letterbox open and close as the letters were pushed through, six or seven at a time. The pile of letters on the mat would grow higher and higher, and she would will the postman not to stop until it had hidden the chalk mark on the door which represented the highest point of the previous day's delivery. Then, after the postman had passed on, mumbling, she would select a handful of letters from the pile, and wander backwards and forwards, from front step to garden gate, opening and reading them. All around her, on both sides and across the road, the front gardens of her neighbours would be sprouting people. Their multi-flora wrap-over pinafores and housecoats of brushed pink nylon would bob and curtsey in the weak morning sunlight, as they weeded beds, hung out dusters, shook rugs or repositioned milk-bottles. Hetty would not be the one to speak first, but if any of these hardy hybrids wished to pass the time of day, she was at her most affable.

It seemed as if almost every family north of the Trent had some member gone missing – improvident uncles, impoverished aunts, fathers, mothers, daughters, sons and a large number of Old Age Pensioners who had last been seen clinging to the back of a bus and waving their pension books. The letters were sorted in what had once been the spare room, but was now Geoff's, since Geoff refused to return to his mother, and his father, who was Hetty's client, had left his lodgings. Proposals of marriage were pinned up on the wall of this room. The score by the end of the first week was 'Geoff 8. Hetty 3.'

Some of the letters were humorous, a few vexing, some were from people who just wanted a letter back, many were disturbing, but mostly they were moving. Hetty had not known that there were so many sad people in the world. It was strange that she had spent three weeks in London, and not made that discovery.

18
Showing a Leg

___

'Is Mr Shawcross at home?'

'Mr Cross is. Yes.' Edith waited. It was she who had been forced to open the door to the visitor, and having been forced, she would do it right.

'May I see him, please?'

'He's busy at the moment. Would you like to come in and wait?' She made way for him to enter. There could be no doubt who he was. One look at his face confirmed for her Hetty's diagnosis of high blood pressure.

'You found us all right, then?' Expecting his son to arrive at twelve thirty for lunch, Frank had locked himself in the toilet at eleven forty-five, ostensibly to study the Racing Pages and come to a decision between Billy the Kid in the three thirty and Tin Soldier in the four fifteen. The time was now twenty past two, and he had been there ever since.

'Wrong bus.'

'Oh!' Having told herself that she must not stare, Edith now found it embarrassing even to glance at him. 'You are

Frank's son, I take it?' From the corner of her eye she watched him nod. 'He won't be long now, I don't expect.' She moved to the door of the living-room, and shouted in a voice which cracked with anxiety, 'Mr Shawcross has arrived, Frank. He's waiting.' Typical of him to leave her to break the ice with a stranger! 'Do have a chair. It's Bernard, isn't it?'

Neither seemed to be able to look at the other. Bernard stared at the fire-grate, which was clean and empty. He lowered himself into an armchair, and felt two lumpy cushions dig into his back.

'You'll have a lot to catch up on. Funny the way things turn out!' She was shuffling sideways, doing a kind of cakewalk to catch another glimpse of his face. 'Frank tells me you were born in Preston Royal Infirmary.' He appeared to be counting how many lumps of coal were in the bucket. 'Safest place if things go wrong, hospital. Not that you were premature or anything, were you?'

'It was Number Seventy-nine. Should have been Twenty-Eight. It took me to the terminal, then I had to wait. Almost fifty minutes.' Fifty years of waiting, and then another fifty minutes. He had almost cried at the Depot, waiting for the afternoon shift to finish their lasagne and chips.

'You've met Hetty, haven't you? Mrs Wainthropp. She had all hers in Prendergast Ward. I expect she mentioned it.'

At nine minutes past three, the bathroom door was unlocked, and Frank emerged, reeking of Edith's lavender water. The front stud of his collarless shirt had been done up, and the toe-caps of his shoes reflected the hours he had spent polishing them. He stood in the corner of the living-room, his arms swinging aimlessly, two scraps of toilet paper attached to his chin by dried blood.

To Edith it seemed as if whole hours passed in silence. The Gunfight at OK Corral could not have matched her front room for tension. Then she noticed that in one of Frank's swinging hands there was a piece of paper, and in the other a roll of five-pound notes.

'Just got to get this on before the three-thirty.' Frank's voice was hoarse and difficult to understand, but Edith was between him and the door before he could begin his move.

'I'll do it.'

'You can't.'

'Why not?'

'Woman in a Betting Shop!'

'No sex discrmination here in Westcliff, is there?' She grabbed the paper and the money, and placed her back firmly against the door. The red-faced man rose to his feet slowly, and turned to face them. Edith linked her arm in one of Frank's, pushed him forward, and said, 'Frank, I'd like you to meet Mr Bernard Shawcross, whom I believe you know.' The faces of both father and son instantly crumpled into silent tears, and Edith untangled herself, and backed away. Before closing the door behind her, she heard Frank say, 'I'd have thought you'd have grown out of that by now.'

Being neither a mother nor any longer a daughter, she was unused to such scenes. Even the father who had repeated himself on silk cards had not returned home to be wept over. It was too late for lunch and too early for tea. She must place Frank's bet, and wander the town until it was safe to return.

Grown men crying! Two faces, one highly coloured and middle-aged, the other merely a setting for two terrified eyes, both crumbling! She had been lucky to escape close personal attachments.

She studied her own face in the window of a shop. Antonioni of the High Street had given her a style he called Roxana. A great deal of tut-tutting had accompanied the snipping, and between the clip! clip! and the standing back to sigh, there had been the kind of broken English only those born within earshot of Romford can aspire to. ''Ave a leetle vi-o-let or a tush of mow-have. Ees so like zee constipated pee 'en now. I no insult; ees true.' She had agreed that her natural hair colouring was dowdy. He had suggested that outside a Public Convenience would look more cheerful – which in Westcliff it would, since the outsides of all the Public Conveniences are planted with flowers, which are changed seasonally. It had gone on for almost an hour, and she had left with mauve hair lacquered into flyaway curls.

Thereafter she had forced her fingers into rubber gloves, and had washed her hair three times in concentrated detergent to remove the colour before Frank saw it. The Roxana perm had also succumbed to the detergent, but the end result had pleased her – muddy grey with the faintest mauve streaks, a straight fringe and two gentle waves above each ear; it was as she had always wanted it. She had watched the mauve ripples move like smoke towards the overflow outlet, and been content.

Best of all was that Frank had said, 'I hope you didn't pay good money for that. He hasn't done anything.' She had bought a new woollen dress and matching cardigan, both of violet, to bring out what was left of the mauve.

She placed fifty pounds each way on Billy the Kid, and left the Betting Shop as quickly as possible. Now she stood outside a jeweller's. The new dress needed a brooch. If she saw something she liked at under five pounds, she might come back later in the week and splash out. The trays of silver and gold charms fascinated her – tophats, flat-irons, poodles and dice, an Eiffel Tower and a pram with wheels that turned for thirty-two pounds. Those wheels wouldn't stay on very long. Hetty's charm bracelet had laddered more pairs of stockings than the Tiller Girls. The trays of rings didn't interest her, not with her hands the way they were. She tried to bring to mind a picture of Frank on their wedding day, not an easy task. She wondered what thoughts had crossed his mind as he had stood before God and placed that curtain ring on her finger, knowing full well that not fifty miles away another woman had been wearing a similar token from him for almost nine years. One bizarre act, which had now gone on for too long to be laughed off! She had not noticed such courage or imagination in him since.

One of Hetty's brothers had given Edith away, and Hetty herself had been the only bridesmaid. The bride's dress was second-hand in Marina Blue, and Hetty had insisted on wearing blue also. The argument had almost ended their friendship, and as usual Hetty had won the compromise, and worn a darker blue, adding so much trimming of silver and gold that she had looked like a plump blue Christmas tree. Frank had borrowed a suit from a funeral director he knew. At least it wasn't the one he had worn for Myra. She remembered cornflowers and mimosa in her bouquet, a few sweet peas, and an arum lily with an injured stem which had waggled suggestively as she moved down the aisle. They had eaten corned beef hash with pickled red cabbage, toasted each other in cider, and thought themselves the luckiest couple in the world.

She had been lucky. Those who knew her had disguised with a generalized good will their surprise that Edith, of all women, should have found herself a husband. Men were still in short supply; the male war babies of the First World War only reached marriageable age in time to be killed off in the next. Hetty had told her later that it had been generally accepted among the concert party (who had performed free at the Reception) that she must have trapped Frank by getting pregnant. The tightness of the second-hand dress, the absence of the bride's mother, and Frank's preoccupied expression throughout, had all helped to fuel this rumour.

From the jeweller's window, she walked slowly to the Public Library. After fifty years she must give them time; they must not be rushed.

'You made fires.'
  'Where?'
  'Where we lived.'
  'I don't remember. What would I do that for?'
  'Newspaper rolled round your fingers. No wood. Then the right-sized pieces of coal. You'd talk to me about the

coal. "This lump's useless. Look at it, full of slate. This bit's like a tommy gun. Bang! bang! you're dead."'

'You mean coal fires?' Bernard nodded.

'I thought you meant arson or something.'

'No. In the grate. There was always a fireguard.'

Frank said, 'You used to climb up and piddle in the coal bucket. Toe-nails the size of lemon pips. Never kept your shoes on in those days.'

'How are your hands?'

'No, that's Edith; she's the one with the rash. What say I find some slippers for you? Take your shoes and socks off, and save the carpet.' Bernard looked round at the bare linoleum with its four small squares of coconut matting, and began to remove his shoes. 'Edith's a bit fussy about her rugs.'

Each was trying to make contact by means of long-remembered extremities, Bernard's memories of his father's hands, Frank's of his dead wife's feet which might be expected to have been inherited by his son. Frank's will was stronger. They talked of feet, moving from varicose veins via bunions into corns. Frank removed his own socks to demonstrate that feet have characters of their own, handed down from generation to generation. Bernard attributed his fallen arches to the wearing of wellington boots at work. Frank rolled up his trouser legs, and the two men walked side by side, backwards and forwards across the cold linoleum, to see whether their feet matched. Neither went so far as to climb into the coal bucket, and Bernard quickly replaced his lovat Terylene-and-wool socks when Edith's cough was heard outside the front door.

Billy the Kid had come under starter's orders, but had been left at the starting gate. Frank, Edith and Bernard had all three missed their midday meal, so tea was taken early.

'We've had a card from Hetty about your son.' Edith passed the pickled beetroot to Bernard, who refused it.

Frank said, 'If he's got any sense he'll be halfway to Australia by now. There's nothing for youngsters here. It's a great life, the sea, if you don't weaken.' In his mind's eye, he saw the jets of water at the Sewage Farm going round and round, and felt a sense of kinship.

'I don't think Geoffrey's the seafaring type. The Isle of Man steamer put him in bed for a week.'

'Young men don't want to be chased all over London by a fat old busybody.'

'She's only doing what she was asked, Frank.'

'We would like him back.'

Edith said, 'Of course you would. Family's family. It's only natural.' Frank was staring at her. Her own child, if it had lived, would never have run off to London. 'It's a worrying time all round, isn't it? You worry when they're babies, then again when they start to walk. Your wife must be out of her . . . ' Bernard's face had grown redder, and he was dripping tea on to the tablecloth. Edith decided to leave the sentence unfinished, and start another. 'School can be terrifying, for them and you. Not knowing what they might catch. Sometimes they grow too quickly, and sometimes not at all. And they blame you for everything, don't they?' Bernard now looked as if he were about to burst into tears. 'It must age you, having children. I don't see how you can help it with all that worry.'

'What would you know about it?' Frank had placed his knife and fork beside his plate, and was shouting at her.

'I'm a woman, aren't I?'

'What's it got to do with you?'

'If he was mine, I'd be worried. That's all I was saying.'

'But he's not yours, is he? Yours died on the hearth-rug, afore it could get out from between your legs. Now you're about to bore this one to death.' He gestured at Bernard who, if there is a stone of dark and dusky red, had apparently been turned to it. No one was any longer eating. 'None of us has had much luck with our offspring,' Frank said to his only son.

'Will you excuse me, please?' There was only the sound of Edith's brightly polished shoes on the linoleum as she left the room and began to mount the stairs one step at a time, her shoulders hunched up around her ears.

Above them, the two men could hear her moving across the floor, and sinking down on the bed. Frank picked up his fork, and moved a slice of beetroot towards a slice of mature cheddar, spiked both, lifted them to his mouth, chewed, swallowed, rinsed away the bits with a gulp of tea, and said, 'I didn't mean anything. Not about you. Except perhaps your blood pressure, and your arches not being a hundred per cent.'

'That's all right.'

'Your mother was a fine woman. Only her and me just couldn't see eye to eye. All that was nothing to do with worry about you. No blame. Except mine. I'd better go up to her. You'd think, after all these years, she'd let sleeping dogs lie.' He pushed back his chair. 'Did she have much illness before she died, your mother?'

Bernard looked at the gnarled fingers pressed against the white tablecloth to stop themselves shaking. Were these the hands, ingrained with coal dust, which had once made the backs of his legs sting? 'It was over quite quickly.'

'That's a blessing, at least.'

Left alone, Bernard took off the borrowed slippers, and put on his own Hush Puppies. It was in his mind to go for a walk on the sea front while matters upstairs were repaired. He liked the ugly woman who had taken his pretty mother's place. He needed time to reassure himself that what he felt was anticlimax not disappointment, to adjust to the fact that this selfish self-opinionated old bigot was the person he had dreamed about all these years, that there had never been even the desire for a sports car, mannequins and holidays in the South of France, that this could really be the person his mother had waited for all those years and wasted her life for, that the blood which circulated with such difficulty through his body, pushing its way through the hardening arteries, had come from this man. When displeased with him, his mother had always said, 'Like father, like son,' and so he had made for himself the image of a father who had raced through life at speed and knew how to handle even the most expensive women. She would say to him despairingly, 'You're wet as a paddling pool, our Bernard, and twice as shallow,' and inside his head he would reply, 'like father, like son,' holding up in defiance the golden image he had made out of two grey words, 'disappear' and 'disappoint'. *Like father, like son!* The only real pleasure Frank had shown in this meeting after fifty years apart was during the time they had spent barefoot, walking side by side across the linoleum.

She had hung a coat over the wardrobe door to obscure the mirror, had snatched the lavender bag from beneath her folded underwear, clutched it to her face, and rolled on to the high bed, pulling the eiderdown up around her. She had removed her teeth, to watch them subside slowly in a tumbler of diluted peroxide. The three-legged Bambi lay on its side, shivering in the draught from the curtains. Any other woman might have tipped the glass bowl of Angel Delight over his head, and left the house to seek out other battered wives.

If she had fought back years ago, she would not feel so flattened now. Mice scraped out messages to each other behind the skirting board. They had been there since Hetty's last visit. Her and her midnight feasts! 'I knew it wouldn't be easy. Difficult to make allowances when we're all three on edge.' He was lying on the bed next to her with his shoes off. 'Can't leave him on his own too long. He's just as much right to be upset.' What had he been doing with his trouser leg rolled up? He was too old to join the Masons without telling her. 'We should have had a baby of our own. That would have helped.'

On the wall the crinoline lady made of silver and gold paper winked at her from behind glass. The mauve Roxana hair-do had cost £13.50. The violet dress, which she might never wear again and which was creasing, scrunched up like this, had been £15.95 and the cardigan £12. Forty-one pounds and forty-five pence spent on an afternoon of either being ignored or snapped at. If it had been her own son standing on the doorstep after fifty years, she would not have sat on the toilet with the racing paper, leaving someone else to make small talk.

'I'm still hungry, aren't you? I'd sent everything in my stomach to the Sewage Farm before he arrived. Then we didn't even get to the pudding.' What was she doing here, a grown woman of seventy something, hiding from her husband under the eiderdown at seven o'clock in the evening, while he lay beside her, trying to pretend that nothing had happened? Why was she incapable of waving two fingers in his face, and making a rude noise? She could have blown the whistle on him years ago, when Hetty had come waltzing in to say, 'You do know Frank's married you bigamously, don't you? He's got another wife over at Garstang who says she'll never divorce him.' If she'd made a complaint right there and then, instead of spending a week running back and forth to the toilet being sick, and then keeping it to herself for the next eight years, they'd have sent him to prison and out of her life. Or later, when he was involved in the Black Market, an anonymous letter or telephone call might have tripped him up and cooled his heels. What had they been doing, those two, with their shoes off and trouser legs rolled up? They could hardly have been playing 'This Little Piggy Went to Market', not just before tea.

'Come on, girl, we're too old for this. You with your Roxana Rainbow Curls, and me with my best collar missing. I want you to come down and watch me make the fire. He's a bit tricky to talk to.'

Listening to him making promises and excuses, trying to cajole her out of the warmth the eiderdown now afforded, she saw from behind closed eylids the last years of her life floating towards the overflow outlet. This sense of hurt and injustice was not a new feeling; it was in fact so comfortable, so lived in, that she could not imagine what might replace it. She was an ugly woman of average intelligence, who had cultivated self-pity into an emotional reassurance. No, she was not that easy a pushover. He would have to try a bit harder if she were to be expected to leave the warmth of this eiderdown and put her teeth back in.

19
Raising Capital

It was a problem. They needed a hundred pounds fast. Hetty studied the tealeaves left in her cup, and attempted to concentrate her thoughts. Robert carried the local paper from breakfast table to WC, and from WC to armchair, wrapped in undemanding thoughts to do with Brussels sprouts and raised beds. She had ransacked his pockets twice, and found no more than twelve pence and something which might once have been a radish. She wondered how many of what were now multi-national companies had begun with the liquidity problem she now faced.

'You're worth more to me dead than you are right now, did you know that?'

'I do now you've told me.'

She watched his eyeballs move from side to side as he pretended to read. Holding the paper up in front of his face, and making noises to signify an attitude to the world outside, was all make-believe. He had no more idea of where Nicaragua was than she had. He collected their pension, and paid the bills. He had taken over the household finances back in 1953, when Hetty had arrived home carrying a television set on which to watch the Coronation, and they had spent the next six years without a roast on Sundays until it was paid for. Now they had separate accounts with the Trustee Savings Bank, and Hetty was allowed pocket money.

'Better watch you when you make the cocoa, then, hadn't I?'

'A hundred pounds is nothing these days.'

'You're fretting over nothing, then.' He overacted getting out of the chair, and then shuffled away, pulling around him the cardigan she had knitted him five Christmases ago. Fifty Christmases ago he had run a mile in under six minutes, and presented her with a lucky charm bracelet. One by one the charms had dropped off.

Of the hundreds of letters requesting her services as a tracer of missing persons, only three had contained money. A Mrs Lillium of Chester and a Mr Radlett of Stalybridge had sent her cheques for five and seven pounds respectively as travelling expenses to go and see them, and a Mr Y. P. Herbert of Preston had sent one for twelve pounds as 'an act of faith'.

But these were cheques, and Hetty's overdraft was already above her limit. If they were paid into the bank, they would be instantly swallowed up. Making them over to Robert would have the same effect, since she owed him ninety-seven pounds which he obstinately refused to write off.

Geoff had suggested steaming the first class stamps off the stamped addressed envelopes. There were a hundred and forty-six of these, which at seventeen pence each should fetch £24.82 at the Post Office. The stamps would be legal tender, he said, even without glue. Hetty enquired at the Sub-Post Office on the corner, queuing for fifteen minutes to make the enquiry, which, even though she made it in a hoarse whisper, was the subject of intense interest to the queue behind her, to be told that the Post Office was only prepared to pay in stamps for stamps.

Geoff himself was still in residence. As the letters had begun to arrive, Hetty realized that she would need assistance, and he had offered his services in return for his keep, a share in any profits and his name on the letter-head, so they had shaken hands, and ordered a thousand sheets of headed notepaper with envelopes to match. That was another twenty-five pounds to find.

Hetty mounted the stairs with a mug of tea and four rounds of toast and marmalade. 'If I borrow a cycle, could you ride over to Preston with a letter?'

Sleep-drenched, undersized, pimply, sixteen-year-old Geoffrey Shawcross, junior partner of Wainthropp and Shawcross, Private Investigators, Missing Persons Found, roused himself from thoughts of masturbation and sat up in bed to receive his breakfast. His first question was incisive and to the point.

'What?'

'We're going to tell Mr Y. P. Herbert that we'll find his little Tommy provided we get a hundred and fifty pounds in cash up front.' The junior partner rubbed his eyes. 'Then we've got your hundred pounds and fifty over to get our show on the road by tonight. But you'll have to make it to Preston before the banks close so that he can get the money out. A cheque's no good to us.'

'How far is Preston?'

'Oh, about twenty-eight miles, but it shouldn't take you more than an hour; it's mostly downhill. I'll ask about brakes when I get the bike. It'll be a girl's, but you don't mind, do you – one of those sit-up-and-beg doodahs; the old post-mistress had it for years. If the chain hadn't got caught in the spokes halfway down Sheer Brow, she'd still be pedalling it today.'

Geoff tried to imagine how much pedalling there would be in twenty-eight miles. 'Has it got gears?'

'I should think so. It was just the chain Dora couldn't master. Everyone round here had a complete set of her oily fingerprints. She'd never have been able to go in for robbing banks. Do you the world of good; you'll come back bursting with leg muscles. Get Y. P. Herbert to write down everything he can remember, every detail about Little Tommy's last days before he disappeared, all his habits, his likes and dislikes, any strange men he may have been seen talking to, and don't forget a photograph. Get back here by four, and we can catch the five thirty.'

'Where to?'

'First stop, P. Lillium of Chester, then J. Radlett of Stalybridge. Those too mean to send money will have to wait their turn.'

'What about paying my hundred pounds?'

'We can do that tomorrow at Westcliff. I had a word with the sergeant there once, and found him most helpful. We'll have a few days' rest with your grandfather, and then start work on Little Tommy and the other two.'

'Three at once?'

'It's a waste to do all that walking round London just looking for one person. Three at a time cuts down the odds and saves on expenses. Here, you'd better take this twelve p with you in case you have a puncture.'

It had not occurred to Geoffrey Shawcross, Private Investigator, that twenty-eight miles mainly downhill on the outward journey would become mainly uphill on the return. He left the house at ten twenty, and did not reach it again, exhausted, until six forty. His opinion was that four slices of toast and marmalade had been an inadequate foundation for the day's work. It had been difficult to persuade Mr Y. P. Herbert to hand over £150 in cash to a sixteen-year-old with one stud in his nostril and another in his ear, but Geoff had taken with him a clipping from the local paper, showing Wainthropp and Shawcross together, posed in the front room, and in the end Mr Herbert, who had grown increasingly affable during an interview which had extended itself over three drinking clubs, had agreed to a fee of fifty pounds a day up to a limit of two hundred, and Geoff had signed a receipt for a hundred and fifty pounds in advance.

Little Tommy proved to be a forty-year-old man with a badly fitting toupée. He had last been seen waving goodbye from a train pulling out of Preston Station. If located, he was not to be approached, but kept under surveillance, and Y. P. Herbert was to be telephoned immediately.

'I think it's something criminal.' They had caught a later train, and were halfway to Chester.

'Rubbish! I don't do criminals. I made that quite clear

to the media.' Hetty held the photograph at arm's length, and squinted at it. 'Anyway we've taken the money now. Didn't he give you a surname?'

Geoff consulted the notes. 'I should have written these myself. He was drinking vodka-and-lime with beer chasers. It's rather difficult to read. Phelan – Little Tommy Phelan. He wears a hair-piece and sings "Danny Boy" whenever possible.'

'Shifty little eyes! We'll start by searching all the pubs in Kilburn.'

'What do you think the "Y" stands for?' Hetty looked at him. 'Y. P. Herbert. I just thought it might be a clue.'

Robert had, as usual, been left with instructions. He was to stack the incoming letters in Geoff's room, and any telemessages were to be kept handy, and read to her when she phoned. If anyone asked, she was away on a case, but would consider bookings for the forthcoming months, and if anyone should be particularly desperate, Robert should offer his own advice, which would be that a deposit in advance always secures preferential treatment, postal orders preferred. Robert had nodded thoughtfully during the briefing, but had not displayed any of his usual relief at being left for a while to a quiet life, and afterwards he had gone to the freezer, and counted its contents in front of her. Hetty had wondered whether he might be sickening for something, and had felt obliged to ask, 'We're not feeling sorry for ourselves, are we?' to which he had replied, 'Go on. Make your fortune. Just remember that ninety-seven pounds of it are mine.'

He would be all right. After a good sleep, he would not even remember she had been home. He always responded to her voice on the telephone by asking who was speaking.

'I'm a dynamo when I get going,' said Hetty to her junior partner, as the train rattled over the points outside Chester.

They took a taxi from the station. They had finance now for their enterprise, and speed was an investment. Mrs Lillium showed them her daughter Beryl's bedroom, left exactly as she herself had left it (except for dusting and the vacuum) two and a half years ago on the day she had been due to sit an O Level in English Literature. The half-read copy of *The Mill on the Floss* still lay open on the bedside cabinet.

'I can't believe George Eliot was responsible. She loved books about the countryside. Very shy, and hardly spoke to anyone, let alone strangers; she'd blush if the television newsreader looked up at her. It's as if she's been swallowed up by one of those blackspots in space.'

'Holes.'

'Pardon.'

'Black holes. Solar chasms.'

Hetty glared at Geoff. To be corrected is never consoling, and Mrs Lillium had not yet agreed a fee.

'Geoffrey's bound to be invaluable in this case, being close to Beryl's own age, and of course he knows London inside out from his own experience of it. Was Beryl involved in any fringe religions at all? Moonies? Harry Krishna? Seventh Day Adventists? Did you, for instance, have Jehovah's Witnesses coming to the door?'

'She admired the Salvation Army, though she wasn't musical herself.'

177

'And you've had no ransom demand?'

'Not unless they telephoned while we were out.'

They took from Mrs Lillium twenty-five pounds in cash, which was all she had in the house, and a cheque for £225 as an advance against five days of intensive search. It had occurred to Hetty that a cheque made out to Wainthropp and Shawcross need not be swallowed up by any overdraft, but could be used to start a banking account in London for the firm. At Coutts.

They phoned for a cab, and caught the last train to Stalybridge, and arrived at the home of Mr Radlett, again by cab, not long after midnight. He seemed unwilling to answer the doorbell, which had to be rung many times, while they waited outside in the rain, and surprised them when he finally did so by wearing pyjamas and a dressing-gown, carrying in one hand a foam fire-extinguisher, in the other a large kitchen knife. He himself was greatly surprised to find that the midnight intruders were neither burglars nor the police, but a rotund lady and an undersized teenager.

He was a bachelor in his late forties, given to retiring early with a good book; it had been some hours since he had finished chapter five and turned off the bedside light. Indeed, he did remember writing the letter and enclosing seven pounds to defray the cost of a visit, but somehow he had imagined that there would be a telephone call or a reciprocal letter to arrange an appointment at a time mutually convenient.

'Time is money, Mr Radlett. If we waited for the GPO, we'd all be paupers.' Hetty plonked herself in the most comfortable chair, wondering whether Mr Radlett was the

kind of man who drank Dubonnet. Geoffrey's thoughts
ran more to steak and chips.

'You make it sound expensive.'

'I tailor my fees to suit the client. Now, if you were
to switch on that electric fire to get a little heat in this
room, and perhaps throw in a tot of something from
what looks like a drinks cabinet over there, I might be
tempted to treat you as a person deserving of special
consideration.'

The fire was switched on, but what had looked like a
drinks cabinet turned out, when unlocked, only to contain
photographic equipment. 'These were my father's lenses.
I think there may be a bottle of whisky in the kitchen. I
don't drink myself.'

Geoff said, 'I'll look, shall I?' Those four pieces of toast
had ceased to sustain him even in memory. There might
be cold baked beans in the kitchen, or even a chicken leg.
'You give my partner the details, and I'll see what I can
find.' He hurried from the room, and soon the little
terraced house resounded with the distant crunching of
Jacob's Cream Crackers.

'My father's hobby is portrait photography, but
Stalybridge isn't well served with models willing to pose
for him. There was a German lady came in from time to
time. I told the neighbours that she came to cut his corns.
My father used to get frustrated. He'd tell me he was off
to take it out on the hills. That was his joke, you see.
Mountains, hillocks, rubbish tips, on would go his boots,
and he would stomp, imagining that he was stamping on
the female form. I never dared take him anywhere near a
cemetery.'

'Did he go often? To the hills?'

'Often. But he always returned. Some of the hills were quite close, and he would return the following day. Others were further. He had the most wonderful time in Scotland one year, stomping on peat. It was there he met this widow, similarly inclined. She had an exceptional figure. They walked the hills, and took pictures of each other. He didn't at all mind having to kneel to eat his meals when he returned, and the bruises soon disappeared.'

'I'm surprised you want him found.'

'He is my father. It's just been the two of us since mother died. We don't always hit it off, but blood is thicker than water. If he has fallen down some glen or other, or even been horribly mauled by stags, I ought to know, if only to cancel his subscription to all these Swedish magazines which keep arriving.'

Hetty explained that her plans did not include the mountains of Scotland, not immediately, nor even the Lake District. But in London, and particularly in Soho, a district about which her knowledge was already extensive, there were hundreds of photographic models of all nationalities and colours. She considered it at least an even chance that a frustrated elderly photographer might have extended his stomping grounds to include that area, and for a nominal retainer she would take the photograph of Mr Radlett Senior with her, and flash it around.

'Do you really think so?'

'I'd stake my reputation on it. If this is really cooking whisky, it's very good. Just let me have a photograph now, and be good enough to telephone a minicab, and in view of your kind hospitality and the amount of cold sausages and yoghurt consumed by my partner, we shall be prepared to make you a special price.'

On the night train from Manchester to London, Geoff expressed his surprise that they were not to begin their enquiries at once. They had another twenty pounds in cash and a cheque for eighty from Mr Radlett, making five hundred pounds in advances altogether, and the sooner they began to earn them the better; he could pay his hundred at West End Central. But Hetty explained that she also had a debt to pay. She had changed five ten-pound notes into fifty one-pound coins, and she intended to stuff them into one of his grandfather's cushions.

20

Support Stockings

'Don't worry, I'm not stopping. I've just popped by to pay my debts, and deliver your grandson to you.' Hetty saw Bernard Shawcross's highly coloured face peering at her over Frank's shoulder. 'Well, isn't this nice? Three generations of Shawcrosses! Where's our Edith?'

'In bed. She's not very bright.'

'Wants taking out of herself, I shouldn't wonder.' Hetty sailed over the doorstep, past the two men, and was emptying her pockets of one-pound coins on to the kitchen table. 'Find a nice safe place for these. There should be fifty. Took you long enough to send them. Now you can have the pleasure of counting them. Tell Edith to get her bum off that bed. I shall want her down here, wearing something loose and totally ravishing by the time I get back. The lunch is on me.'

Then she was gone, leaving the three men silent. Geoffrey had wanted to say, 'Don't leave me,' but she was too quick for him. The old man looked at him in an unwelcoming way, as if to say, 'Another mouth to feed!' and began to count the coins, stacking them in piles of five, and grunting as each stack was completed. His father seemed at a loss. Well, Hetty had that effect on people.

'When did you last see your mother?' Geoff shrugged. 'Does she know you're safe?' Geoff nodded. It was his lethargic nod. In his father's presence he could feel lethargy coming over him like sleeping sickness. He sat down. The cushions were lumpy. It was as if all the excitement of his London adventure and the press coverage which followed it had happened to someone else. Yet here he was; he was somebody; he had a job as junior partner in a firm of Private Investigators. Nobody else in his form at school would have achieved more than a Government Training Scheme to wash cars. He was an adult. He had matured sexually. Until his trip to London there were parts of his anatomy which had caused him nothing but embarrassment and guilt. Now he had discovered exciting uses for them. The two Bristol girls had not laughed at his efforts, but had exhibited positive appreciation in the way of sighs, squeals, bites, scratches and the insertion of fingers up his rectum. Could his father not sense the difference?

The old man was offering him tea. 'What's that?' He was pointing at the stud in Geoff's left nostril. 'He's not half-caste, is he? Is it so you can tie him up and take him for walks?'

'Did Mrs Wainthropp mention how much I owe her for finding you?'

Geoffrey was about to shake his head, but he remembered that, as junior partner, he had responsibilities to the firm which were greater than mere family affection.

'We've given you our lowest rates for being our first client. Two hundred and eighty-three pounds, inclusive of accommodation expenses and mileage. We'd appreciate settlement within one calendar month.'

Bernard Shawcross took from his pocket his note-pad accounts-book, found the section headed 'Still to Pay', and wrote '£283. Mrs H. Wainthropp. Safe return of Geoffrey.' The entry looked ludicrous just below '£1.72. Shoe Repairs' and '29p to Jack for chocolate biscuit at Tea Break (do not repeat)'.

Frank said, 'What do you mean – "we"?'

'Wainthropp and Shawcross, Private Investigators. I'd give you our card but they're still at the printers.'

'Where did she get the money to pay me back?'

'We've taken on a few more clients. People who are genuinely desperate to get their relations back can usually be relied upon to find some of the cost in advance.' Geoff addressed this remark to his father, but Bernard's thoughts were lost in a maze of mental arithmetic.

As the morning progressed, Frank and Bernard excluded the third Shawcross from what had clearly been an ongoing conversation about the good old days of ten Woodbines for sixpence and beer for threepence a pint. Geoff closed his eyes, and took what ease he could among the lumpy cushions, wondering whether he was to go as short of food on this day as the one before. At twelve thirty Hetty returned, wearing a coat and skirt of bright turquoise and a large floppy hat of salmon-pink straw, both purchased from Mother and Bride of the High Street. She acknowledged Geoff's grimaces and whispered request to get him out of there with her new mother-of-the-bride smile and the instruction through clenched teeth to get back in there and sit on his nest-egg. Then she was bouncing up the stairs, like some hippopotamus in a Disney cartoon, yelling, 'Edith, get your knickers on!'

Soon she reappeared, bringing down Edith, who looked reluctant and ill. Geoffrey stood by the living-room window, and watched the two women walking away from him, down the street hand in hand, with Edith bouncing off the hat which was already losing its shape. They might have taken him with them; he was the junior partner. He hoped Hetty did not intend to abandon him.

His father and grandfather continued their conversation as if they had never left it. They had reached 1957, ten years before Geoff was born.

'Edith started drawing the pension. Or was that '57?'

'It was the year I had boils. They gave me iron.'

'The boils?'

'The doctor. He gave me iron *for* the boils. Mother was very poorly too that year, with her circulation.'

'She always had chilblains. Flat feet too. Never saw her out of carpet slippers, not in my day.'

'Couldn't seem to keep herself warm.'

'Sat on top of the fire, browning the insides of her legs.'

'Support stockings.'

'What?'

'I got her some of those thick support stockings. Very warm.'

Frank Cross's flow of memories seemed momentarily halted. He stared in silence at the empty grate, then said, 'Did she really wear those things?' He shook his head.

'Why on earth would she want to do that?'

'They were a great boon. Often, you know, she'd talk a bit when she got really tired – silly imagined things; she seemed to think her legs were hollow. "I'm empty inside, our Bernard," she'd say, but she wasn't hungry; it was something different. But she could feel the support stockings all the time. We made a joke of it; we said they were all that held her together.'

The old man seemed to be miles away. 'Thick stockings on those feet?'

'She was over sixty then, dad.'

Frank Shawcross turned to his grandson, Geoff, who was by now asleep. 'I didn't know your grandmother then, you see.'

'How long have you been hiding under the bedclothes?'

'Only a few days.'

'Since Bernie Beetroot's been here?'

'More or less. It seemed better if I kept out of their way.'

'Waste, all waste! You'll get more than enough peace and quiet when you kick the bucket.' Hetty separated the tip of her fried scampi with her teeth, and tossed it back into the basket. 'I'll bet you haven't even been out to change your library books.'

'When I've read them, I just start at the back and work forwards. That way I can imagine it's a different story.'

'What do they find to talk about?'

'They're working through their lives since Frank left. Frank's got up to 1948; Bernard's at 1957. It's funny hearing your past described by someone else. I don't remember having pneumonia in 1946. You feel excluded.'

'How do you know what they're saying, if you've been keeping out of the way?'

'Oh, I don't go down. I put a glass tumbler against the floorboards.'

'When's he due back in the Halifax deep-freeze?'

'Monday.'

'Good!'

'He was talking about giving it up, and moving down here to be near Frank in Frank's last years.' Edith had ceased pretending to eat, and was rearranging her scampi into patterns. 'They've kept the fire blazing until after midnight sometimes, sitting there with their shoes and socks off. Mostly they talk about Myra. Frank wants to know everything that happened after he left home, what she said about him, whether she had any men friends, even what she wore, particularly on her feet. Bernard's memory is amazing. He was describing a pair of court shoes she bought for VE day. I don't want to cast blame, Hetty, but it is your fault. "No harm in finding out," you said, "A discreet enquiry commits nobody." Now it's all gone wrong, and as usual I'm the one left holding the . . . ' She left the sentence unfinished.

Hetty leaned forward irritably, and exchanged Edith's basket of scampi for her own, which now contained only tips. 'It's all gone wrong because you let it.' She began to eat the lightly nibbled scampi in Edith's basket. 'These won't come back to life, you know, and you're not Scarlett O'Hara, to leave expensive luxuries on your plate. I've had to accept money in advance to pay for these.' Edith took up one of Hetty's discarded tips, which were all that remained in the basket now before her, and touched it lightly with her front teeth, as Hetty continued the harangue. 'You must be the world champion at standing back and letting things go wrong for you. I've been pulling you out of holes you've dug for yourself ever since that day you arrived on our doorstep in a thunderstorm and borrowed my skirt and blouse. A woman of your age being jealous of a corpse! I've never heard such – ' She had attempted, while still in full flow, to take a gulp of wine and a mouthful of French bread. Combined, the two activities brought on a coughing fit. Edith managed to rescue the wine-glass before the occupants of the next table received more of the House White than they had paid for. 'But don't worry. I found him, and I'll think of something to keep him out of harm's way. He won't get a job down here, and his wife's not a well person.'

After that the talk somehow turned to Hetty herself, to publicity, to fame and how she intended not to allow it to spoil her, and of her resolution to remember old friends. Fillet steak, artichoke hearts and croquette potatoes came and went, Hetty finishing what Edith could not quite manage in spite of its deliciousness, while Hetty itemized the peculiarities of her new clients and speculated as to what the persons they sought might be up to.

Then coffee came, and Hetty once more paid some attention to her oldest friend. 'You've done something daft to your hair.'

Bernard Shawcross left his father and the woman with whom his father lived, and reluctantly returned to Halifax and the Lean Price Wholesale Butchery. He had promised to come back as soon as was feasible, since his life now had a new focus and meaning. He would write every other day; his note-pad accounts-book already contained calculations adding the cost of postage and stationery to his weekly outgoings. Meanwhile he would make plans against the time when he could cast aside the wellingtons and thermal socks, and make his newly focused and meaningful life in or near Westcliff-on-Sea.

Frank and Edith tried to return to their usual routine, but found that their hearts were not in it. Both felt that they had been changed by Bernard's visit. It was not Bernard himself who had brought these changes, but the memories of his mother; it almost seemed as if More Life Myra herself had descended on them for a visit, nor did it feel to Edith, as she watched Frank's faraway look and noted his lack of interest in the contents of the rubbish bag, as if Myra had yet left. Often Edith found that she had to repeat what she had just said, only to be ignored a second time.

Frank had aged. He had aged as people often do, suddenly. The walks along the sea front for his bowels' sake became trips to the end of the road and back. He forgot where he had put things, and what he was looking for, and when he had last seen his teeth.

In her own mind Edith still blamed Hetty for finding what should have remained lost, Hetty the scatterbrained who had cajoled and persisted, for her own reasons not for theirs. Hetty the easily bored who required distraction, Hetty the unwilling to be a nobody, who had wished to make her mark and become someone, had left Frank almost gaga and Edith lost, empty and afraid. If Bernard

Shawcross were able to fulfil his promise, to apply for a position in frozen meat somewhere near Westcliff-on-Sea and get it, Frank might become lost for ever down Memory Lane.

21
Snake's Eyes

Hetty and Geoff settled in at the Silver Birch Hotel. So far they had been seduced by their own publicity. Both had managed to forget that Hetty had been a singularly unsuccessful private eye, that even when she had been almost within touching distance of her subject, she had failed to recognize him, and that their mutual discovery of each other had been by accident, not by her design. She had, Geoff found, no better plan than to walk the streets again, and hope to be lucky again.

Geoffrey's mind was more organizational. The three subjects must be sought in three different and appropriate areas. They would show photographs of Mr Radlett Senior to the staff of shops selling photographic equipment, scour the pubs of Kilburn for the Irish tenor, and he himself, in the character of an Old Boy who had made good and found employment, would return to the Night Shelter as a first step towards Beryl Lillium.

The Night Shelter people were congratulatory but unhelpful; they did not keep records of their transients and their confidentiality was absolute. The YWCA had no record of Beryl Lillium, nor did the Salvation Army. The assistants in the camera shops said they were sorry, but so many old gentlemen were like that; they couldn't tell one elderly satyr from another. 'Danny Boy' had been sung in all the pubs of Kilburn, but by tenors other than Little Tommy. Was it a serious crime he had committed, this fellow with the Brillo pad stuck on his head, or was it just him being an Irishman?

'Clueless,' Hetty said. 'We've got three people to look for, take our pick of any of them, and we've not a clue between us.' Fame was slipping away from her, as it had so many times before in her life, and even Dubonnet could not revive her spirit. She decided that she had better invest some of the firm's money in a telephone call to Mrs Lillium.

She telephoned Mrs Lillium, and accused her of holding out. Did she really want her daughter found at all, or was she employing Wainthropp and Shawcross as window-dressing for the neighbours? Mothers and daughters had secrets together; they confided in each other. What little secret confidence from her daughter had so embarrassed Mrs Lillium that she was trying to hide it from those who were her only hope of getting Beryl back? 'Oh, I know it's sad when it's one of your own, but if you don't tell us, you can't expect us to help you.'

Mrs Lillium became tearful. Beryl had never confided. She had lived in her own world. Her mother had thought that she was at that age, and would soon grow out of it. 'We're a very close family. I don't think she felt excluded or anything.'

The girl had left home. There must have been a reason. Had she ever been to London before?

'Not since she was eight. We took her to see the Christmas Illuminations in Oxford Street, and then a pantomime at the Palladium. She met Father Christmas in Harrods, Selfridge's, Debenhams and John Lewis.'

'Four Father Christmases in one day! Did anything else unusual happen?'

'Not that I can remember. She was sick on the Circle Line, and she screamed a lot when we had to leave the zoo because they were locking the gates.'

'She's fond of animals, then?'

'Not particularly. We spent most of the time in the Reptile House.'

'Snakes?'

'Oh yes, she's mad about those. Didn't I tell you? She's got ever so many books on them. I moved them out of her room because they gave me goose-pimples while I was vacuuming. I think the only time we did disagree was when she wanted me to buy her a Diamond Python. I mean, they can grow to ten feet long, and how do you know you're going to be able to find enough rats and mice to keep them happy?'

The glass-fronted cages were brilliantly lighted. Some contained branches of gnarled wood and little pools of stagnant water. One had a glossy rubber-plant in a plastic pot, but no reptile; there was a notice informing the public that this cage was unoccupied, in case they should linger in front of it, hoping for something particularly virulent to appear. Before other cases, art-students sat, resting their behinds on the hand-rails, sketch pads on their laps, BB pencils or felt-tipped pens at the ready, their feet covering the name-plates of the reptiles in the cases, and schoolchildren ran among them, lifting up the feet to read the name and shout them in the general direction of other schoolchildren, all of whom wore coloured plastic anoraks against the heavy rain outside, and carried packed lunches. Single-parent families pushed occupied and unoccupied single and twin pushchairs. One man whom Hetty took to be an estranged husband spending his three-hour ration of monthly access kept touching his child, as if trying to cram the whole month of physical reassurance into these few hours in a public place among creepy-crawlies and the rain. He stood before three glass cases containing the Green Mamba, the Leopard Gecko and the Short-Necked Skink, caressing his offspring's shoulder and reading aloud a passage about the incubation of eggs from the white card on the nearest case. '*Most Reptiles are independent of their parents immediately they are born or hatched. Baby venomous snakes have fully functioning venom glands and fangs.*' Another father in thick spectacles crouched and swayed, sliding his nose along the surface of the glass behind which a Puff Adder did likewise; it was not clear whether the man was imitating the snake, or the snake the man. The man's seven children stood at a little distance behind him, trying to disassociate themselves from his antics.

'He's pulling faces back at me. Look! he's rocking with me now. They do that to music where he comes from.'

'Dad, Leonard needs to go somewhere in a hurry, and we haven't got to the Birds of Prey yet.'

In fact, the aviary usually containing birds of prey had been emptied for redevelopment, and the bears had been sent on holiday to another Zoo until the Mappin Terraces had been redesigned. Geoffrey Shawcross could have told the children this, for Geoffrey had read all the notices outside, as he stood in the rain, which ran down inside his collar and seemed to be collecting in puddles around his waistband. His job was to stand watching the outside of the Reptile House while Hetty and Chalky searched the interior. Was it always to be like this? Geoffrey outside in the wet being prodded by the umbrellas of passers-by while Hetty remained warm and watched the show?

None of the keepers recognized Beryl Lillium from her photographs. There were a few nutters who came almost every day to stare at the cobras, but she was not one of them. Girls of that age and development were not common in the Reptile House. If she had visited recently, they would have remembered her.

It had cost the firm of Wainthropp and Shawcross, with their associate Chalky, a total of ten pounds fifty pence to enter the zoo, and it was money down the drain. Since they were already there, however, they might as well see the rest of it. Chalky had noticed that the Zoo was prepared to allow the general public to adopt some of the animals, though not to take them home – a sealion for £2,000, a lion for £1,500, a chimpanzee for £500, a flamingo for £90 and a Slow Loris, for £60. He could not remember ever having seen a Slow Loris, and felt drawn to the breed for being so frugal in their demands.

The Elephant House brought on Geoffrey's asthma, and they had to leave; it had been the same at the circus when he was younger, and had been taken as a treat. He would have mentioned it earlier, but had hoped it would not come up. At the Monkey House Hetty suggested that he should remain outside again, but he was by now shivering violently and insisted on warmth. He would stand well back, and try not to breathe. This whole visit to the Zoo, on which Hetty had pinned such hopes, was clearly going wrong. She stared at an elderly female chimpanzee, on her own in a cage with one youngster. Some of the £500 adoption fee must have been spent on providing her with props, with which to entertain the public – three plastic dustbin-lids, some synthetic straw, a paper sack and the remains of a cardboard box. While the young chimp swung from an iron climbing-frame, dropping handfuls of straw to watch it fall, the elderly female sat in a corner, covering her rotund figure with the paper sack, adjusting the cardboard box on her head, and pulling faces at the spectators. 'Look at her,' Geoff said sourly. 'She's like you. She wants to be somebody.'

They sat in Phillida's room, watching *Crime Watch*. Beneath the signed photograph of Lord Louis Mountbatten, a woman police constable, dressed identically to a recent victim of rape, was walking through gorse on the edge of a golf-course, hoping to jog the memories of any viewers, who might have been close by on the night in question.

Phillida said, 'I wonder how they come to London, these young people.'

Geoff said, 'Bus, I suppose. I did. You can't afford the train if you're running away.'

The WPC turned to avoid a bunker. An actor dressed as

the rapist and carrying what may have been a Number
Four Iron, was seen to follow her. 'Right!' Hetty shouted.
'Got it! Atta-girl!'

'Eh?'

'Forget about the Zoo. Back to basics. We follow girls
from Bus Terminals, and see where they go to.'

So they spent the next day following girls from Bus
Terminals, and seeing where they went.

Geoff's girl, who looked about fourteen, got her suitcase
from the boot of the coach from Newcastle and South
Shields, and sat on it. Ten minutes later she was picked up
by a man with silver sideburns, wearing a mohair suit.
Geoff followed them in a taxi to Compton Street, where
they ate foreign food, and then in another to a side alley
off Curzon Street and a door marked 'Bel Canto Voice
Production', where they remained for two hours, pro-
ceeding thereafter to Her Majesty's Theatre, again by
taxi, where the girl was auditioned for a tour of *The Sound
of Music*. Total cost in taxi-fares £11.60. None of the
drivers would give a receipt.

Hetty's girl was a tall blonde teenager, who walked her
round the Natural History Museum and the Victoria and
Albert before window-shopping in Oxford Street and
swimming twenty lengths at the Tottenham Court Road
Baths. She then returned to the Coach Station to use the
other half of her Daystretcher Return. There were no
taxi-fares; they had walked everywhere. Hetty's feet had
swollen and she didn't want to talk about it.

Phillida said, 'Well, I told you all it was a rotten idea.
Every time I set foot outside, I remember why I hardly

ever leave this room. London's a mess, and that's upsetting when you've known it as well as I have. I disown it. It's quite horrible out there, and you won't get me further than Fortnum's ever again.' She had followed a girl of about sixteen, with dyed black hair which looked as if it had been cut with a knife and fork. The girl's legs were like chopsticks, she had difficulty walking in high heels, her tights were laddered, and she had to stop every few minutes to haul them up. If ever there was a subject for a television documentary on teenage runaways, this girl was it. She had drunk three cups of tea at an ABC and downed some pills with them, and had circled some of the small ads in the evening paper. She had left the evening paper on the table, and Phillida had attempted to grab it, but some horsy bitch in a tweed hat had reached it first. 'They're as mean as sin, the women around South Kensington. I've noticed it before. Anyway I followed her to Piccadilly Circus, where somebody seems to have boarded up the statue of Eros. There's a sign on it, saying "Murphy. Eros Resiting and Refurbishing". You can't turn your back on anything these days. Refurbishing! They'll have had that poor little boy done over by David Hockney. I felt quite faint, so I went back to Fortnum's for one or two little tit-bits, and came straight home.'

'What about the girl?'

'Oh, I watched her shoplifting in Boots. It's so depressing. In my time, it was only worth owning things if one had had to save up to get them. Anyway there are depilatory creams these days for under-arm hair. She didn't need a battery-shaver.'

'But you didn't see where she went?'

'Took up with some gentleman from the Middle East. They'd obviously met before. I imagine she comes down at least twice a week. I had to take an aspirin and lie down for the rest of the afternoon.'

Chalky's girl had been about fifteen going on forty-seven and he had followed her from Victoria to Trafalgar Square on foot. He could tell she was a stranger because she carried an *A to Z* street directory. In Charing Cross Road she had entered a photographic studio called Gerald's.

'A photographer!'

'But she was a girl, not a randy old gentleman.' Chalky had counted five, and followed her in, but she and her suitcases had vanished. 'No one there but Gerald, and he trying to kid me he about to close for lunch. I ask what he charge for Wedding Groups, but he don't do weddings, only theatre and artistic.' Chalky had cast around for some object of study which would keep him in the shop until his subject reappeared, and found a drawer with a sign reading 'For Adults Only'. The photographs in the drawer were Gerald's sideline, and they were all for sale. There were black girls rubbing themselves against coconut trees and tied to pirate ships, brown girls with strings of onions leaning against the Eiffel Tower, girls of all colours with animals of all sorts, blonde girls with huge busts being examined by doctors for what Chalky assumed to be cervical cancer. And a girl with very white skin and eyes modestly downcast, who was kissing a python next to a sign reading, 'New Forest. Keep Britain Tidy'.

'That's it,' Hetty said.

'What you mean, "That's it"? You giving me notice because I lost my subject?'

'It's a clue. That photograph of the woman kissing the snake. What did she look like?'

'We're trying to trace a girl, and we wondered if you knew the name of this one here with the snake?' The man behind the counter shook his head. 'Wasn't it you took this picture?'

The man continued to shake his head, and Chalky intervened. 'Now, come on, Gerald! You tell me this is your side-line.'

'Selling 'em, not taking 'em. I can't do work like that. Haven't got the facilities. I buy them by the gross, assorted poses. Them as don't turn over fast enough, they swap for new ones. She's been in that drawer, oh, must be three months; she'll end up in the North somewhere, where they're not so discriminating. I like her meself; it's a good picture – "Keep Britain Tidy". I like a bit of humour now and again.'

'What's she doing in the New Forest?'

'She's not in the New Forest; she's in the studio. Where would you find an inch of space to take a picture like that in the New Forest if the sun was out?'

'Your supplier would know who the photographer was.'

'Might.'

'How much would this picture cost with the name and address of your supplier scribbled on the back?'

'An arm and a leg. And they'd both be mine.' Gerald busied himself with stocking the shelves. As far as he was concerned, the conversation was clearly over.

Chalky said, 'That little girl I follow in here yesterday. Fourteen, I think she say her age was. She come in here, go through that door maybe, and never come out. You got any snaps of that girl? Your own work?'

Gerald's stocking of the shelves seemed to consist of taking packets of film from one area, blowing dust off them, and putting them back in another. He paused in this activity, thought for a moment, then turned to face them, and spoke decisively.

'Look, it's this snake girl you're after, right? Well, that picture was taken in a London studio, I'll stake my life on it. Now, if she's handy with snakes she'll most likely be working the clubs. Try the Strip At Ease; they're mostly animal acts there. One wrestles with a leopard, there's a donkey that farts to music, and there's bound to be at least one snake act. Now piss off, and leave me to earn a crust, will you?'

They stood outside the Stars and Strips, a fat old woman, an elderly black man and an undersized teenager in a cotton windcheater advertising *Star Wars*, which had absorbed so much water that, although the rain had stopped, he was a walking cloudburst in himself. They stood there, avoided by punters, putting the photographs of the club's attractions under their investigative scrutiny.

Their problem was simple. In these photographs, the animals had been given prominence, and the naked girls took a supporting role. A highly manicured poodle rested its front paws on a pair of naked breasts, but the owner of the breasts had no head. A brightly coloured cockatoo caressed a nipple with its beak, but only the lower half of the nipple-owner's face was in the frame. There were snakes with arms and snakes with legs and even some

203

pubic hair standing on a ladder while a snake looked up at it. Even the donkey with its hoof poised above a complete head managed to cast the shadow of that hoof on the performer's face.

Geoff went to consult the uniformed doorkeeper, and returned.

'What's this one say?' Geoff shook his head. 'Did you show him your birth certificate?'

'He said I was jail bait. An open invitation to Mary Whitehouse to pull on her cardigan and rush hot-foot from her cocoa to the nearest magistrate. And anyway I'm too wet.'

'I suppose it's up to me again as always.' Hetty had visited four Strip Joints already, starting with the Strip At Ease, and it was only nine thirty. The shows had varied in length from twenty minutes to an hour, and she had sat through them all, being pinched and stroked by elderly male punters and being forced to sip alcohol at three pounds fifty a tot. She had seen nothing of Beryl Lillium, and was beginning to suspect that the Lillium advance had already been spent.

Inside the Stars and Strips she sat with her overcoat covering her thighs, which were still sore from the attention they had received earlier, attempting to ignore the leers and whispered promises of a good time made to her by the club's geriatric clientele.

The lights were lowered, and from a tape-deck somewhere came the sound of a breathy flute playing gems from *Scheherazade*. A pin spotlight took a few moments to find its position in the middle of the dark curtains, from between which a woman's arm was extended, beckoning the audience to come closer. They would readily have done so, but their chairs were bolted to the floor, and Hetty gained the impression that some of the older ones had been strapped in. A second arm slid snakelike down the first. The two arms coiled round each other, and were then withdrawn. The pin spot moved jerkily downwards to discover that a leg in a fishnet stocking with a frilly garter had been extended through the curtains. There was a drum-roll, and the spotlight went out, flashing on a second later to show that a second leg had joined the first, and that the only covering on this leg was a three-year-old Carpet Python coiled around it. Hetty felt the hair on the back of her neck moving. It was not the lascivious touch of a geriatric punter, but a genuine *frisson*. She was close, so close; she knew it; she must be. The legs were gyrating to the sensuous sound of the flute, and the hips above the legs gyrated, and strings came in to join the flute, and the music built towards a crescendo. Then the lights went off again, and the curtains were pulled apart, and elderly sighs could be heard from all over the room, and all the lights came up together to reveal, totally naked in the centre of the tiny stage, except for one fishnet stocking, a frilly garter and a python, the performer herself.

She stood there, her eyes cast modestly down, as the sleepy python began, in time to the music of *Scheherazade*, to explore the crevices and orifices of her beautifully matured body. She was the shy and only daughter of Mrs Lillium of Chester, and the firm of Wainthropp and Shawcross, Private Investigators, had scored a bullseye.

22
Cushioning the Blow

There had been no reason for it, none that one could see. He had simply been crossing the road, his left arm held high to inform the traffic of what he was doing, one moment a Senior Citizen in motion, the next an untidy heap in a dangerous place with out-of-focus faces staring down at him. Capability left him, like a gas lamp being turned out, the glow descending until the mantle is left grey-white, fragile as the shell of a blown egg.

The pains in his head and chest had made him hold his breath, and this he wrongly assumed to be the reason he could not speak to ask what was happening. There had been no fright, no fall downstairs, no heavy meal followed by violent exercise; he had eaten no pork pies tasting of caramel, drunk no more than his usual pint of beer, won no more than forty-two pounds at the Betting Shop. It had just happened, for no reason.

The out-of-focus faces had worn expressions which he took to be accusing, since he was blocking the road and causing congestion in the High Street. Mouths moved in some of the faces, and no sound came out. He was back at school, at the end of his first day, being told to leave his desk. 'Get up, boy! When I say "One!" you stand up, is that clear? "Two!" you put your left leg over the seat. "Three!" your right leg joins its partner. "Four!" face the lane between the desks. "Five!" you march on the spot. "Six!" you step forward and keep going until you're through the school gate. Left! right! left! right! UP, boy, I said; you're not sitting there all night.'

Finally two of the out-of-focus faces had lifted him on to the pavement to stop the motorists blowing their horns, and a third face had undone several buttons of his shirt.

Then there had been the hospital. He had cried every night he had spent in the Observation Ward until finally they had seen the point he was trying to make, that his grief was out of place in public. As Visiting Hour approached, they had tried to warn him with looks, then asked outright for promises of good behaviour. 'Selfish to get everyone in a state, howling silently like that.' He had wanted to tell them that the silence of the howls was not intentional, and had kept those parts of his face over which he had control stretched wide and creased like the boy in the old advertisement before he is given what he most wants, a bar of Fry's Chocolate. Finally they had got his message. They had allowed him home.

Now he lay in a makeshift bed downstairs. They had tried with him; he would give them that. They were a necessary evil, which others might need, but he had Edith. Stiff backs and high-church faces! Squeaky shoes on composition floors! What did they think his eardrums were made of? – asbestos?

How long was it since he himself had last attended church? Riding in the pony-and-trap crushed between the bony knees of his brothers, the frizzy hair of his elder sisters brushing his face, his tiny bottom bouncing on what little of the seat he was allowed. Pains in his stomach from the strain of wanting to break wind and trying to hold it back. 'Not on God's day, Francis, please!' Then the combined smells of mints and mothballs, brilliantine and musty clothes, and his arms aching from trying to keep the hymnbook at an angle which suited his father.

The hospital smells had been just as bad – floor polish, boiled cabbage and fouled linen, some of it his own. No wonder the visitors, holding bunches of flowers up to their faces, had darted through the swing doors like greyhounds leaving their traps. Now the floor polish and boiled cabbage were gone. Edith fed him baby foods from tins so small she had to balance them on her nose to read the labels, and there was never time for her to dust, let alone polish.

Edith might be old, but she could cope. They hadn't experienced her strength in bed. Even all-in wrestlers would appeal to the referee if trapped inside those thighs. It had been her pretence, even a game they played, that she refused him intimacies, but skilful fingerwork could excite old memories, and she was a terrier when roused.

Now Edith came and went, and there would be no more grappling for position, no more of that. They had shown her how to give him blanket-baths, and had advised her to warm the room first. He had watched her holding the mantel for support, staring at the ashes in the grate, and pondering the daily miracle of how fire is made. Finally she had bought firelighters. Nothing was sacred.

She would lean over him, dabbing at him as if he were a precious ornament, sponging his body bit by bit, and his thoughts would be years away, watching his elder sister light the fire in the copper in the backhouse to give them all their Friday-night bath. There had been real and natural smells then. He could almost taste the smoke as it blew back into his sister's face, the smoke of rotten bean-sticks, old socks, candle grease, chicken feathers, birds' nests, dried potato peelings, old boots worn to the uppers, anything they'd been able to find or steal and hide, ready for Friday night. Four of them, sitting on the scrubbed wooden draining-board, eight legs dangling inside the boiler, paddling in heated water and touching each other's feet as they waited their turn to be scrubbed. 'Frankie's got a boil on his bum. Give him some of that iron.' Out-of-focus faces with heads back laughing, small toes wriggling to insert themselves between other small toes.

It was odd that he could remember those toes, and yet in hospital he had not known who Edith was until she had sat on his good side, and placed her fingers between his, gripping them with such force that, if speech had been going to return to him, it would have happened there and then. The nurse had said, 'It's your wife come to see you, Mr Cross. Now perhaps you'll stop pulling silly faces,' and he had looked at Edith and thought, 'Thank God for that. I do remember something. I remember you shouting at me that if I didn't find my teeth and get properly dressed instead of staring out of the window you'd have me certified into a home.'

He had looked at her, and known her to be his wife,

though why he had picked such an ugly one he had not been able to imagine. Slowly other aspects of the woman had returned to him, such as her strength in bed, and now, as he watched her trudging upstairs or shuffling down them one at a time, he knew that she was willing her shoulders to relax from the hunched position, for hunched shoulders spelt resentment, and that was now taboo.

He remembered his wife, and much about her habits, and he remembered leaving the house, and going to the pub and on to the Betting Shop, but before that there was a blank, years of nothing until he reached his childhood. They had told him that other parts of his memory might return slowly and in bits. He had to accept that what had happened to him was not a minor stroke, not minor by any means, and he was lucky to have survived it. The only reason he was being allowed home was because he was making himself and others iller where he was. He had signed a piece of paper. Edith had guided his good hand. He had not recognized the signature as his, but then it was she who had done the writing.

Just as he watched her, he noticed, so she watched him, almost as if he were not really her husband, but that she had decided to pretend he was for the sake of peace. She watched as he took the spoon into his mouth, and shuffled the food to his good side. She watched for his nodding or blinking (he had a choice) when the food was safely past his windpipe. She watched him dreaming, and sometimes asked, without any hope of reply, what he was thinking about. She watched his face for a change of expression as she hoisted his buttocks to slide the chamber pot beneath them. The pot was always too cold, killing any inclination to fill it, and her adjustments to his genitals were performed with less reverence than he would have wished.

She had opened the door to a young policewoman, who had asked if she were Mrs Frank Cross, and suggested that they should make a cup of tea together. Edith had recognized her as a WPC she had sometimes seen on duty outside the Library. All Edith's questions had been met with others, such as where did Edith keep the sugar and did she mind if the young WPC slipped her shoes off for a couple of minutes, since they were new and giving her gyp. Edith had watched without protest as the policewoman, shoeless, tidied away everything sharp, putting the breadknife into the oven and the potato-peeler into the fridge. It was probably some kind of game for the television. There would be hidden cameras in the garden.

She allowed herself to be led into her own living-room, placed in the centre of her own settee, and propped with lumpy cushions. Tea was brought to her. She discovered that her hands were shaking and that she had become quietly hysterical; she would not be in at all the right frame of mind to appear on TV.

The WPC chose another cushion, and began to pummel it vigorously. The stitching had not been designed for such treatment. It might explode, scattering paper currency all over the room. She began to wonder if this was indeed the WPC from the Library or a mugger in disguise. The disguised mugger balanced the cushion in her hands, as if about to make a guess at its value, then threw it to the ground, and sat on it, smiling up at her hostess as if house-calls of this nature were the part of her job she enjoyed most.

'Tea all right?' Edith had nodded, although in both colour and taste it resembled treacle. Having achieved her approval, the tea was immediately taken away again, and the WPC had begun to explain why she was there. Out of the many words of the explanation the only ones Edith had taken in were 'husband', 'stroke' and 'hospital'.

Then she had sat on a wooden bench for what seemed like hours, watching white-clad figures come and go through swing doors, until at last two of the figures had taken her arms, supporting her on either side as if she were a legless cripple, and guided her to a room in which a sleeping man with a twisted face lay beside machinery. She had asked where Frank was, and they had told her that this was he.

She had stopped on the way home to telephone Hetty, not knowing what else to do, but Robert had yawned back down the phone at her, and sighed, and seemed stuck for words, and had later said, 'Oh, hell, what a mess!' as if someone had just dropped a jar of jam. Hetty was not due to phone him for another three days. He had no number for her, as she was moving about. Her last postcard had contained no news, just a shopping-list on the back of a photograph of an orang-utan with instructions to restock the deep-freeze.

The house had been as she had left it. She had bolted the door behind her before replacing the sharp utensils where they belonged. Then she had sat on the settee between cushions placed strategically by the WPC just in case she was the fainting sort, and stared at the empty grate, wanting a fire but thinking it to be a waste for one person, who would probably be going to bed soon. At the hospital they had told her that waiting was the worst part, and she had omitted to ask them which part was the best.

She had spent five days alone, visiting the hospital only to be told that there was no change. Then Hetty had arrived. At first Edith had thought that the knock on the door was someone come to tell her that it was all over, but Hetty had stood there on the doorstep wearing a tartan trouser suit with beret and pom-pom, had embraced her violently and immediately began to weep enough for the two of them. 'All over? No such luck, love. It's only me.'

They had lighted a fire at Hetty's insistence, and sat before it drinking the gin and Dubonnet she had brought with her, until they both felt more reconciled to the situation. Hetty told Edith of the finding of Beryl Lillium, and of reuniting her with her mother on Platform Eleven at King's Cross Station. Mrs Lillium had seemed more envious of her daughter's appearance and situation than relieved to discover that she was still alive, but she had settled her account and put Wainthropp and Shawcross back in funds.

The Women's Collective who owned several fifty-pence peep-shows, where men stood in small booths and peered at women dancing naked, had remembered having trouble with one old gentleman in hiking boots, who had kept trying to smuggle a pocket camera into one of the booths. One of their members had agreed to do private posing for him, but so far Hetty had been unable to locate either the old man or his model, since they were thought to be on a working holiday somewhere in the Alps.

Three more clients had been taken on, and there seemed to be some prospect of finding Little Tommy in a pocket of Irish at Willesden, who were given to holding Musical Soirées. It was an eventful and satisfying vocation, and Hetty confessed that she had considered applying for a Small Business Expansion Grant.

Over the next few days they had visited the hospital together, where Hetty asked questions of the staff and generally informed them how things were done in the North, particularly in the Prendergast Ward of Preston Hospital, where she had suffered three confinements. Frank remained the same, neither in nor out of the world, while Edith sat beside him, sometimes talking quietly, sometimes trying to read, sometimes just watching for signs of life, and Hetty wandered the hospital corridors, visiting other patients who lacked visitors or discussing the latest form of laser surgery with those she took to be surgeons. As the days passed, Edith noticed Hetty becoming more and more impatient. She put this down to Hetty's need to return to London and continue her career.

On the sixth day of her visit, Hetty had almost sprinted to the hospital, dragging Edith behind her. She marched through the hospital and into the ward, bent over Frank's bed with her mouth close to his ear, and shouted, 'Come on, you ugly bugger! Jump off now, or you'll end up at the

David Cook

terminus.' Frank had opened his eyes, and Hetty had
taken the credit. With Frank awake, she had felt free to
continue her work, though she had returned to Westcliff
when it became necessary to convince the authorities that,
if allowed home, Frank would have a responsible and able
person looking after him. 'If the selfish bugger wants to
die in his own home, why shouldn't he? I'll supervise.
Edith was a nurse, you know.' And it was true that, for a
short period before her marriage to Frank, Edith had
worked as a kitchen assistant in a Mental Hospital, though
the only professional qualifications required had been a
loud voice and a strong back.

She had stayed to help with Frank's arrival home, and
had spent the best part of a fortnight settling him in. She
had shouted at him as if he were deaf, and had got more
response than Edith had seemed able to get. She had
taken pleasure in helping to wash and dress him ready for
his trips in the wheelchair. It was Hetty who had invented
the game of sliding the racing paper under his good hand,
and then rushing to place a bet on whichever horse the tip
of his index finger pointed to. The success rate of this
apparently random selection had been amazing, and had
been increased if the selection was made while Frank was
on the pot, which was how he himself had always done it,
retiring with the racing paper to the WC, which concentrated his mind. The winnings had been divided equally,
allowing Hetty to open a Building Society Account and
Edith to knock together three more cushions to contain
her share.

Frank's eyes showed no sign of pleasure at his achieve-
ments. Edith kept a running total, and added it to the

216

figure of £32,624 she had found scribbled on a scrap of paper taken from his waistcoat pocket. 'That makes thirty-seven thousand, eight hundred and sixty-four we're sitting on now.' The eyelids lowered to tell her that she had done the sum correctly, but there was no approbation. Instead she sensed that he would have liked to reprove her for squandering the money on firelighters and mauve hair.

Soon Hetty had taken to gazing out of the window and doing little running steps as she pushed Frank's wheelchair round the flowerbeds in the Park. Edith had realized that the time had almost arrived when she would be on her own again. She had remembered the days of solitude, loneliness and apathy between Hetty's visits before Frank had been brought back home. Now, far from seeming empty, the house was full of him. His smell was different from the smell she had remembered and liked. It would be the special food in little tins, she supposed. Mashed swedes, strained plums and creamed spinach were bound to take their toll; she had never been able to savour the smell of milk-fed babies. The house was full of gear more to be expected in that of a nursing mother – plastic bibs, mugs with spouts, nappies for wiping his face, three chamber-pots. and there were creams, antiseptics and disinfectants also, but these were for herself, for the hands she had kept hidden inside gloves every time she had visited the hospital.

Her routine was set now. Breakfast and its aftermath took an hour and a half. Then they would wrestle to get him into his wheelchair, and she would push him to the Park. Back again for lunch, which took until three thirty, and then they both slept, she in the chair, he in his bed. After that they listened to the radio or watched television until his gaze began to wander round the room, and he began to pluck at his covers, sliding them on to the floor to gain attention.

It was like retrieving a rattle for a baby, the motions repeated many times until she gave in. This was the time when hugs were needed, reassurances and promises demanded by eyes and the insistent fingers of his good hand. No, she would not leave him. How could he think of such a thing? No, she would not put him in a Home. How could anyone but she put up with such a spoiled old ram? Wiping away the tears which would otherwise make his cheeks sore, pressing gently with her fingers to close his protruding lower lip, which often made him look like an old sheep chewing turnips, she swore she loved him more than ever now, vowed that he was her baby boy, her darling sweetheart. She would keep him alive until they both could go. They would go together or they wouldn't go at all, and that was all there was to it.

If the weeping persisted, somehow she would take him from the bed and slide him along the floor to the rug in front of the fire. After seven weeks she had lost half a stone in weight, and her hands itched continuously.

Edith cradled Frank's head on her lap, and arranged what was left of his hair. On the television screen, a mousy bank clerk removed his spectacles, threw away his umbrella, and jumped into a white sports car crammed with women who had too many teeth, to speed along a narrow mountain road. Sitting on the rug before a fire which was in, and certainly not out, she felt the skin between her fingers break, and a trickle of blood landed upon her baby's head.

23
Double-Glazed

As the two men gazed at each other, the clock could be heard marking off each second. The living-room stank of old sweat, of stale urine and weak antiseptic. The younger man waited a little longer, and repeated the word he had already used three times. The word was 'Dad', and he murmured it as if asking a question, for the lines on the older man's face had formed themselves into a shape unfamiliar to him. They were tangled screwed-up lines, pointing every which way, around eyes too bright and anxious.

He took another step forward, and spoke again softly as if in church. 'It's all right. I'm not going to bite you.' The anxiety in the old man's eyes became stronger with each word until it turned to fear. 'I'd have come sooner if I'd known. I've been waiting for a letter from you.' A faint sound emerged from the old man's lips, the sound a dog makes as it scratches at the door to be let in, halfway between a whine and a yelp. The expression in the eyes suggested that if help did not come quickly the head containing the eyes would explode. 'Do you know who I am? It's Bernard. We met some weeks ago. We talked for a long time about Mother and what it was like after you left us.' One side of the old man's mouth moved, the lips opening and closing as the sound became more piteous and more urgent, and to this sound was added other sounds from within his stomach, sounds like those a cistern makes when clearing its pipes of air. 'Are you hungry? Do you think he might be hungry?'

Edith shook her head. There had been no time for her to warn the visitor that his father could no longer speak. She supposed that it would have been correct to have written to him, informing him of the situation, but there had been so many other matters to see to, many of them not at all correct. Besides, she had assumed that the visitor's own son, Geoffrey, would have been told by Hetty, and the news been passed on sooner than this. She had wondered why letters had continued to arrive every other day, but they had been addressed to Frank and not to them both, and she had saved them, unopened.

'I don't think he knows who I am.'

'It's impossible to say what he knows. Most of his memory has gone. Hetty was here. She helped me with him for a while. He's known her for almost fifty years, but I think he believed she was someone from the hospital, he was so well behaved.'

'He looks terrified.'

'Yes, you just have to get used to it. Anything out of the ordinary frightens him. But if he were really as frightened as he makes out, he'd be dead by now. The fear would have killed him.'

'Is there nothing you can give him to calm him down?'

'If you sit here with me, and take your jacket and your shoes off, he'll know that you haven't come to take him away. That's what he fears most.'

They were whispering about him. Why was Edith being so chatty with this red-faced man? Was he a Social Worker? He had noticed a lot of them in hospital, Social Workers, always being over-familiar, trying to insinuate themselves, using first names without so much as a by-your-leave. It would be like a Social Worker to call a complete stranger 'Dad'. In the hospital they'd been middle-class women mostly, educated bitches pretending to be something they weren't. They all looked as if they'd been through a depression and were lucky to have come out the other side.

Now the man had taken his shoes off. And what was she thinking, letting a stranger clean the grate out and fetch the coal? Claims he's been here before. They think they can tell you anything when you've lost your memory. What was all that about Mother? He can't be old enough to remember her; she died just after the war, April 1919. Surely he couldn't have meant Edith. Did they call old women 'Mother' the same way they called elderly men 'Dad'? 'We talked about what it was like after you left us' – presumably he meant the unconsciousness, that time in hospital. Well, Frank or 'Dad' or whoever was back now, so this man could stop padding about the place as if he owned it, sneaking sideways glances as if he expected 'Dad' to disappear in a puff of smoke.

Now he was at the window, pressing his face against it,

then wiping his eyes with a hanky. Yes, it does bring tears to your eyes, that icy blast. Had Edith finally decided after all this time that they needed double-glazing, and got someone from the DHSS to come round and test that draught from the window? He had to be here to test for something, fiddling with the fire like that in his bare feet. Why hadn't he taken out his tape-measure? Angling for a cup of tea, no doubt.

It was warmer in the Park sometimes than it was in this room before Edith got the fire lit, and there you could break wind whenever you wanted. If she'd only realize how difficult it was to hold on to wind and everything else when you'd only got one buttock functioning normally, perhaps she wouldn't make so free with those accusing looks. Good! They were lighting the fire. Now, you red-faced block, stop pissing around, and get that tape-measure stretched across the window.

'I kept your letters, if I can remember where. I expect you'd like them back. He did enjoy reading the ones that arrived before his stroke. They made him very thoughtful.' From a drawer, Edith produced twenty-four unopened letters.

Bernard Shawcross had put a great deal of thought into what he wrote to his father, and since he had promised to send a letter every other day, a major proportion of his evenings had been spent in literary composition. Replies had arrived at the rate of one a week in his father's large bold hand. Most of what both men had written had concerned the past; current affairs were rarely mentioned, and nothing of interest happened at Bernard's place of work. Bernard had discovered that, if he lay on his single bed with closed eyes and concentrated, he could recall almost photographically even the smallest details of his childhood. Thereafter it was simply a matter of transferring into words what he had seen in pictures. He had described the decoration he himself had applied to his Easter egg in 1948 and the purchase of his first pair of long trousers, which had been in Southport in a thunderstorm; they had been of grey flannel, with enough material in the turn-ups to lengthen them twice a year until he was sixteen.

'One of them has two stamps on.'

'Yes, I thought it might be a bit heavy.' This bulkier envelope contained twenty-five school reports, each copied from the originals he had kept in a biscuit tin for posterity. The quality of the work on which they reported was neither one thing nor the other, and the word which had most frequently been used was 'average', but he had thought they might give his father yet another clue to the personality of his lost son.

With the reports he had included a short note of his own, beginning, 'Moment of truth! Not many boys get the chance to hide the enclosed from their father for over forty years. I "Could Do Better" at Maths still, even now, and Country Dancing isn't ever going to get me an "A".' Yes, he had discovered that he could make jokes with his father in letters. That had been a step forward.

Now the time he had found to write those jokes would have to be filled by something else.

24
Exit Laughing

The shoe-box in which Edith stored her old photographs and postcards also contained a copy of *Woman's Own* for March 13th, 1937, and a selection of sheet music which had once been Hetty's, but which she had discarded. There was a short story in the *Woman's Own* which Edith had particularly enjoyed, and which she sometimes re-read, a knitting pattern she had never got round to using, and the offer of two almost-free gifts; with a birthstone ring for ninepence came a free horoscope, and with a commitment to subscribe to *Woman's Own* for thirteen weeks came nine table-mats of pure Irish linen with lace borders. Among the song-sheets were such old favourites as 'Beat Me, Daddy, Eight to the Bar', 'When Budapest Was Young', 'The Little Boy That Santa Claus Forgot' and 'Be Like a Kettle, and Sing'. The last of these had brought Hetty considerable acclaim at Methodist Chapel Daffodil Teas.

Sitting on the hearth-rug, with the shoe-box beside her and her back resting against the seat of the armchair,

Edith was able to support Frank's back with her chest as she showed him the contents of the shoe-box.

He had been particularly lively all day, spitting out his food so that it landed at her throat and ran down the inside of her dress, refusing to have anything, even pyjamas, covering his body, and attempting with little jerks to slide the bed and himself closer to the window. There were other ways in which he seemed to be improving, for he had suddenly rediscovered the ability to laugh. As an expression of mirth it was not totally convincing, since its sound was more like that a starter motor makes when the battery of the car is flat, but it was an addition to his other noises, and seemed to suggest that he could distinguish between a photograph of Edith aged three and a half and a cartoon postcard about the Boxer Rebellion.

She turned the pages of *Woman's Own*, stopping at any pictures which seemed to give him pleasure. Almost all the advertisements were for soap, sanitary towels, corsets or laxatives. How simple life had been in those days!

'"How Mary Norman Became an Alura Lovely". She doesn't look any different to me than she did before. What do you think?' Frank chuckled. It was difficult in this position for her to see whether his eyes were focused on what she was pointing out, but at least he was calmer, and as long as her own arms and legs didn't go numb with the weight of him, they would be all right for an hour or two. She had built up the fire to last.

'Look, it says, "Why had they never told her? Men thought Gladys was just a good-time girl until . . . "' Frank chuckled. 'Just your cup of tea, she was, even using the wrong kind of face-powder. Now here's one for me. "She was in utter despair. A victim of anaemia and nerves." Here's another of mine, "Three times a day after meals. Wash up with Hudson's Concentrated Soap."'

Frank's good hand was touching the back of one of Edith's, signalling that he wished to hold it.

'How can I turn the pages, with you holding on like a great baby?' She allowed her hand to be held, and rested the magazine in his lap. Frank's chuckle grew louder and more aggressive. For a while she suffered his fingernails digging into her palms, and rested her cheek on the back of his head, remembering an unsuccessful attempt to cut those fingernails when she had been unable to keep his good hand still.

Frank's grip loosened, so that she was able to reposition her own hand, and hold his. 'Look, there's Mary Evelyn's Coconut Pyramids again. We only tried those once. They kept getting under your teeth.' With her free hand she put the magazine aside, and began selecting photographs from the shoe-box. 'There's Hetty and her brothers doing "Is You Is or Is You Ain't My Baby" at our wedding reception. This one's of me minus the top of my head. You took that with Robert's Box Brownie. And this is my mother before she was married. I've no idea what colour her dress was there. She did tell me once; I should have written it on the back. Everything came out sepia in those days, even the aspidistra. What's the matter? Have we fallen out? Don't you want to hold my hand any more?' Frank's hand had slipped out from inside hers, and was resting on the rug. 'Don't go to sleep on me yet, or I'll never get you back to bed.'

Edith leaned forward to try to see whether his eyes were closed. His head had slumped forwards, and as she tried to shake him awake she discovered that she was suddenly very frightened.

He had gone. For another hour she remained where she was, holding him tightly to her with one arm under his chin to support his head, while her free hand continued to lift photographs from the shoe-box and hold them in front of him.

'This is one of you and me with that greyhound of yours, the one that ate one of your socks and was ill for a month. Here's Uncle Len in his Fire Warden's uniform . . . Nesta Ridley, pretending to hold up Blackpool Tower . . . I can't make this one out. Don't know who it's of any more . . . Hardly worth keeping it now.'

A crowbar loosened the bolt, and the weight of the fireman's shoulder did the rest. The front door parted from its hinges and landed on the coconut matting, raising a cloud of dust. Hetty had agreed to take full responsibility, though she had not expected the firemen to arrive complete with engine, nor that the Brigade's Fan Club, who now lined the street, should turn out in such force.

'Do you ride everywhere with that thing? I said on the phone, clear as day, it was only one tiny front door I wanted shifting. You didn't have to dress up for it.'

Frank's bed downstairs was unoccupied, which Hetty thought just as well, considering the size of the audience now gathered around the doorway and peering in through the window.

In the kitchen the scraps of food on the unwashed

dishes had hardened, suggesting that they had been waiting for attention for some time.

On the stairs there was a smell, which grew stronger as they climbed, so that the leading fireman stopped, and suggested to Hetty that she should wait down below. Hetty shook her head, and covered the lower part of her face with her hand.

In the bedroom, the fireman pushed aside the glass fairing of Bambi which lay in a pool of condensation on the sill in his haste to get to the window and open it. The fairing landed on the floor, and was broken.

Both bodies lay on their sides facing each other, and at first it was thought that both were dead, for Edith could not be roused, and did not move. Her arms were cold, and did not respond to Hetty's tugs. Only the lightest of pulses at her neck and wrist indicated that she was still alive.

There was no resistance when Frank's body was removed from inside her arms, but for some time afterwards those arms remained extended, forming a circle, the position they had held for four days and nights.

Edith had decided that Frank's body could not be left where it was on the rug by the fire, and that, even if she managed to get it back on to the narrow bed downstairs, she would be unable to lie beside him as she had promised. She had spent two and a half hours dragging him to the bottom of the stairs, and pulling him up. As she had attempted to climb backwards, her fingers dug into his armpits, his weight had pulled her forwards, and several times she had almost fallen on top of him. She had allowed him to die needing a shave and his fingernails

231

cutting, and, once upstairs, had been too exhausted to attend to either.

She had promised that they would go together. Promises should be kept. Hetty, paying one of her flying visits and calling the Fire Brigade when nobody answered her knocking and shouting, had prevented her from keeping hers. Now it was too late.

She watched Hetty dismiss the last and youngest of the firemen by patting his bottom. She watched the doctor writing out Frank's death certificate, and listened to him telling Hetty that she, Edith, was suffering from hypothermia and mild catatonia, and needed hospitalization, and to Hetty's reply that hospitalization was one sure way of killing this patient off. She tried to convince herself that she was still part of real life, if only just, and not a character in some play or film of which Hetty was the star, who wore all the best costumes and spoke the best lines, while Edith played some incompetent chambermaid suffering from dropsy.

First Hetty lied, then switched to attack. The lie – that she was Edith's sister and would decide what was best for her nearest and dearest. The attack – where had the doctor been during these last few days, how come it had been left to Hetty, a professional woman living three hundred miles away, to call the Fire Brigade and have the door knocked in? She was the only person the patient would now trust, and she must follow her conscience, sacrificing her career and nursing her sister to the bitter end. Edith thought that if the bitter end was what Hetty anticipated, she might have done better to have let matters take their course, but she did not speak her thoughts, closing her eyes modestly instead, and allowing Hetty to pose in the doorway for a round of imaginary applause.

After a week of carrying trays of food up and down stairs, of making conversation and getting no response, and of trying to sleep next to Edith in the ruts of the mattress made by Frank's body, Hetty decided it was time for her to put her foot down.

'If you don't want me sleeping in this bed, you've only to say. It's no fun for me either, you know; you're not exactly Ronald Colman. But I'm not sleeping downstairs, and I'm not lugging that bed back up to the spare room on my own. I could go to that nice little hotel, where they're used to me, and get off-season rates. The people there talk to each other. They say "Thank you," when they're given breakfast in bed. Sometimes they make up whole sentences like, "I wonder whether I might have a refill of this delicious tea." They don't just stare out of the window, holding their cups aloft, like someone not a million miles away, and they don't stay in bed all day wearing suffragette nighties. They dress up of an evening, and sit round the bar drinking Snowballs and complaining what a dump Westcliff is. There are some nights, our Edith, when you can walk to the bathroom and back without me now, and if you can get that far, you can blooming well slide down those stairs. So I'll get the fire going, and we'll have some music out of the radio or find those old seventy-eight records, and then we can have a dance.'

Hustled into the violet two-piece and cardigan, and bustled downstairs, Edith sat by the fire, and watched Hetty dance to the tune of 'Two Little Girls in Blue', her bosoms bounding like tennis balls in a sack, and sweat running down the side of her face and dripping from the end of her nose. Candles had been lighted, to make a party atmosphere, and cheese biscuits, crisps and peanuts were on hand to accompany the gin and Dubonnet. The room still had a faint smell of sickness, and the joss-sticks Hetty had lit to disguise it were not entirely successful, particularly since the smoke kept getting in her eyes. Also Frank's bed still took up much of the room, so that Hetty's space for dancing was limited.

'What say I phone the Fire Brigade? Ask them if they'd like to come to a party?' Edith placed another lump of coal on the already blazing fire. 'You go on like that and we shall need them. When was that chimney of yours last swept?' No response, not even a shrug.

Hetty eased her imaginary partners into the veleta, the military two-step, the waltz and the foxtrot. She formed an imaginary circle for the Hokey Cokey. she filled the whole room with imaginary guests, most of whom were taken over to meet Edith in the hope that one of them might find favour.

'I'm not sure if you know Avis Longbottom, Edith. Avis bleaches the tripe over at Willenshaw's, don't you, love? Isn't that a beautiful dress she's made herself – very nineteen twenties! Beer bottle tops pressed into chammy leather, isn't it?' Edith was not amused.

The heat and the smoke and the exhaustion caused by her attempts to keep the party going, combined with the handfuls of cheese biscuits and crisps, eaten too fast and shaken up vigorously by dancing, were making Hetty queasy. She was drunk, and might not make it up the stairs. It was all Edith's fault for being such a wet blanket. No party she could remember at which Edith had put in an appearance had ever recovered from the handicap of Edith's solid shoulders and downturned mouth. Excusing herself to her imaginary partner, Hetty crossed the room to the record-player, moved the pick-up arm back to the beginning of 'Life is Just a Bowl of Cherries', straightened her back and, weaving slightly, approached Edith's chair.

'All right, ratbag, I still have one or two tricks up my sleeve. We know what's got sniffling Edith's knickers in a knot, don't we? We know why she's looking like a carrot half scraped. Here!' She removed the two cushions behind Edith's back, and slung them across the room, then dragged out the one she was sitting on from beneath her. Then she collected every cushion she could find, ripped them open, and poured their contents into the centre of the bed.

'You work, you slave, you worry so. But you can't take your dough when you go, go, go. Life is just a bowl of cherries.' The record was finishing as Hetty, singing along to it, emptied the last cushion, and turned towards the figure by the fire. The room was beginning to revolve. Well, let it.

'There you are. He's come back to you. Shall we wrap him in a sheet for the cremation?' Edith did not reply. Steadying herself against the bed, Hetty found the four corners of the sheet, brought them together, and attempted to tie them into a knot. Still no movement, except for the room, which Hetty stopped revolving for a moment by holding her breath. In that moment, a speck of light glinted on Edith's cheek below her left eye, then another larger speck.

Hetty left the bed, and moved towards her, holding on to furniture as she went. She kneeled down in front of the armchair, with one of her own arms resting on Edith's shoulder. 'That's a start, girl. For God's sake, let them come.' The specks of light moving down Edith's cheek multiplied, and her lips trembled. 'I'm sorry for breaking the door down and spoiling your plan, but you are my oldest friend, and I expect to be consulted on these things. It won't hurt him to wait a bit longer for you to join him. There can't be much to rush about for where he is.'

Thinking she was about to be led up to bed, Edith allowed herself to be helped to her feet, but Hetty turned to the record-player, and started it again.

'Come on! You can be the woman; I'll lead.' Holding on to each other for support, the two women moved slowly round the room in time to the music. 'I'd no intention of burning that money, you know. I reckon we should spend it as quickly as possible, don't you?'

25

Distinguishing Marks

She needed a complete change. She must take a holiday, a long one, away from it all. Eastbourne was suggested. Bournemouth was said to be quiet. Lytham St Anne's was at least a possibility. She would not benefit, would not return to her old self, unless she stayed away from Westcliff for a month or more. If she was sick of the sea, there were the Welsh Valleys, the Scottish Highlands or the Lake District. Her mind required distraction, but she should avoid over-excitement. Herne Bay seemed an ideal choice.

None of these suggestions brought any positive reaction from Edith. Hetty threatened a World Cruise, and asked the travel agent whether P and O had any special concessions for OAPs.

The travel agent was a double act, a husband and wife who worked harmoniously side by side behind the counter, and took it in turns to bring each other mugs of Instant Coffee. They grew warily used to the presence of the two elderly ladies standing before the rack of travel brochures and blocking everyone else's view.

'Well, you can see all you'd want to see at Morecambe in half a day, and still have time to die while you were trying to find a lavatory.' This was the fatter lady; the other never spoke until one day a fresh brochure offering Rentavilla Holidays in Northern Italy was placed in the rack. Even then she did not actually utter any words, but acted for the first time in a positive way which indicated preference. She removed the brochure from the rack, placed it in the hands of the fat lady, and pushed her towards the counter, where the husband and wife waited, wearing lookalike smiles.

The picture on the cover of the brochure showed an open window in a whitewashed room, through which could be seen a hillside covered with pines. The travel agents had considered this picture a poor introduction to a country where so many other things are on offer. They felt it their duty to point out that much of Tuscany is far from the sea, that English food and comforts are not easily to be found inland, and wouldn't a package tour be simpler all round? But the taller woman's eyes never left the picture, and it was clear that her wishes were paramount, for the fat one proceeded to remove wads of notes from somewhere deep inside her undergarments, remarking only, 'We'll have it,' and then to her companion, 'I'll say this for you, our Edith; you don't do things by halves. You do realize we're going to have to cook for ourselves, and it'll be a bugger getting those Eyeties to understand plain English whenever we run out of sugar.'

The husband and wife had seemed a little disconcerted at

being paid an advance from Hetty's underwear. It was
agreed that since neither Hetty nor Edith fancied restitch-
ing fourteen cushions, they would risk Frank's displeasure, beamed at them from the hereafter, and put the
money in a bank.

'She wants one of those accounts where you don't pay
charges if you keep something in it. She'll want a cheque-
book and credit card and another card for getting cash out
through that hole in the wall. She'd also like to know what
interest you pay on money deposited.'

'Well, at present for sums over as little as two hundred
pounds, we pay seven per cent.'

'What about for sums as little as forty-two thousand,
seven hundred and sixty-three?' Hetty emptied two car-
rier bags of banknotes on to the manager's desk.

'Oh, that will do very nicely here with us. Eight and
three quarter per cent when forty thousand remains on
deposit.'

Hetty took back some of the notes. 'Better make that
forty-one thousand. I think we're about to spend the rest
quite soon.'

'All this cash is rather unusual. Might one be permitted
to ask . . . ?'

'Where we got it? Certainly. We emptied the attic, and
had a car-boot sale.'

'I was going to ask whether either of you has ever had a
bank account before.'

'Oh, yes. I'm with the TSB, and she's with the DHSS.'
The bank manager joined Hetty politely in laughter, and
pressed a button on his desk. Some responsible person
came in from an outer office, and began to count the

money and form it into piles. As he flicked through the notes, it seemed to Edith that Frank's portrait was stamped on every one.

'We'll need some Traveller's Cheques and Italian money.' The manager nodded. 'By noon tomorrow.' The manager seemed about to demur. 'Of course if there's a problem, we could try our luck on the other side of the street. We have to leave the country quickly. For tax reasons.'

More polite laughter. 'I don't think there need be any delay. We are dealing in cash, are we not?'

As they left the bank, Hetty said to Edith, 'Isn't it nice how money always makes people smile a lot?'

Beach wear was bought (though they would be nowhere near a beach), and cocktail wear and casual everyday wear, and new suitcases to carry it all in. Hetty bought suntan lotion in bulk and two jumbo-sized tubes of insect repellent. They packed English tea-bags and soft toilet paper and Instant Coffee and tins of baked beans, discovered that the suitcases were too heavy to lift, and began to weed out some of the beach wear. Then Hetty remembered that neither of them held a passport.

The friendly bank manager advised them how to proceed, and five yellowed and brittle scraps of paper were found, which when Sellotaped together constituted Edith's birth certificate. Robert was telephoned, and instructed to search for Hetty's in a biscuit tin marked 'Strictly Private' hidden behind the cistern.

The flight to Pisa was changed, and changed again. If they waited for the passports to arrive by post, they would wait for ever. They went to London, and sat in the Passport Office at Petty France.

During their wait of two and a half hours among anxious Asians and first-time holidaymakers, Geoff, who had been summoned to meet them off the train to carry their cases, gave Hetty an up-to-the-minute report on the activities of Wainthropp and Shawcross, of which he was temporarily the only active partner, and received instructions. He had found Little Tommy under a completely new and well-fitting toupée, singing 'The Rose of Tralee' in a Working Men's Club at Turnham Green, had informed Y. P. Herbert, and received the impression that the one hundred and fifty pounds advance made after the sixth vodka-and-lime was now regarded by Mr Herbert as a once-for-all payment; they were unlikely to get the last fifty. Mr Herbert's Christian names were Yorick Percy. 'I always knew he had a skeleton in his cupboard,' said Hetty.

The firm had two new subjects. One was a thirteen-year-old from Salford who collected credit cards as once children of his age had collected cigarette cards; nevertheless his parents were worried, and the boy had left home. The other was a forty-two-year-old Elvis Presley lookalike from Hebden Bridge. Hetty suggested that Geoff should start at Harrods and move on to the juvenile Courts for the first. The second would be more difficult, since the English-speaking world contained so many Elvis Presley lookalikes, but there must be theatrical agencies which dealt with them.

Their names were called, and each was given a shiny new passport. Edith's occupation – Widow. Born Rochdale

241

24 Aug. 1908. Height 1.73 m. No distinguishing marks. Facial hair was not a distinguishing mark, since it could be at least temporarily removed. Hetty's occupation –Private Investigator. Born Blackburn – Hetty kept her thumb over that bit. Height 1.59 m. Distinguishing marks – appendix scar, scar from removal of gallstones, rabbit-shaped birthmark above left nipple.

Edith said, 'I thought we were going on a holiday, not to enter Miss World.'

'I like them to know who they're dealing with. Passports can get stolen, you know. They'd have to suffer to use this one again.'

26
First Aid

The village was very small, of not more than sixty houses, not all of them occupied. Some of the unoccupied houses were ruins, being allowed slowly to fall to bits. Others had been renovated by psychoanalysts of various nationalities for use as holiday homes. It was one of these houses, four-bedroomed and with a well-maintained swimming pool, which had been rented to Edith and Hetty.

There was no restaurant or trattoria, no bar, not even a shop in the village, which was at the top of a hill, and reached after driving half an hour up a very narrow road, all hairpin bends, with rocks on one side and precipices on the other. This road continued past the village, winding downhill for a short while and then climbing again an even higher hill to an even smaller village, and then stopped. There were no psychoanalysts at all in the second village. They had all run out of puff.

Some of the land close to the village was terraced, but the growing of vines had long ago been given up, since the wine was not of good quality, and there is too much wine

243

in Italy. Mostly what one saw from the windows of the village houses were pines.

The village had a church, of course, with a tower and bells. Four loudspeakers were placed one at each corner of the tower, and the bells were on a record, or perhaps a tape. The recording was of considerable age, and at least one of the bells seemed to have cracked. Each summons to worship would be prefaced by a prolonged hiss and crackle, as if the bells had to clear their throats before sounding off.

The bells sounded more on Sunday than on a weekday. The weekdays had their own distinctive sounds. At six am there would be a concrete-mixer, the exact location of which they had not yet been able to discover, but the likelihood was that it would be doing something renovational to a psychoanalyst's house. At six forty-five, a procession of cars and scooters hooted its way down the hill, as those villagers in work left for the shoe-factory in Lucca. At seven fifteen the industrious Signora Bugatti switched on her circular saw, which was even now, at five past nine, working towards the fulfilment of her ambition to supply the whole of northern Italy with logs for the winter.

'You'd better make the most of that forest of yours while it's still there. She's slicing through it at a rate of knots.'

Edith, in a dressing-gown of purple towelling, emerged from the house, and surveyed her new world from each corner of her very own private balcony, before feeling the side of the teapot to discover whether the tea Hetty had made was still warm.

'That was a joke. Rate of knots – wood. Not bad for this time of the morning, considering last night.'

Requested to do so, Edith did consider last night. 'Yes, you were well away. If you'd had any more to drink, I could have claimed for you as another Wine Lake.'

'It helps me sleep. All this lazing around, I'm not used to it.'

'Look at those mountains.'

'I have. I was sitting here at seven, watching the dodgem cars leave for work.' Hetty began weeding among the marigolds, geraniums and roses with black-spot which were fighting each other for space in the large terra-cotta pots. At her feet enormous ants ran busily about, picking up the bodies of their fellows whom Hetty had squashed earlier, and carrying them away to be eaten by the next generation. 'I shall have to have another go with that spray.' She gave over weeding, and tilted her face to the sun. Later she would cover her nose with tinfoil to prevent burning. 'What's on the agenda for today?'

Hetty knew well enough that there was nothing on the agenda for that or any other day beyond sunbathing, swimming in the pool, and going for a walk around tea-time. To go out of the village would require the summoning of a taxi from the little town in the valley; it had to be summoned anyway when they made their twice-weekly visit to the shops, adding considerably to the overall cost of their purchases. The life suited Edith very well, but Hetty was already becoming restive.

'Buon giorno! buon giorno!' The village priest was waving at them from his balcony, his house and the church being just across the way. Behind him the knobbly tiles which covered the roofs of the village houses, and which looked to Hetty like the illustrations to books of fairy-tales remembered from her childhood, ascended the hill-side, packed tightly together. Television aerials projected from windows and balconies like the teeth of so many swordfish. The largest of the aerials, a shark among swordfish, projected from the priest's house.

Hetty turned to wave back to the priest, and since she was wearing a very tight bathing costume and had been repairing the zip at the front, he blushed and went hurriedly back indoors. 'Do you suppose he watches Dallas?'

Edith inhaled the fresh morning air, and squinted upwards, checking the sky for clouds. There were none. 'I think I'll scramble some eggs.'

'Good idea. I'll have three.' Just at the outskirts of the village there was a little shed, perhaps five feet by four, and they had promised its inhabitant that they would not eat bacon during their holiday. They had conversed with him through a hole left by a missing plank; it was his only access to light as well as to conversation. He was said never to be let out of the hut, since exercise would make him slimmer, and Hetty nursed a secret plan to buy him from his owner and find him other accommodation. This was not mere kindheartedness; she wished to be released from her promise, since she had begun to long for the taste of good lean bacon.

In the kitchen, Edith sang a tuneless breathy song about the thoughts of a young girl as she waves goodbye to her soldier husband after one night of love. The sadness of the song was not expressed in the singing. Edith was happy, and did not care who knew it. The untroubled pace of life in the village filled her with a calmness she could not remember having felt before.

Hetty applied a thick layer of Sunscreen to a patch of red on her left shoulder. Soon Giorgio would arrive to clean the swimming pool, and she would go down and lie on large floor-cushions set by the verge, and talk to him while he worked. Meanwhile she watched a lizard sauntering across the balcony, ignoring the ants. Every so often it would stop to lift alternate feet off the hot tiles.

'That creepy's lifting its leg again, our Edith. Do you think it's got bladder trouble? It doesn't seem to be able to leave a puddle.'

It had become a running joke that Giorgio always warmed the pool for Hetty. They had been told that the village boys must not be allowed to use the pool, but had not expected Giorgio, whose job it was to maintain the pool and its pumping engine, to include himself in this general exclusion. On the first day of their stay, when Giorgio and his mother, who kept the house clean, had stood by the pool with folded arms, waiting for approval, Hetty had nudged the nineteen-year-old Giorgio playfully, and said, 'Well, get your knickers off, then. I'm not getting in until you've warmed it up a bit.' Heads had been shaken, expostulations made in Italian, meaningful glances made towards the windows of houses overlooking the pool, but Hetty had threatened to be damned before she would swim in a pool from which the servants were excluded. There were programmes on British television devoted to exposing such outrages. Edith had remained silent, and Giorgio's mother had backed away as one in the presence of the possessed, and the passiveness from one woman and uneasiness from the other had together provoked Hetty into shouting, 'When I pay the rent, I say who swims,' and pushing Giorgio into the pool fully clothed.

Now, at the mere cost of a new wristwatch, a convention had been established that if Hetty appeared while Giorgio was cleaning the pool (as she always did), he would finish his work, retire modestly behind the little concrete box in which the pumping engine was kept, remove shirt and jeans to reveal the bathing trunks he wore underneath, then execute a perfect swallow dive and swim several lengths, some underwater. He was as sleek as an otter, and as beautiful; when he smiled, his teeth were like the snow in sunlight. He had not been properly employed for nine months, since being made redundant at the shoe-factory.

Hetty sat in sun-hat and sun-glasses, sticky with Ambre Solaire, watching Giorgio swim from behind a paperback copy of *Gone With the Wind*. She had read the first twenty pages four times. She wondered whether it was too soon to open an Italian branch of Wainthropp and Shawcross. Perhaps when she had studied the language a little more closely.

'How about finding boyfriends for me and Edith, Giorgio?'

Giorgio, treading water, poked a finger in one ear to free it of wax. 'Mi scusi?'

Hetty consulted her Italian Phrase Book. There were sections on 'Enjoying Your Stay', 'Moving Around', 'If You're Ill' and 'Shopping'. Boyfriends ought to be in

'Enjoying Your Stay', but most of that section seemed to be about reading menus and visiting churches. 'Boy-friends.'

'Scusi?'

'Signora Cross, Signora Hetty, vorrei uomo.' Incom-prehension. Hetty performed a mime of linking arms and walking out, of placing her head coyly on an imaginary shoulder, and of removing an imaginary hand from her knee.

Giorgio applauded from the shallow end. 'Bravo.'

'Uomo amico.'

'Giorgio you amico.'

'I meant someone more in our own league. Even if you were to shine a strong light in my eyes, and I had to own to fifty-eight, I'd still be old enough to be your grandma.'

'Scusi?'

Hetty had provided herself with a small dictionary as well as a Phrase Book. She consulted it for 'grandma'. 'Nonna. Me nonna.'

'Si, si.' Giorgio was delighted that Hetty was a grand-mother. The village approved of grandmothers, and in-cluded a great many. She would probably wish to show him photographs of her grandchildren later, and he would have no objection to that. It was a pity she had not brought some of them with her. Summer visitors, when they were families, did sometimes include teenage girls, with whom Giorgio had made friendships in the past, though such friendships never lasted longer than the visit. He submerged again, and conversation flagged.

The tea-time walks taken by Hetty and Edith were not

long walks, but they involved a fair amount of exercise, since half the distance was always bound to be uphill. The house they were renting stood on the far side of the village where the road ran on higher. Between their house and the pig there was another dwelling, larger and more modern than theirs, with pink stucco walls and railings of wrought iron painted orange. This house also had a swimming pool, and the garden surrounding it had been lovingly tended instead of going to waste as the psychoanalyst's garden had been allowed to do. On the washing-line, a woman's flimsy undergarments could be seen. Hetty had counted five pairs of briefs, none of them larger than a man's glove. Occasionally the owner of these briefs, a young woman of outstanding beauty, had been sighted, but never for long and only at a distance; she kept indoors. But all day and almost every day, in the swimming pool itself, a bald fat man would be sitting, supported by the inflated inner-tube of a car, and reading a newspaper he never seemed to finish. In the evenings the house would be visited by men in expensive automobiles, and then loud music could be heard, and the sound of raucous Italian male voices shouting phrases which Hetty doubted could be found in her Phrase Book.

Usually when they passed the house Hetty would wave, but the fat man never responded. Then, after a conversation with the pig, the two women would go on up the road, and Edith would pick wild flowers. Cow parsley, campion, poppies and mallow grew in profusion on the verges; there was a tiny campanula, and a snapdragon gone wild, and something which looked like valerian, but more hairy. There were elderberries already in late July, which Edith considered forward, and always the scent of pines, sometimes faint, at others almost overpowering.

The walk in the other direction was similar, but for Edith a little less seductive, since it might be considered as the beginning of their journey back to England when at last they would have to make it. This walk took them past the Public Wash-house in the village square, which consisted of a series of shallow troughs containing grey stagnant water and a smaller trough into which water from a pipe ran continuously. They had never seen any of the village people washing clothes in any of the antique stone troughs, but once a woman in a headscarf had emerged from a house nearby carrying the rubber floor-mat from a car, and washed that under the flowing water.

The third walk was through the warren of steep alleyways which made up the village itself, and this was Hetty's favourite, being shorter and more full of human interest. At almost every corner there was a private shrine to the Madonna. Chipped plaster figures carrying plastic dolls leaned beside nightlights in chrome or gilt holders and small bunches of flowers in jars which had once contained anchovies or (Hetty would have guessed) fishpaste. At the sides of some of these shrines children's drawings had been attached and left to weather.

The brochure had promised them 'the real Italy', so the villagers they saw must be the real Italians. Most of them seemed to be women of their own age, who sat in doorways or on balconies, wearing cotton print frocks not unlike Edith's own. The women chatted to each other while they knitted or sewed; the houses were so crushed together that such conversations, across an alley or between adjacent balconies, were easy. Windows and doors stood open all day to catch what breeze was going, and with the breeze came music from radios tuned to different stations. One woman had a pocket handkerchief of a garden, packed tightly with plastic gnomes.

The women were not large, but they all looked as if they had been used to hard work. Some had tight perms, but none had coloured their hair. All had olive skins, and some had tufts of facial hair. Some of them nodded and smiled at the two visitors who ascended the cobbled alleys cautiously and with many stops for breath. Among these women, Hetty stood out. Edith did not. It was almost as if Edith had been a real Italian all along, out of place in Westcliff, but unremarkable here.

The few men to be seen were also elderly. These men nodded shiftily and made a great play of busying themselves. In the evenings they might allow themselves to be caught standing about or chatting, but their daytimes were fully taken up with finding things to do. After all, *they* were not on holiday, and no one really retired here. One such old man Hetty and Edith had found in a back yard, his own back turned away from passers by, skinning some small animal. At his feet had stood a dog and cat, side by side, watching every stage in the process with total concentration. The animal losing its pelt could no longer be identified. Edith had supposed it to be a rabbit, Hetty that it might once have answered to the name of Tiddles.

This afternoon, on their return from the tea-time walk, the two women noticed that their garden gate was open. Although the garden and the pool were behind the house, they were reached by a gate from the road itself, and this gate was protected by a notice that the property inside was private, and was supplied with a large padlock. Giorgio insisted that the gate should be locked, although Hetty often forgot.

Tea had been taken before the walk, and it was too soon for drinks. This was a dead time, a time when Hetty might get irritable unless they were careful. As the two women entered the garden they heard a small stifled cry as if some animal were in pain. 'Sounds as if something else is just about to lose its fur coat,' Hetty said.

Apart from the swimming pool and the little shed for the pumping engine, the garden consisted of a patch of grass containing many weeds, three walnut trees, a pergola on which a halfhearted vine was being trained, and an electric pylon with cables which almost brushed the balcony. There were said to be small scorpions living in the grass, but the only scorpion Hetty and Edith had seen so far had been in the bathroom, and Edith had killed it with a slipper.

Hetty paced the verge of the pool, trying to decide whether she should get changed and have another swim. The water made gentle slurping noises as it spilled out of the overflow to be recycled by the pumping engine. Edith was examining the vine on the pergola which masked the shed, and which seemed to be suffering from something akin to leaf-curl.

'Have you ever looked inside?'

'No, what's in there?'

'Just Giorgio's pump for the pool, but he polishes every inch of it. He's particularly proud that it was made in Elizabeth, N.J.'

253

'What's the N.J. stand for?'

'How should I know? Maybe it's after our own dear queen. Elizabeth, No Jokes.'

The door of the little shed was open. Edith looked inside.

'Hetty! Come here quickly. And take your belt off. I need it.'

Edith was ripping a piece off her own dress. Had she gone mad? Then she was in among Giorgio's machinery. Hetty ran, loosening her belt. Edith was bending over something which seemed to be caught up among the cogs and wheels. She grabbed the belt from Hetty, who now saw a pair of tiny feet with one shoe missing. There was blood almost everywhere, pints of it. Hetty felt faint.

'Get an ambulance. Quickly. Use the phone.'

'We can't use the phone. It's got that lock on it. No outgoing calls.'

'Next door, then. Hurry. She's lost a lot of blood.'

'I know. I can see most of it.' Hetty ran over the stumps of thistles and nettles to the fence beyond which was a piece of common land before the garden of the pink-stuccoed house began. She could just make out the bald head of the fat man in its usual position, bent over the newspaper as he sat like Buddha in his inner-tube, moving slowly in circles on the surface of the pool.

'Help! We need help. Phone an ambulance.'

The newspaper was lowered, the head lifted, and the face stared moonily at the rowdy Englishwoman who was jumping up and down, waving both arms. Hetty rummaged in her pockets, dropping her Phrase Book into a clump of unmown nettles. Howling with pain, she thrust her arm in up to the elbow to retrieve it. Fortunately the section headed 'If You're Ill' had a subsection for accidents. She must control her hysteria, and speak slowly and clearly to the fat man, stressing all those parts of each word marked in bold type. Otherwise he might decide to ignore her, might even get away from her altogether by deciding to swim under water where even the most perfectly pronounced words would not reach him.

She did not even know whether he could hear her. Passing by on the road, she had never bothered to check whether he wore a deaf-aid. 'Che STA-toh con een-chee den-tay.' The inner-tube was still, the moony face still turned in her direction; he was listening. 'Kee-a-MA-tay oon am-boo-LANT-sa.' There was a pause. Even the air seemed to be unnaturally still. Then the fat man began manoeuvring the inner-tube further away from her, paddling with both hands towards the other end of the pool. What was he doing? Had she frightened him, was he trying to get away from her? She tried again. 'Am-boo-LANT-sa. Pronto! Per fa-VOH-ray.'

The man looked back at her. He was nodding; she was sure. He had lifted a flabby arm, and nodded. He was out of the inner-tube now, and clambering out of the water. She realized that he must have paddled to the shallow end because he could not swim.

Then almost at once he was with them in the garden, still wearing wet swimming trunks. He had not telephoned for an ambulance, which would take at least half an hour to reach them up the narrow road, but had brought his own car, and drove them to the hospital immediately and at breakneck speed, with Edith cradling the unconscious

three-year-old girl in her arms in the back seat, and Hetty
sitting next to him, eyes closed, gripping the dashboard.

Now the house was full of people. Upstairs Edith was
receiving congratulations. The festivities might go on all
night. Hetty, still trembling even after several glasses of
wine, had taken herself off into the cellar, where she sat
leaning against the ping-pong table among the hundreds
of empty wine bottles kept by the psychoanalyst against
the day when he might have a *vendage* from the wine on
the pergola. She was trying to persuade Giorgio to climb
out of the empty wine-cask into which he had crawled to
hide himself.

It seemed that several weeks ago the little girl had taken
to following him wherever he went. She must have followed him into the garden, and hidden to avoid his displeasure, and decided to investigate the pump-house after
he had left. As Hetty and Edith had entered the garden,
hers must have been the faint cry they heard. The machine
had been left running, since a timing device would stop it
automatically. Two of the little girl's fingers had been
crushed, and a vein severed in her elbow, so she would
certainly have bled to death had Edith not applied Hetty's
belt as a tourniquet. At the hospital they said that the
English signora had without doubt saved the life of the
little girl, who would, thanks to her and to Heaven, soon
be in good health again, and restored to the village, her
fingers only slightly scarred.

Presents had been brought, pots of honey, vegetables, a
freshly killed cockerel (so that the mornings would be
quieter in one respect at least), a gallon of wine. Signora

Bugatti had brought logs for the fire, which they were hardly likely to need. There were cakes, and dishes of pasta, and something cooked in a crock which may have been the small animal they had seen skinned. The priest had looked in, and blessed them both. There were lighted candles in the little shrines all over the village, and a great coming and going of villagers at the house of Signora Cross and the friend of Signora Cross. (None of the villagers could manage Wainthropp.) Nobody appeared to wish to give any credit to the fat man, or to be very interested in the part he had played, and he himself had disappeared next door, presumably to change out of his swimming trunks, the moment they had returned from hospital. Hetty and Edith had not seen him since.

Finally Hetty managed to persuade Giorgio that living indefinitely inside a wine-cask would deform his physique, and that this deformity would please no one, least of all the Madonna, who had been so generous in the proportioning of it. Furthermore it would be unfair to Edith and herself if they were forced to spend the rest of their holiday swimming in a pool coated with creepy-crawlies, simply because Georgio had decided to adopt a new way of life. So he left the cask, and accepted a large gin-and-tonic, and was reunited with his tearful mother, who had been drinking steadily upstairs to dull the pain of her only son's absence. And after a while, when even those rejoicing villagers who had come and gone several times had gone for the last time, Hetty lowered herself on to a sofa where, through the door, she could watch Edith rinsing wine-glasses under the kitchen tap, and said, 'It helped, of course, you having been a nurse.'

'I wasn't a nurse. I worked in the kitchens. Somebody was always cutting themselves.'

'Nicks and grazes, not whole arteries.'

'It was a Mental Hospital, and the cook was manic-depressive. Many's the morning I've found her with her head in the oven. It would have been a poor do if I hadn't learned how to bandage the odd wrist while I was there.' Edith was examining the skin between her fingers, and realizing that she had not needed to apply ointment to them for quite some time.

Hetty helped herself to another nightcap. If she didn't sleep tonight, after all the excitement, she never would. She said, 'Funny nobody wanted to thank the fat man for what he did.'

'Perhaps he has Mafia connections, and they're frightened. Come to bed; it's another day tomorrow.'

27
Two Fingers

Edith sat on the edge of Hetty's bed peeling a peach for their breakfast. She had also brought two lightly boiled eggs and a very large pot of tea. Neither woman had yet been able to persuade her false teeth to perform successfully on the rock-hard bread delivered to the village by van every other day.

'It's only a hangover. It will pass.' The combined sounds of the concrete-mixer, the recorded bells and the saw drowned out Edith's words. Hetty replaced the wads of cotton wool in her ears, and concentrated on lip-reading.

'If you wanted to go home, I'd be all right on my own. Giorgio and his mother would keep an eye on me. There's not really enough life for you here, is there?' Hetty smiled weakly, and accepted half a peach. One of the eggs had cracked while being boiled. It looked like a sea anemone, and the smell of it was doing strange things to her stomach.

Staying in bed all morning was not Hetty's idea of how best to spend her holiday, but her first attempts to stand were unsuccessful, so she resigned herself to being bored until her knees recovered. She drowsed fitfully, re-arranged the cracks in the ceiling into a drawing by Picasso, and marvelled on the change in Edith's person-ality, the new pleasantness, the confidence, the considera-tion for others, all qualities acquired since Frank's death. Hetty decided comfortably that she herself had been responsible for Edith's acquisition of these excellent qual-ities.

At eleven o'clock Giorgio poked his head round the bedroom door, and presented her with a mug of coffee and a fistful of wild flowers. 'Nonno,' he said mysteri-ously. 'Nonno. Domani,' tapped the side of his nose, and went out again. Hetty lay considering this enigmatic pro-nouncement for a while, and just as she had sneaked out of bed to change her nightdress in case there were any more visitors, Edith appeared again with a lunch of minestrone soup and salad.

'If I'm to be treated as a film star, I might as well dress the part.' The noises outside had stopped for lunch, so she took the cotton wool out of her ears and began spraying perfume under her arms. Edith quickly covered the food with a paper napkin.

'Well, what's the great world outside doing?'

'We've been invited to take tea next door.' Hetty stopped spooning soup, and adjusted the piece of spaghetti hanging from her lip. 'I went round to thank the fat man for helping us yesterday, and to borrow their phone to find out about flights back for you. The young woman seemed delighted to have a visitor. I don't think she sees many other women. She can speak English, learned it from one of those records, French and German as well, so she made the call for me. Then as I was leaving, a funny thing happened. Do you want some of this grated cheese on your soup?'

'What funny thing?'

Edith spooned her soup slowly, and gazed towards the window. The taste wasn't quite right. It needed something, but she couldn't decide what.

'What was funny?'

'As I was leaving the house, Giorgio saw me. He went very strange, flinging his arms about, shaking his head, mumbling. He kept trying to drag me towards the church. I told him I was a lapsed Congregationalist, but he insisted on lighting a candle.'

Hetty began to giggle. She had asked Giorgio why he didn't also maintain the pool next door, and he had shaken his head many times before performing a series of mimes. First there had been a woman hitching up her skirt and winking, then someone sleeping and waking up to count money. Hetty had guessed the Tooth Fairy, 'Denta Fata'. Her guess had not pleased Giorgio, who had become first sulky, then impatient, and had mimed smoking a cigar, driving a fast car, and mowing down battalions of imaginary enemies as if it were a punishment. Then, in the face of Hetty's continued incomprehension, he had performed the hitching-up-skirt mime again, and Hetty had said, a little too loudly for his comfort, 'I see. She's on the game.'

'Only what I still don't understand,' she said to Edith, 'is what the Tooth Fairy's got to do with it.'

'See how you feel about going. We needn't stay long.'

261

Hetty settled into finishing her soup. Edith's cooking was something else which had improved. She felt better already.

Edith said, 'I think you'll like her. She's the most beautiful young woman I've ever seen.'

Between lunch and tea-time, Edith lay down in her room. The room was white with no pictures on the walls. The windows had brown wooden shutters. They were open, and outside there was bright sunlight, and a view of pines against a clear blue sky. She lay naked on the bed, with closed eyes.

She did not achieve near-silence, but the noise of the recorded bells was intermittent, and the concrete-mixer and the electric saw would not begin again until three. She lay on her back, her arms resting gently on her belly, and proceeded to empty her mind.

One cannot go to emptiness immediately. She began with pictures of her childhood, beginning with a wooden duck on wheels, which made a noise like a football rattle when it was moved. Then there was a monkey on a stick, dressed in cotton pants and a bolero which she was never allowed to remove, even for washing. The monkey went through the motions of climbing, but never seemed to get anywhere. Not until its clothes had become unhygienic did it achieve the heights for which it struggled, being placed in the hands of Guy Fawkes on Bonfire Night. Behind closed eyes, Edith watched the monkey burn. It did not suffer, but blazed away merrily to ash with its stick.

Then there were dolls, none of which had made any serious claim on her affection. Her outright rejection of a black doll caused a small pang of guilt even to this day. There had been picture-books, some of which had pop-up sections of forests and buildings which soon became un-glued, and later there were story-books, chosen by her mother, of middle-class girls who had fallen from grace. Usually they were able to regain it by saving kittens from drowning or presenting their savings to a blind beggar.

At school she had compensated for her own lack of beauty by physical strength, protecting younger daintier girls from being bullied. Quite large boys had backed away at the sight of Edith's clenched teeth and long arms swinging. Later she had met Hetty, five years younger, small and fat, but desperately aspiring to daintiness. Hetty had certainly needed protection from boys, and even young men, often against her will. Their friendship had been cemented in those days. The cement had set. Hetty was still her friend, her only friend, but she could do without Hetty now.

Back through the drifting piles of sepia photographs. Back through the pictures in *The Illustrated London News* – the Arrest of Mrs Pankhurst, the Sinking of the *Lusitania*, the Landing at Gallipoli. Somewhere on the edge of consciousness, her mother pointed to the door, somewhere Frank was grunting as he sifted through gar-bage in a black plastic bag. She ignored them, giving herself to sepia and to childhood. The wooden duck crawled towards her across the floor, smelling of sandpap-ered wood and pines, the monkey ascended to Heaven from the burning hands of Guy Fawkes, the pages of *The Illustrated London News* fluttered and rustled like the branches of the pine trees which once they had been. She reached out towards Mr Ramsay MacDonald and became a part of Nothing.

The young woman's name was Maria. The fat man was Alberto. He sat uncomfortably in striped blazer and cricket flannels, sipping tea while the women talked without constraint about furnishing fabrics and the garden. Hetty and Edith were shown the house, in which every object gleamed, and one of whose bedrooms contained a round bed with satin sheets and a mirror in the ceiling. They were enthusiastic about all they saw. As they were leaving, Maria said, 'Alberto has an interest in a restaurant. If you were free this evening, we would like to take you there.'

The restaurant was a Night Club, with facilities for gambling. Edith and Hetty wore the cocktail dresses they had bought in Westcliff. Maria wore emerald green satin, and was greeted like a celebrity; nobody in her party was allowed to pay for anything. After the meal, the two women were presented with gambling chips with which to try their luck. Hetty lost hers swiftly, and returned to Maria at the table.

'I don't see how Alberto can make a profit at this rate.'

'It is all public relations. They will charge a few drunks a little more for the privilege of being thrown out.'

'Our Edith's doing well. I suppose that means the price of brandy has just shot up.'

'Someone has to be seen to win. It is all carefully accounted for. What made you choose this part of Italy for your holiday?'

'Edith's kinky about mountains and Christmas trees. I

usually prefer a dip in the sea and a bit more life. This evening's a real tonic for me. I like being with people. The village is nice, though. And the villagers seem friendly, don't you think?'

Maria put her glass down carefully. 'I think you know that they are not friendly towards me. I also think you know why. One cannot blame them. Alberto suffers more than myself. He would like to take walks and go to church, but they stare at him, or go into their houses and slam the door. He is very sensitive. The garden and the pool have become his prison. When there is time, we get into the car and drive somewhere we are not known; then he is happy. But one cannot spend one's life running away.' They watched Alberto leading Edith away to cash her chips. 'Is it true the little girl will be all right?'

'Two fingers were badly crushed.'

'Two fingers are very important to a woman.'

'She can always gesture with the other hand.'

Both women laughed. Maria made a gesture with two fingers towards the exit. 'Back into your churches, you little people!' Both sipped a little more brandy. 'This has been a lovely evening. Look! Even Alberto is laughing.'

'Do you ever come to England?'

'Sometimes I visit Knightsbridge. Usually I stay a month, and work; it helps to pay for Christmas.'

'I work in London a lot myself.'

'What do you do?'

'I find lost people. Missing persons. I'm a private investigator. Don't laugh; I've been doing very well.'

'I'm not laughing; I think it is splendid. Alberto's cousin, Giovanni, has been missing six months. He also lost some fingers. Three. They arrived one morning in a parcel. We kept them in the deep-freeze, but when he returned home they were of no use to him, so we buried them under the vine. Soon after that he went on his travels. Maybe he is in London also; we don't know.'

'I'll keep an eye out for him.'

'I do not think he wishes to be found. I think he would make one-finger gesture to you, Hetty.'

Hetty choked on her brandy. 'When you get to my age, anything's better than being ignored.'

Next evening at seven pm Giorgio stood on the doorstep between pots of busy lizzie, glancing nervously over his shoulder. He was wearing a suit and a tie. At seven minutes past seven an elderly man, also wearing a suit with a tie and clutching a large lily, was to be observed coming up the road towards the house. Since he was the victim of a tubercular cough, he could be heard as well as seen. He stopped at a little distance from the house in order to polish his shoes on the backs of his shins. Hetty, Edith and Giorgio all waited while he did so. The old man seemed reluctant to proceed further.

Giorgio made the introduction. 'Questo e mei zio, Federico.' Giorgio beckoned the old man to come forward, and he did so very slowly, holding out the lily at arm's length as if it were a white flag. The lily was pointing towards Edith, but her hands were full of plates, so Giorgio turned his uncle on the spot to face Hetty, and the flower was offered a second time. Hetty accepted it, and dropped a curtsey to break the ice. The old man nodded, and the effort of doing so brought on another fit of coughing.

'Giglio.'

Hetty smiled coyly, and passed her Collins Gem Italian Dictionary to Giorgio. He looked up the word, and showed it to her. 'Giglio', as so frequently with Italian words, was not pronounced as it was spelled. It meant 'lily'.

'Thank you, Federico. Very thoughtful. You'll find I'm a bit giggley-oh myself when I've had a few. Do come in and see the view.'

Giorgio's mysterious remark of the day before had been explained. He had decided that, during their conversation by the pool, Hetty had been asking for a grandfather to be her boyfriend, and, having none, had persuaded his uncle, who would usually at this time of the evening have been inhaling something medicinal, to come for a meal.

Hetty discovered herself to be experiencing one of her very rare bouts of embarrassment. It was clear that Edith intended to busy herself in the kitchen as much as she could, since she did not regard herself as responsible, and was only taking part in the charade under protest. As the four of them sat sipping pre-dinner drinks, Hetty racked her brain for conversation. With her Phrase Book on her knee, she flicked over the pages. 'Your First Questions' seemed an appropriate section; she could leave the answers to take care of themselves. But when she came upon, 'When is the next train to Rimini?' she began to giggle and had to close the book. What conversation there was consisted of Giorgio speaking to Federico in Italian and Hetty asking Edith if she could help in the kitchen, to which question the only answer she received was 'Don't you dare.' For the rest of the time, Hetty watched the old

man and his nephew, smiling graciously the while, to
indicate perfect understanding and approbation. It was
her view that, in years gone by, Federico might once have
looked like Rossano Brazzi, but now that time and
weather had had their way with him the person he most
resembled was Harold Macmillan. After several weeks,
they went in to dinner.

Now time could be taken up in passing plates and
dishes, and there was music to fill the silences. The
records left by the psychoanalyst for his tenants were all
classical. Edith's choice of *Thus Spake Zarathustra* as an
accompaniment to the *spaghetti ai funghi* greatly reduced
the need for chit-chat.

Both women wished that they were able to converse
with the old man from the mountains. They wanted to
reassure him that they were not *femmes fatales* and had
only wished to meet someone of their own age. Both
sensed that in his own village he might once have been
thought of as a ladies' man, and both felt a strong impulse
to trim the frayed threads from the cuffs of his shirt which
now dangled over his plate, collecting gravy. He ate
slowly, causing them to fear that the size of the meal might
be overfacing him, but this was not so; he was merely
prolonging his enjoyment. He drank moderately, savour-
ing the wine, which was the best that the supermarket of
the town in the valley had been able to supply. He nodded
his approval of their choice of wine, and they nodded their
pleasure in accepting his approval. Hetty, having failed to
find 'Bon Appétit' in her Collins Gem Dictionary, lifted
her glass and pronounced the words 'Godersi la Vita!'
which looked as if they might mean 'Enjoy life', wishing

Federico the success and fortune which his appearance indicated he had lacked up to now. As always the unfairness of this saddened her and made her emotional, and she drank a little too quickly.

With the meal completed and the dishes cleared, Edith made a short announcement, some of which she hoped Giorgio might be able to convey to Federico. She said that both she and Hetty were honoured to have him as their guest, and that if she were younger she would certainly learn to speak Italian, not only because it was a beautiful language to listen to, but also because she would like to know more about the Italian people she had met. She ended by suggesting that Federico might like to talk about himself and his life, and that Giorgio could translate a word here and there wherever possible, and they would get the gist of it. Hetty clapped her hands in agreement, and patted Edith's knee, grateful that she had come up with such a brainwave.

Unfortunately Giorgio proved unable to translate any of Edith's speech. Challenged, Hetty turned to the Phrase Book and the Dictionary, and after much struggle produced the words 'Federico discorso egocentrico' supplemented by such a variety of gestures and facial expressions as could never have been anticipated by those who had compiled those works. And Federico understood. After a few moments with his head back and his eyes closed, he indicated by pointing to himself and imitating the rocking of a baby that he intended to begin the story of his life at a very early age.

Bach had long ago succeeded Richard Strauss on the turntable, and now Chopin took over from Bach, to be followed by Porpora and Albinoni, as the seventy-two-year-old Zio Federico, once a worker in the vineyard in the days when the vines were still cultivated, long a widower, who lived in a house outside the village and further up the mountain, with no company but an old horse, spoke of a life which had never ventured outside a radius of forty miles. Giorgio sat entranced, forgetting his duties as a translator, and translation would in any case have been an intrusion, for Hetty and Edith were listening to the sound of the old man's voice, and creating their own history for the guest whose face reflected the pains and pleasures of each of his many years.

When he spoke of craftsmanship, they understood him easily by the way his hands moved, and when of arthritis, they understood that well enough too. His description of his wife working side by side to build a house was also understood; for the rest, their understanding went below the surface. He spoke of humility and humiliation, of anger at injustice and occasional revenge, of saving to buy overcoats and shoes, of the deaths of children and of bad winters and ruined vines. He spoke of good years, when sick children recovered, harvests were bountiful and the television set repaired. Now he was alone with his horse, who stank, because she was old also, and the food he could afford to give her was sub-standard. Edith and Hetty nodded and smiled. The old man was relaxed and enjoying himself. It was all in the past. What was most important was to have survived. The world beyond these mountains would have troubled him. He felt complete, had lived well, and now only wished to die painlessly in his own garden.

Finally he smiled wistfuly, shook his head, wiped his eyes, and said, 'Io ero molto romantico. Adesso il tempo e contro di me.'

'He was very romantic. But now time is against him.'

28

Tidying Up

At four thirty every day Edith and Alberto would take a walk through the village together. No villagers crossed themselves or ran indoors. Little children did not dart inside the church to hide between the rows of chairs. They nodded and smiled at Signora Cross, and eventually took to answering Alberto's cheery greetings.

Alberto was very happy. Hetty consulted Maria. 'What do you feel about it?'

'Alberto never knew his mother. She died at his birth, and he was brought up in an Orphanage. She would have been the same age as Signora Cross. Mothers are very important to Italian men.'

'But for you it must be like finding your mother-in-law has just moved in next door. You know she intends to stay here? She's forever doing sums on bits of paper to work out how long she can afford to live.'

'Alberto is not my husband or lover, and never has been. He idealizes women too much ever to be a successful suitor. We are friends and business partners. I am very pleased for him.' Maria paused, then added, 'You have not spoken of how you feel.'

Hetty thought for a moment. 'Homesick. I'm the one with itchy feet. Luckily I know a good chiropodist. I shall go back, and sell Edith's house in Westcliff, to top up what her husband left her. It should be enough if she can only get that head-doctor to extend the tenancy.'

'Oh, he will be back in the autumn, I think, with his wife. Head-doctors from all over the world gather every August in Vienna to read papers and commit adultery in the city of Sigmund Freud. Then they spend a month of domesticity in their second homes before resuming their practices in London, Paris or New York. But that will not matter. Before then she will have moved in here with us. We stray dogs must stick together.'

Two days later Hetty boarded a plane to London, and was met at the airport by Geoff, who informed her that Phillida Meadowhite was refusing to leave her room, but Chalky was visiting her every day with take-away meals. Letters requesting the services of Wainthropp and Shaw-cross had dried up, and his view was that another burst of publicity was needed. Hetty pinched him on the bottom, and told him not to fret. She was home again, and about to put her thinking cap on.

Robert was in bed with a cold when she reached home. The freezer was empty, the kitchen piled high with un-washed plates, and the electricity had been cut off be-cause he had lost the bill. As she poured him a whisky from the duty-free bottle she had bought on the plane, and climbed into bed beside him, he asked how long she intended to stay this time.

'Just as long as I feel needed. Why? Have you missed me?'

'Now and then.'

One afternoon in October, a client of Maria's, a man of money and good connections to whom it would be unwise to deny favour, arrived with a friend. Alberto was away that afternoon on the business of the restaurant, and the friend was left downstairs to wait without company. He grew bored, and decided to explore the house. Upstairs in one of the bedrooms, a small room with bare whitewashed walls and a view of pines, he found a naked woman lying on a bed. Congratulating himself on his good fortune, he began to approach the bed, then stopped because, although it was clear that the woman was in her way beautiful and her face bore an expression of ecstatic peace, it was also clear that she was old. Curious, he took a couple of steps closer, and a further matter became clear to him, which was that the woman on the bed was dead.

Maria telephoned the number Hetty had left with her, and the bewildered Robert took and passed a message. Hetty flew back to Italy for the funeral, which was attended by the whole village, anxious to say farewell to their friend.

The lapsed Congregationalist was buried, as she would have wished, with the full rites of the Catholic Church. Hetty did not object. She wept, but this was seen by the villagers as entirely appropriate, and most of them wept also, especially Alberto. Hetty herself, on her return to England, sent, in gratitude and as a memorial to her friend, a brand-new recording entitled *Church Bells for Every Occasion*, and this has given such pleasure that it is indeed played on every occasion, sectarian as well as ecclesiastical, ringing out to announce the arrival of the Bread Van in the village as well as the Beginning of Early Morning Mass.

Bernard B. Shawcross inherited £65,000. Hetty was left a collection of clothes three sizes too large for her and a shoe-box containing sepia photographs, including one of herself at the age of fifteen singing 'The Little Boy That Santa Claus Forgot'.

Maureen O'Brien

DEADLY REFLECTION

'A tale of obsessive love meeting willing victim . . . an escalation which gathers horrid and chilly momentum' Frances Fyfield in the *Evening Standard*

Jenitha Wren wants a husband. Someone who'll come home every night and still be there in the morning. Someone to cook for in the evenings. When a well-intentioned friend introduces her to Thomas, a handsome if taciturn Dane, she dares to hope she's found him.

Together, the two journey to Thomas's birthplace, a remote spot on the Danish coast, to meet his family. It is a bizarre household, steeped in an atmosphere of unease. Feeling increasingly isolated, Jen realises she has systematically cut herself off from all those who care for her. And she is forced to confront the bleak truth that her wilful blindness may have led her into mortal danger.

'Atmosphere and characterization take over and the mystery unfolds to its inevitably tragic end' Susanna Yager in the *Daily Telegraph*

'A beautifully paced atmospheric chiller' *Liverpool Daily Post*

'A story of real depth and heart-stopping suspense. There isn't a literary novelist alive who can match O'Brien for psychological verity' Matt Coward in the *Morning Star*

FICTION / GENERAL 0 7472 4374 3

THE JOURNEY IN

JOSS KINGSNORTH

In this absorbing novel, Joss Kingsnorth explores the world of the artist, and the conflicting loyalties which many women will recognise as their own, with sensitivity and acuity.

At the much-heralded opening of her husband's new exhibition, Hester Eliot realises she is shockingly disillusioned with Robert's work. And, physically exhausted after a miscarriage, she has begun to question her own talent as a painter.

When a friend offers Hester the use of her cottage in the little estuary town of Coombe Ferrers in the West Country, Hester hopes it will give her the opportunity to disperse the dark clouds she has been holding at bay; the chance to mourn her mother, who died before her time, and the child, who never had a time. In doing so, Hester will recover her freedom.

'The Devon scene is set most beautifully in this excellent first novel. Joss Kingsnorth is . . . one to watch' *Dartmouth Chronicle*

FICTION / GENERAL 0 7472 4560 6

A selection of bestsellers from Headline

LAND OF YOUR POSSESSION	Wendy Robertson	£5.99 ☐
TRADERS	Andrew MacAllen	£5.99 ☐
SEASONS OF HER LIFE	Fern Michaels	£5.99 ☐
CHILD OF SHADOWS	Elizabeth Walker	£5.99 ☐
A RAGE TO LIVE	Roberta Latow	£5.99 ☐
GOING TOO FAR	Catherine Alliott	£5.99 ☐
HANNAH OF HOPE STREET	Dee Williams	£4.99 ☐
THE WILLOW GIRLS	Pamela Evans	£5.99 ☐
MORE THAN RICHES	Josephine Cox	£5.99 ☐
FOR MY DAUGHTERS	Barbara Delinsky	£4.99 ☐
BLISS	Claudia Crawford	£5.99 ☐
PLEASANT VICES	Laura Daniels	£5.99 ☐
QUEENIE	Harry Cole	£5.99 ☐

All Headline books are available at your local bookshop or newsagent, or can be ordered direct from the publisher. Just tick the titles you want and fill in the form below. Prices and availability subject to change without notice.

Headline Book Publishing, Cash Sales Department, Bookpoint, 39 Milton Park, Abingdon, OXON, OX14 4TD, UK. If you have a credit card you may order by telephone – 01235 400400.

Please enclose a cheque or postal order made payable to Bookpoint Ltd to the value of the cover price and allow the following for postage and packing:

UK & BFPO: £1.00 for the first book, 50p for the second book and 30p for each additional book ordered up to a maximum charge of £3.00.

OVERSEAS & EIRE: £2.00 for the first book, £1.00 for the second book and 50p for each additional book.

Name ....

Address ....

....

....

If you would prefer to pay by credit card, please complete:
Please debit my Visa/Access/Diner's Card/American Express (delete as applicable) card no:

Signature .... Expiry Date..............